THE UNKNOWN CHEKHOV

STORIES AND OTHER WRITINGS

Translated and with
an introduction by
AVRAHM YARMOLINSKY

The Ecco Press
New York

PRINTED IN THE UNITED STATES OF AMERICA

The Ecco Press logo by Ahmed Yacoubi

An Unpleasantness first appeared in *Charm* and *Boa Constrictor and Rabbit*
in *Harper's Bazaar*. The first nine chapters of *The Peasants* are reprinted in somewhat
revised form from *The Portable Chekhov*, edited by Avrahm Yarmolinsky,
Copyright 1947, by The Viking Press, Inc., N. Y. C.

Library of Congress Cataloging in Publication Data
Chekhov, Anton Pavlovich, 1860-1904.
The unknown Chekhov.
(The Tales of Chekhov ; v. 14)
Reprint. Originally published: New York : Noonday Press, 1954.
Published simultaneously in Canada by Penguin Books Canada.
1. Chekhov, Anton Pavlovich, 1860-1904—Translations, English.
I. Yarmolinsky, Avrahm, 1890-   . II. Title.
III. Series: Chekhov, Anton Pavlovich, 1860-1904.
Short stories. English ; v. 14.
PG3456.A15G3   1984   vol. 14   [891.73'3]   86-29240
ISBN 0-88001-142-4 (pbk.)   891.73'3 s

Second printing, 1988

The editor is deeply indebted to his wife Babette Deutsch, for her unstinted help in preparing the text.

contents

2 other writings

introduction

The first performance of *The Cherry Orchard* took place on January 30, 1904 (N.S.), the forty-fourth anniversary of the playwright's name day. A mortally sick man, he dragged himself to the Moscow Art Theatre for the occasion, which was turned into a public celebration of his silver jubilee as a writer; he died several months later. Active as an author for a relatively short period, and, furthermore, handicapped by tuberculosis throughout his adult life, Chekhov nevertheless produced a rather large body of writing. Virtually all of it was published during his lifetime. Of the few pieces that appeared posthumously, several were first printed in the definitive edition of his works and correspondence, the twenty volumes of which came off a Moscow press between 1944 and 1951.

Besides this scholarly edition, several others have been issued for popular consumption. If, as it appears, Chekhov —along with other writers in the liberal tradition—is being widely read in the Soviet Union, one may take comfort in the thought that the humane values which have such a precarious existence there may be finding nourishment. In any event, his work must be a relief from what should be called the unliterature that has been produced to official specifications. For he was the least dogmatic as he was the least politically-minded of men. He owed allegiance to no ready-made ideology, no class, no party, no institution, be it of Church or State. The only dictates that he recognized were those of his own conscience. His concern was always with the man, the woman, the child, as a person. To portray them simply, inwardly, and, above all, honestly, was, he believed, his whole duty. His performance of it has long been the admiration of readers far beyond the confines of his own country—and of theatregoers as well.

Chekhov's last and best known play was the first to be Englished. The translation, entitled, all-too literally, *The Cherry Garden*, was published in New Haven "under the supervision of the Dramatic Department of *The Yale Courant*." Since then, all of his writings for the stage, except for a variant of one skit, have become accessible in English, most of them in more than one translation. This cannot be said of his fiction, one of the twin pillars on which his great reputation rests.

At the start of his career he turned out a great deal of copy for the comic papers. Much of this work has remained, deservedly, untranslated: it holds little that would bring a smile to the lips of a foreigner. Aside from these trifles, he composed some four hundred and fifty narratives which have left an indelible mark on the art of the short story.

The distinction of having been the first, in the area of English speech, to discover Chekhov the story teller apparently belongs to a New York periodical: *Short Stories, a Magazine of Fact and Fiction*. The issue for October, 1891, carried a tender and thoughtful piece from his pen, largely interesting for its insights into the workings of a child's mind. At least a dozen years were to pass, however, before his tales began to gain some attention in the English-speaking countries. His vogue did not assume large proportions, particularly among the sophisticates, until the first World War. It was then that *The Tales of Tchehov* started appearing simultaneously in London and New York, the initial volume coming out in 1916, the thirteenth and last in 1922. The text was turned into English by that diligent, if by no means irreproachable, translator of the nineteenth-century Russians, the late Constance Garnett. These volumes contain two hundred narratives, the greater part of Chekhov's best.

During the years that followed, renderings of not a few of the stories that had been left out by Mrs. Garnett found their way into print. Yet in the summer of 1953, when work on the present collection was begun, scores of stories were still inaccessible in English, some of them comparable to those that have become a part of the literary heritage of the West. Wholly unknown were Chekhov's journalistic writings, as well as his book on the island of Sakhalin and its penal colony. The reader is offered here a selection from all of this material.

The stories—these form the bulk of our book—appear in the order in which they were published. This is roughly also the order in which they were composed. Regrettably, such an arrangement is lacking in *The Tales of Tchehov* and, indeed, the contents of the volumes seem to have been grouped at random. This circumstance, coupled with the inaccessibility of much of Chekhov's early work, has tended to obscure his growth as a writer. One of the striking facts of his literary biography is that the man who started out as a hack, carelessly and frivolously exploiting a comic vein that was not of the richest, eventually developed into a conscientious and responsible artist, an author of major stature.

"Oh, with what trash I began," he observed one day in

a retrospective mood, "my God, with what trash!" He supplied the public prints devoted to wit and humor with jokes, lampoons, aphorisms, advertisements, mathematical problems, captions for cartoons, Liliputian essays, miniature stories—all calculated to raise a laugh and be forgotten. And yet, from the first, among these facetiae there turned up sketches and narratives of a different stamp. There was clowning in these, too, and there were irritating stylistic mannerisms, implausible situations, loose ends. Nevertheless, they evidenced a genuine sense of fun, a satiric verve, an eye for revealing details of appearance and behavior, an ear for living speech, signs of that "talent for humanity," compacted of understanding and compassion, which is Chekhov's signature.

The comic spirit dominates many of the early pieces— those written during the years 1880 to 1887—that are included in the present volume. Like "A Horsey Name" and "Chameleon," which have long been available in English, "Vint" has amused generations of the author's compatriots. There are bits of pure comedy in "Perpetuum Mobile" and in "The Skit," which pokes fun at the cowardice of petty officialdom, a favorite target of young Chekhov's satirical thrusts. "Two of a Kind," although the work of an apprentice, presents an amusing situation that has a certain novelty. "The Village Elder," while scarcely more than an anecdote, has a robust, indigenous quality; indeed, it comes close to being the kind of minor masterpiece that could have been written by the author of "The Jumping Frog." The absurd stupidity of the protagonist in "Women Make Trouble" is much like that of the peasant in the somewhat earlier "Malefactor," a story of which Tolstoy spoke admiringly. Himself the son of a serf (who, rising in the world, became a grocer), Chekhov was not inclined to idealize the *muzhik* or sentimentalize over him.

The first version of "Boa Constrictor and Rabbit" was

entitled: "For the Information of Husbands; a learned paper." This was barred by the Censorship Committee on the ground that the subject was "immoral" and that, though its tone was facetious, the sketch contained "indecently voluptuous scenes and cynical allusions." The editor of the weekly to which the condemned squib had been offered informed the author of the official verdict, adding, in jest, that it served him right. "To revenge myself on the censors and on those who maliciously rejoice at my misfortune," Chekhov wrote in reply, "I have formed, with my friends, *A Society for the Promotion of Cuckoldry*. The statutes have already been submitted to the proper authorities. I have been elected president by a vote of thirteen to four."

Chekhov had been scribbling away for half a dozen years before he bade farewell to the farcical. He never lost his taste for comedy, and long clung to the notion of resuming his former manner. Indeed, as late as 1892 the author of "The Steppe," "The Name Day Party," "The Duel" contributed four items to the comic weekly, *Splinters*, in which much of his early work had appeared. "A Fragment," the first of these contributions, is included here. It is noteworthy that Chekhov depended a good deal on grotesquely substandard speech for his effects and that he displayed great ingenuity in inventing funny names for his characters. His humorous stories, therefore, are peculiarly apt to suffer from the hazards of translation.

Occasionally the youthful author tried his hand at writing of a serious cast. Such an attempt was "Because of Little Apples," with which our collection opens. Indignation fashioned this immature, derivative, yet obviously promising sketch of a sadistic country squire, one of the very first pieces that Chekhov published. "Two in One," the next inclusion, is notable for its flash of insight into the psychology of "the little man" in a hierarchical society. There is comedy, but no light-hearted banter, in "Worse and Worse." It is worthy of comparison with "Sergeant Prishibeyev," a squib immensely popular in Russia, which furnished the language with a synonym for a one-man vigilance committee, and which only recently became available in English. "Drowning" might be a sketch of a derelict by Maxim Gorki, with the rhetoric squeezed out. In "Saintly Simplicity" humor is blended with pathos, an element that so markedly tinges Chekhov's mature work. Pathos, indeed, dominates "Other People's Misfortune." In this story the author for the first time deals with the economic ruin of the landowning gentry—a theme that will continue to haunt him until he builds *The Cherry Orchard* around it. Here is one of the many pieces in which he put in practice his maxim that an author must be "humane to the tips of his fingers." To turn to "The Lodger" is to find a study of a type, representatives of which throng Chekhov's stories and help to make them actual to a mid-twentieth century audience: men and women betrayed by weakness into a cruelly frustrating situation and unable to break out of the trap.

In May, 1886, Chekhov wrote to his brother Alexander, who had literary ambitions: "In descriptions of Nature one must seize on small details, grouping them so that when the reader closes his eyes he gets a picture. For instance, you'll have a moonlit night if you write that on the mill dam a piece of glass from a broken bottle glittered like a bright little star, and that the black shadow of a dog or a wolf rolled past like a ball." Again, a character in *The Sea Gull* says approvingly of Trigorin, the novelist: "With him, the neck of a broken bottle glitters on the dam and the mill wheel casts a black shadow—and there before you is a moonlit night." These passages have often been quoted in commenting on Chekhov's device of evoking a natural scene with one or two telling details. As a matter of fact, he had used this very description in a story composed two months before he wrote the letter quoted above, namely in "Hydrophobia," which until now has not been accessible in English.

The piece is of interest for another reason: in revising it many years after it was first published, the author gave it a new ending, which is printed here along with the original one. In the first version there is a definite conclusion treated in a rather conventional manner. The later version disregards the reader's natural curiosity as to the outcome of the accident and ends on an unresolved chord. Here is a pointed illustration of the change in Chekhov's handling of his material. The young storyteller by no means disdained what he called "a good plot." Only in his maturity did he lean toward narratives that, as Galsworthy put it, were "all middle like a tortoise."

It is surprising that "An Unpleasantness" has not hitherto attracted the attention of translators. This tale belongs to the period when Chekhov was well past his apprenticeship. Reprinted many times, it was included in the edition of his collected works that he prepared in his last years in accordance with an exacting, if not unexceptionable, standard of literary merit. "An Unpleasantness" has more substance than many of his tales and the narrative interest which he was often content to forego. It has, beyond that, the psychological acuteness the reader has come to expect of him. Rooted in his experience and perception of life, it occupies a significant place among the stories that present the *intelligentzia:* oversensitive, cerebral, often inept and futile, yet when "it thinks and feels honestly and is capable of work," as he wrote in his notebook, the source of "the strength and salvation of the people." In concentrating on a specific social problem, notably the lamentable lot of the doctors employed in zemstvo hospitals, the narrator also manages to bring home a larger truth: that something is rotten in the state of Russia. The shadow of his country's destiny lies, however lightly, on these pages. The nature of the evil, and how it can be done away with, is clearly not his affair. Programs of action, systems of ideas meant little to him. The only credo that he formulated was couched in the most general terms: "My holy of holies is the human body, health, intelligence, talent, inspiration, love, and absolute freedom—freedom from force and falsehood, no matter how the last two manifest themselves." This offhand statement from one of his letters has often been quoted, and deservedly so. The fact that he starts with the human body reminds us that it is the credo of one who was a physician as well as a writer. The entire passage is a secularist's confession of faith in his fellowmen.

The present volume is the first to offer an English translation of another substantial narrative that could also have been called "An Unpleasantness." Written in the winter of 1897-98, while Chekhov was staying in Nice for his health, it belongs to the period when the measure of his gifts was fully evident. A magazine editor had asked him for "an international story" with a foreign locale. Such a piece, he replied, he could compose solely in Russia. "I can write only from memory," he added; "I never write directly from life. The subject must pass through the sieve of my memory, so that alone what is important or typical remains there as on a filter." And he sent the editor "A Visit to Friends," the visit in question being to an estate near a station within a two hours' ride from Moscow.

The decay of the landowning class figures in this story, as it does in "Other People's Misfortune." But while in the earlier piece the sad predicament of the Mikhailovs, faced with the loss of their patrimony, is treated with compassion, no sympathy is wasted on the similarly circumstanced family of gentlefolk in the later story. (The attitude toward the world of the feckless landed gentry reflected in *The Cherry Orchard* is at bottom an ambivalent one.) A tale of disenchantment that mixes melancholy with scorn, "A Visit to Friends" has a certain astringency about it. Discernible here is the note—muffled, it is true—that is heard now and then in Chekhov's later work and that sounds clearly in "Betrothed," the last story from his pen. It is the motif of revolt. It bodes not only yearning for a renewal of life, but the rejection of compromise, the breaking away from a stuffy, confining existence ruled by stupidity and injustice.

"Peasants" is an example of Chekhov's humane art that the fewest of his narratives surpass, or, indeed, equal. The recent publication of a sequel to it, even though incomplete, is therefore something of a literary event. The newly disclosed text, a precious, if slight, addition to Chekhov's *oeuvre*, is offered here together with the story of which it is a continuation. He had apparently planned a large canvas, which was to deal with the lower depths both in urban and rural life. Characteristically enough, in the end he limited the scope of the tale and therewith cut it down to a kind of novella. It remains a major contribution to his anatomy of Russian society. He was a short-winded writer. Or perhaps he saved his breath to sing a greater number of songs, like the bird in Daudet's fable that he quoted in his notebook.

Half a dozen unfinished stories are printed in the recently published definitive edition of Chekhov's writings. There are particularly compelling passages in the fragment that takes as its title the medical term: "De-compensation." It was one of the last pieces with which he was occupied. If its completion does not present the challenge of *The Mystery of Edwin Drood*, it nevertheless offers a grateful opportunity to the perceptive Chekhovian.

The two versions of "On the Harmful Effects of Tobacco," with which Part II of this book opens, illustrate the change that came over Chekhov's writing with the passage of time. The original version, which dates from 1886, and which is here for the first time offered in English, is straight farce. In the second, composed sixteen years later, the farcical verve is somewhat toned down, and toward the end of the piece the henpecked husband abandons his absurd posturings and, breaking down, allows a brief view of the ugly actuality.

The two short pieces that follow the "Monologue for the Stage" afford a glimpse of an aspect of Chekhov's work which is new to his foreign public. From the first, the youthful humorist tried his hand at journalism, and for over two years, while living in Moscow, contributed a fortnightly correspondence to a weekly in the capital. These breezy, gossipy, often biting paragraphs—he did not flinch from muckraking—touched on everything, from the unsanitary condition of the tenements to women's fashions. Even as an established author, he would occasionally write a theatrical notice, an obituary, an editorial, for a leading Petersburg daily. "Moscow Hypocrites" and "Good News" exemplify these later pieces. In the first he speaks up, and vigorously, for the Moscow sales clerks against their employers. His remarks about the Russian national character in "Good News" must be read in the light of his belief that he belonged to a sterile, spiritless, Laodicean generation and lived in "a flabby, sour, dull time." This belief weakened as the country emerged from the doldrums of the eighties and early nineties, and felt the stir that preceded the abortive revolution of 1905-06.

The last two inclusions are bound up with a puzzling episode in Chekhov's life. On May 3, 1890 (N.S.) he left Moscow and made his way across Siberia, reaching Sakhalin, Russia's Far Eastern prison island, on July 23. The Trans-Siberian Railroad was yet to be built, and if he traveled some of the way by rail and steamer, he covered many of those six thousand weary miles by coach. "Across Siberia" is a forthright record of a part of this journey, set down while he was on the road and dispatched in instalments to a Petersburg daily. He was rather dissatisfied with these sketches, finding that they said more about his own thoughts and feelings than they did about Siberia. But the account does not strike one as unduly subjective. The emphasis is on the external world—both the natural scene and the men and women who people it. Of course, the personal note is unavoidable in writing of this kind, and one is grateful for it, since all that Chekhov left behind by way of autobiography is what may be gathered from his letters to intimates. Besides retailing his day-to-day experiences, the author occasionally voices his private opinions and beliefs, such as his opposition to life sentences for criminals, his faith in Siberia's glorious future.

His homeward journey, by way of the Indian Ocean and the Black Sea, furnished a glowing contrast to the miseries of his trip to the bleak island and his stay there. Late in December he was back at his desk in Moscow. The three months that he spent on Sakhalin he occupied himself making an intensive study of the penal colony there. This was not perhaps what alone had prompted him to undertake the arduous journey, one that, given the state of his health, was hazardous as well, to that man-made inferno. Before his departure he had given his friends several conflicting and rather unconvincing reasons for his venture. It is not impossible that, as David Magarschack, his latest biographer, has surmised, he was really running away from a passionate involvement with a married woman. It is nevertheless certain that a strong motive was his desire to acquaint the public with the lot of a segment, perhaps the most wretched segment, of Russia's convict body. He knew that in the prisons throughout the country numberless men and women were being depraved and destroyed "carelessly, thoughtlessly, barbarously," as he put it in a letter, and he blamed not the authorities, but himself and all his compatriots. Hence he felt it to be his duty to try, single-handed, as was characteristic of him, to advance the cause of prison reform. What could be more effective than telling people truthfully what he saw with his own eyes of the workings of the system? He belonged to a generation that had not lost faith in the power of enlightenment. "Man will become better," he wrote in his notebook, "when you show him what he is like."

The fruit of Chekhov's investigation of convict life on Sakhalin was not a tract, not a pamphlet but a rather poorly organized, if sober and candid book: a cross between a personal memoir and a lumbering sociological monograph. In addition to pages that might have come from Dostoevsky's *House of the Dead*, it contains thumbnail sketches of individual convicts and settlers, as well as population statistics, weather tables and other geographical data, and scraps of historical information. After having been serialized in a monthly, the work came out separately in 1895. It does not seem to have been instrumental in improving the condition of the convicts. It is noteworthy that Chekhov made no attempt to use any of this material in his fictions. He built "with the blocks quarried in the deeps of his imagination and on his personal premises," as Henry James declares the artist must. Siberia and Sakhalin were not Chekhov's personal premises.

"Yegor's Story," with which our volume concludes, is an excerpt from *The Island of Sakhalin (Travel Notes)*, but a thing complete in itself. It is a piece of documentary writing, innocent of any attempt to tamper with the facts or to reshape the raw stuff in hand. The uncouth talk of the convict is rendered in all its earthy crudity with dictaphone faithfulness. The peasant in question is rather unlike the tillers of the soil whom Chekhov usually pictures. The man is caught in the machinery of the state, but he is not crushed by it. A solid figure, calling to mind Platon Karatayev in *War and Peace,* he has a toughness and resilience that one has learned not to expect from Chekhov's characters. Yet this unvarnished true story bears a curious resemblance to the narratives of his invention. There is something about it that is essentially Chekhovian. It is not so much a certain inconclusiveness, due to the doubt as to whether Yegor is guilty of the murder for which he is serving time or is the victim of a miscarriage of justice. Rather, it lies in the fact that these few pages, as unemphatic as they are honest, reveal the cruel power of accident, that they leave with the reader a suggestion of the inherent pathos of man's lot. Is this a case of life imitating art, Chekhov's art?

Avrahm Yarmolinsky

1 stories

because of little apples

Somewhere between the Euxine Pontus and the Solovetzki Islands in the White Sea, at certain degrees of latitude and longitude, on his own black earth, a landowner by the name of Trifon Semyonovich had been dwelling for many years. His acres numbered 8000. His estate was, of course, mortgaged and for sale. It had been put on the market before Trifon Semyonovich developed a bald spot, but it had not been sold yet, owing to the gullibility of the bank manager and the resourcefulness of Trifon Semyonovich. Sooner or later the bank would fail, because Trifon Semyonovich, like so many others of his kind, pocketed the loan, but paid no interest, and on the rare occasions when he did pay something on account, he made a great ceremony of it.

If this world were not this world, and things were called by their proper names, Trifon Semyonovich would be called by the name given to bears and wolves. Frankly, Trifon Semyonovich was a beast. I invite him to agree with me. If this invitation reaches him (he sometimes reads *The Dragonfly**), he will probably not get angry, for he has

* The weekly in which this story appeared. *Ed.'s note.*

some intelligence and he may indeed fully accept my view. What is more, in gratitude for my not having revealed his surname, he may even display his generosity by sending me a dozen of his tart winter apples in the Fall. I shall not mention all his virtues: to do so would require a tome the size of Eugène Sue's *Wandering Jew*. I shall not touch on his cheating at preference, or the tricks he plays on the priest and the deacon, or his horseback rides through the village streets in the attire of the times of Cain and Abel. I shall confine myself to one scene which characterizes his attitude towards his fellowman.

One fine morning—this was at the end of summer—Trifon Semyonovich was walking in his luxuriant orchard. Whatever inspires Messrs. the poets was generously scattered about, and seemed to say: "Here, take it, man! Enjoy yourself, before autumn is upon us!" But Trifon Semyonovich did not enjoy himself that morning: he was no poet and, besides, he was out of sorts because he had lost money at cards the previous night. Behind Trifon Semyonovich walked his faithful servant, Karpushka, an old fellow of about sixty, darting glances all about him.

He is almost superior in virture to Trifon Semyonovich himself. He blacks boots wonderfully, hangs unwanted dogs, steals everything he can lay hold of, and is an excellent spy. The village clerk nicknamed him Hangman, and he is known thus throughout the district. Hardly a day passes without a complaint being lodged against Karpushka by peasants and neighboring landlords, but Trifon Semyonovich pays no attention, for Karpushka is irreplaceable. When Trifon Semyonovich goes for a walk, he always takes Karpushka along: it is safer and jollier. Karpushka is unable to hold his tongue, he is always chattering.

On the morning in question he walked behind his master, telling him how two high school boys in white caps had tried to bribe him to let them hunt on his master's grounds, and how he had refused the fifty copeck piece and how he had sicked Chestnut and Gray on them. When he was through with this tale, he began to describe the revolting habits of the village feldscher [medical assistant], when suddenly he seemed to hear a suspicious rustling sound from the clump of apple and pear trees. He stopped, cocked his head and began to listen. Having convinced himself that the sound was a suspicious one, he tugged at his master's jacket and dashed in the direction of the noise. Trifon Semyonovich, anticipating an incident, started, and ran after Karpushka with an old man's mincing steps.

On the edge of the orchard, under an old, spreading apple tree, stood a peasant girl, munching. Nearby, a broad-shouldered peasant lad was crawling on his knees and collecting windfalls. The green apples he threw into the bushes, the ripe ones he tenderly presented to his Dulcinea on his broad, gray palm. Dulcinea, apparently careless of her stomach, kept munching the apples with relish, and the lad seemed to have no thought for himself and to be concentrating his whole attention on Dulcinea.

"Pick one off the tree!" the girl egged him on in a whisper.

"I'm scared."

"What are you afraid of? The Hangman is probably in the pot-house . . ."

The lad got to his feet, jumped high, picked an apple from the tree and offered it to the girl. But the lad and his lass, as Adam and Eve of old, had no luck with their apple. No sooner did she take a bite and share it with the lad, no sooner did both of them taste the acid on their tongues than their faces lengthened, blanched, were distorted—not because the apple was sour, but because they beheld the stern face of Trifon Semyonovich, and Karpushka's maliciously grinning little mug.

"How do you do, my dear friends!" said Trifon Semyonovich. "You're eating little apples? Perhaps I've disturbed you?"

The lad pulled off his cap and hung his head. The girl began to examine her apron.

"Well, how are you, Grigory?" Trifon Semyonovich turned to the lad. "How are you getting on, my boy?"

"It was only one," mumbled the lad, "and I picked it off the ground. . . ."

"And how are you, sweetheart?" Trifon Semyonovich asked the girl.

She fell to studying her apron even more intently.

"You haven't celebrated your wedding yet, have you?"

"Not yet . . . I swear, Master, we've had only one, and it was—sort of—"

"Very well, very well. You're a capital fellow. You know how to read?"

"No . . . But I swear, Master, we took only one, and off the ground."

"You don't know how to read, but you know how to steal. Well and good. You're not weighed down with knowledge. When did you start stealing?"

"I wasn't stealing."

"Well, and your sweetheart here," Karpushka put in, turning to the lad, "why has she grown so thoughtful? You don't love her enough, is that it?"

"Hold your tongue, Karp," said Trifon Semyonovich. "Well, Grigory, entertain us: tell us a fairy tale . . ."

Grigory coughed, and smiled crookedly.

"I don't know any fairy tales, Master," he said. "I don't need your apples. If I want apples, I can buy them."

"I'm glad to know that you've plenty of money, my boy. Well, do tell us a fairy tale. I'll listen to it, Karp here will listen, your charming sweetheart will listen. Don't be shy, be bold. A thief must be bold. Isn't that so, my boy?"

And Trifon Semyonovich stared spitefully at the lad. The unlucky fellow's face became beaded with sweat.

"You'd better get him to sing a song, Master. The fool isn't up to telling fairy tales," Karpushka interposed in his ugly, thin, tremulous tenor.

"Shut up, Karp, let him tell a story first. Well, go on, my boy!"

"I don't know how."

"Is it possible you don't know how? But you know how to steal? How does the eighth commandment go?"

"Why do you ask me? I don't know. I swear, Master, we've only eaten one apple, and that off the ground."

"Begin the story!"

Karpushka started picking nettles. The boy knew very well what that meant. Trifon Semyonovich, like many of his kind, had a fine way of dealing out penalties to thieves who fell into his clutches. He locked them up in a cellar for twenty-four hours, or flogged them with nettles, or, having stripped them to the skin, sent them off. Is that news to you? There are people with whom such behavior is as common as a cart.

Grigory looked at the nettles out of the corner of his eye, hesitated a while, cleared his throat, and started telling a fairy tale, or rather making up stuff and nonsense. Sighing, sweating, hawking, blowing his nose ever so often, he began to spin a tale in which knights bested wicked old men and married beautiful maidens. Trifon Semyonovich stood listening, without taking his eyes off the narrator.

"Enough!" he said, when finally the lad lost the thread of the tale, and began mumbling whatever balderdash came into his head.

"You're good at telling fairy tales, but you're better at stealing. And you, my beauty," he turned to the girl, "recite the Lord's Prayer."

The pretty girl blushed and, scarcely able to breathe, almost inaudibly recited the prayer.

"Now how does the eighth commandment go?"

"You think that we have taken a lot?" asked the lad, and threw up his hands in desperation. "I'll swear on a cross, if you don't believe me."

"It's a bad thing, my children, that you don't know the commandments. I must give you a lesson. Did he teach you to steal, my beauty? Why don't you answer, my angel? You must answer. Speak! You are silent? Silence means assent. Well, my beauty, because your sweetheart has taught you how to steal, give him a beating!"

"I won't," whispered the girl.

"Beat him up a bit. Fools must be taught a lesson. Give him a beating, my darling! You'd rather not? Very well, then I'll have Karp and Matvey use the nettles on you . . . You still won't?"

"I'm not going to."

"Come here, Karp."

The girl rushed headlong at the lad and slapped him on the face. He smiled sheepishly and tears came into his eyes.

"That's capital, my beauty! Now, pull his hair for him! Go to it, my angel! You don't want to? Karp, come here!"

The girl clutched her sweetheart's hair.

"Don't stand still! Drag him by the hair!"

The girl obeyed. Karpushka was in ecstasies, guffawing and shrieking in his tremulous voice.

"Enough!" said Trifon Semyonovich. "Thank you, darling, for having given wickedness its due. And now," he turned to the lad, "teach your girl a lesson. She beat you, now you give her a beating . . ."

"What things you think of, Master! Why should I give her a beating?"

"You ask why! She gave you a beating, didn't she? Now you thrash her. That'll do her good. You don't want to? You'll regret it. Karp, call Matvey."

The lad spat, hawked, grasped his sweetheart's braid, and began to give wickedness its due. As he was doing so, without realizing it he was carried away, and in his ecstasy forgot that he was thrashing not Trifon Semyonovich, but the girl he planned to marry. The girl started screaming. He kept on beating her for a long time. I don't know how it all would have ended, if Sashenka, Trifon Semyonovich's daughter, had not come running from behind the bushes.

"Papa, come and have tea!" she cried, and seeing what was going on, burst into peals of laughter.

"Enough!" said Trifon Semyonovich. "You can go now, my darlings. Goodby! I'll send you some little apples for the wedding."

And Trifon Semyonovich made a low bow to the miserable culprits.

The boy and girl set themselves straight as best they could and went off. The boy turned to the right, the girl to the left, and they have not met since. If Sashenka had not appeared, the two of them would probably have had a taste of the nettles. That's how Trifon Semyonovich amuses himself in his old age.

His children have taken after him. His daughters are in the habit of sewing onions onto the hats of guests of "low rank" and writing on the back of drunken guests of the same rank: "donkee" and "fool." One winter his darling son, Mitya, a retired second lieutenant, outdid even his papasha: with the aid of Karpushka, he tarred the gates * of a former private, because the man had refused to give the lieutenant a wolf cub, and also because he was alleged

* Tarring the gates defamed the women of the house and was indeed equivalent to the stigma of the scarlet letter. *Ed.'s note.*

to have prejudiced his daughters against the lieutenant's candy and gingerbread . . .

After this, call Trifon Semyonovich—Trifon Semyonovich!

1880

two in one

Don't you believe these Judases, these chameleons! Nowadays it is easier to lose your faith than your gloves—and I have lost it!

It was night. I was riding in a streetcar. As a highly-stationed personage it does not behoove me to ride in a streetcar, but this time I wore my greatcoat and could hide in my sable collar. It's also cheaper, you know. . . . In spite of the late hour and the cold, the car was crowded. No one recognized me. My fur collar made it possible for me to travel incognito. I was riding along, dozing or glancing at the common herd. . . .

"No, it isn't he!" I thought, looking at a little man in a coat lined and trimmed with catskin. "It isn't he! No, it is he! He himself!"

I considered the question, and I believed my eyes, and I didn't believe my eyes.

The little man in the catskin coat was the spit and image of Ivan Kapitonych, one of my clerks. Ivan Kapitonych is a small flattened creature looking habitually crestfallen, who lives only to pick up the handkerchief you drop and to wish you a happy holiday. He is young, but his back is bowed, he sags at the knees, and his arms, like a soldier's standing at attention, are aligned with the seam of his trousers. His face looks as though it had been squeezed between door and jamb, and clouted with a wet rag. It is sour and pitiful; looking at it, you want to whine or break into a mournful tune. When he sees me he shudders, turns pale, turns red, as if I were about to eat him alive or cut his throat, and when I give him a dressing down, he freezes and trembles all over.

I know no one humbler, more submissive, more of a cipher than he is. I don't think there is even an animal more shrinking than he.

The little man in the catskin coat strongly reminded me of this Ivan Kapitonych: the spit and image of him! Only he wasn't as bent as the other, did not seem crestfallen, behaved with familiarity, and, what was more revolting, he actually discussed politics with his neighbor. The whole car was listening to him.

"Gambetta is dead!" he was saying, fidgeting and waving his arms. "This plays into Bismarck's hands. Gambetta, you know, was a sly one! He would have fought the Germans and gotten reparations, Ivan Matveich! Because he was a great man. He was a Frenchman, but he had a Russian soul. A genius!"

Oh, you good-for-nothing!

When the conductor came up to him for the fare, he left Bismarck alone.

"Why is the car so dark?" he attacked the conductor. "Haven't you any lights, eh? What kind of mismanagement is this? The trouble is, there's no one to teach you a lesson. Abroad they'd give it to you! The public wasn't made for you, you were made for the public! Devil take it! I don't know what the authorities are thinking of!"

A moment later he demanded that we all move up.

"Move up! I mean you! Give the lady a seat! You there, you could be a little more polite! Conductor! Come here, conductor! You take the money, so see that people get seats! It's disgusting!"

"Smoking is not allowed," the conductor shouted at him.

"Who made that rule? Who's giving the orders? That's an invasion of my liberty! I will not tolerate anyone invading my liberty! I'm a free man!"

Oh, you worm! I looked at his little snout, and didn't believe my eyes. No, it's not he! It can't be! He doesn't know such words as "Gambetta," "liberty."

"Well, I declare, this is splendid management!" he exclaimed, throwing away his cigarette. "Try and get along with such gentlemen. They are crazy about regulations, about the letter of the law. Formalists, Philistines! It's stifling!"

I couldn't bear it any longer, and burst out laughing. Hearing it, he glanced at me, and his voice quavered. He recognized my laugh and must have recognized my greatcoat. Instantly his back curved, his face fell, his voice died away, his arms stiffened along the seams of his trousers, he sagged at the knees. Instantly he underwent a complete change. I no longer had any doubts: it was Ivan Kapitonych, my clerk. He sat down and hid his little nose in his catskin collar.

Now I stared at that face of his. "Is it possible," I asked myself, "that this crestfallen, flattened mannikin knows how to say such words as 'Philistine,' 'liberty?' Eh? Is it possible? Yes, he does. It's incredible, but true . . ." Oh, you worm!

After this, put your trust in the miserable faces of these chameleons! I no longer do. Enough—you're not going to hoodwink me!

1883

perpetuum mobile

An elderly investigating magistrate, Grishutkin, who had entered the service even before the Emancipation, and Dr. Svistitzky, a melancholy soul, were on their way to an autopsy. They were driving along a country road. The autumn night was pitch dark and rain was coming down in buckets.

"It's vile," the magistrate grumbled. "There's no civilization, there's no humanity, and there's not even a decent climate. What a country! And to think that this is Europe. . . . The rain! The rain! As though it were being paid to come down, the blackguard! Drive faster," he shouted at the man on the box, "or I'll kick your teeth in, you good-for-nothing, blast you!"

"It's an odd thing, Agey Alexeich," said the doctor, sighing and drawing his wet coat closer about him. "I don't even notice this weather. I feel a strange, oppressive dread. It seems to me as if some misfortune were about to overwhelm me. I believe in forebodings, and . . . I'm waiting. Anything can happen. Blood poisoning . . . the death of someone you love. . . ."

"You ought to be ashamed to speak of forebodings, you old woman, at least in the presence of Mishka up there. Nothing can be worse than this. Such rain—what can be worse? You know what, Timofey Vasilich, I simply can't go any farther. For the life of me, I can't go on. We must stop somewhere for the night. Who lives in the neighborhood?"

"Ivan Ivanych Yezhov," said Mishka from the box. "Just beyond these woods, across the bridge."

"Yezhov? Off to Yezhov! I haven't visited the old sinner for a long time, by the way."

They went through the woods, crossed the bridge, and drove into the large courtyard of the manor house of Major General Yezhov, chairman of the circuit court.

"He's at home!" said Grishutkin, climbing out of the carriage and looking up at the windows, which were lit. "It's a good thing that he's at home. We'll eat and drink our fill and have a good night's sleep. He's a worthless fellow, but hospitable, you've got to do him justice."

In the anteroom they were met by Yezhov himself, a little, wrinkled old man, with a face puckered into a bristly ball.

"You've come at the right moment, gentlemen, at the right moment," he began. "We've just sat down to supper and we're having pork, thirty-three in a trice. You know, we have the assistant district attorney with us. He stepped in to fetch me, bless him. Tomorrow we have to drive out to attend a session of the court. There's a session tomorrow. Thirty-three in a trice."

Grishutkin and Svistitzky entered the dining hall. A big table stood there, heaped with appetizers and wines. One place was occupied by the daughter of the house, Nadezhda Ivanovna, a dark-haired young woman in deep mourning for her husband, who had died recently. Next her sat the assistant district attorney, Tulpansky, a young man with side whiskers, and many blue veins in his face.

"You are acquainted?" asked Yezhov, pointing to each in turn. "This is my daughter, this is the district attorney."

The young woman smiled, and screwing up her eyes gave her hand to the newly arrived guests.

"And so . . . as you are fresh from the road, gentlemen!" said Yezhov, pouring out three glasses. "Don't hold back, bless you! I'll have one, too, just to keep you company, thirty-three in a trice. Well, now, our healths!"

They emptied the glasses. Grishutkin had a gherkin and attacked the pork. The doctor downed his glass and sighed. Tulpansky, having asked the lady's permission, lit a cigar, and in the act bared his teeth so that it seemed as if he had a hundred of them in his mouth.

"Well, gentlemen? The glasses are waiting! Eh? District Attorney? Doctor? I drink to medicine! I love medicine. And I love youth, thirty-three in a trice. Say what you may, youth will always go forward. Well, now, our healths!"

They fell to talking. All took part in the conversation, except the district attorney, who sat there, held his peace, and blew tobacco smoke out of his nostrils. It was obvious that he considered himself an aristocrat and despised the doctor and the examining magistrate. After supper Yezhov, Grishutkin, and the district attorney sat down to play whist with a dummy. The doctor and Nadezhda Ivanovna seated themselves near the piano and engaged in conversation.

"You are on your way to an autopsy?" began the pretty widow. "To cut up a corpse? Ah, what strength of will, what iron character it takes to lift the knife and plunge it to the hilt into a dead body, without so much as wincing or blinking an eye. You know, I revere physicians. They are people apart, saintly people. Doctor, why are you so melancholy?" she asked.

"I have a foreboding. . . . I'm oppressed by a strange, dark foreboding. As though the loss of a loved one awaited me."

"Are you married, doctor? You have a family?"

"Not a soul. I'm alone, I haven't even any friends. Tell me, madam, do you believe in forebodings?"

"Oh, yes, I do."

While the doctor and the little widow were discussing premonitions, the host and the magistrate would leave the card table from time to time and go over to the sideboard, which was laden with drinks and appetizers. At two in the morning Yezhov, who had lost heavily at cards, recalled the morrow's court session and slapped his forehead:

"Saints be with us! What are we doing? We're wicked, wicked! Tomorrow at dawn we have to drive to the session, and here we are playing cards! To bed, to bed, thirty-three in a trice! Nadya, time to sleep! I declare the meeting adjourned!"

"You're lucky that you can sleep on such a night, doctor," said Nadezhda Ivanovna, bidding the physician goodnight. "I cannot sleep when the rain drums on the windows and my poor pine trees groan. Now I'll go and bore myself with a book. I can't sleep. In general, if the light from a small lamp on the window sill near my door is visible in the passage, it means that I'm awake and consumed by boredom . . ."

In the room assigned to them the doctor and Grishutkin found two huge beds, made up on the floor, complete with feather beds. The doctor undressed, lay down, and pulled the blanket over his head. The magistrate undressed and lay down, but for a long time kept turning and twisting, and finally got up and began to pace the room. He was a very restless fellow.

"I keep thinking about this little lady, the charming widow," he said. "What a morsel! I would give my life for her! Eyes, shoulders, legs in lilac stockings . . . a hot dish! Wow, what a woman! You can see it at a glance! And to have such a honey nabbed by the devil knows whom—a jurist, a district attorney! By that scrawny nincompoop, who looks like an Englishman! I can't stand these jurists, brother! When you were discussing premonitions with her, he was ready to burst with jealousy. No two ways about it, she's a chic little piece, remarkably chic! One of Nature's marvels!"

"Yes, an estimable woman," said the doctor, poking his head out from under the blanket. "Impressionable, high-strung, sympathetic, so responsive. You and I will fall asleep presently, but she, poor thing, can't sleep. Her nerves can't bear such a stormy night. She told me that she would not know what to do with herself and would have to stay up, reading. Poor thing, that little lamp is sure to be burning now. . . ."

"What little lamp?"

"She said that if a little lamp is burning on the window sill near her door, it means that she's not sleeping."

"She said this to you, to you?"

"Yes, to me."

"In that case, I don't understand you! If she said this to you, then you are the happiest of mortals! Bravo, doctor! Bully for you! I congratulate you, friend! I envy you, but I congratulate you. I'm glad not so much on your account, but because of that jurist, the redheaded cad. I'm glad that you'll cuckold him! Well, get dressed! March!"

Grishutkin, in his cups, was unceremonious with everyone.

"You're inventing all this, Agey Alexeich! God knows what you're saying . . ." the doctor retorted, bashfully.

"Now, don't argue, doctor! Get dressed and off with

you . . . How does it go in *Life for the Czar?* 'And on the path of love we pluck a day as though it were a flower' . . . Get dressed, my dear boy. Come on! Timosha! Doctor! Get a move on, you dolt!"

"Excuse me, I don't understand you."

"What is it you don't understand? Is this astronomy? Get dressed and go where the little lamp is burning—that's all there is to it."

"Strange, that you have such an unflattering opinion of this lady and of me."

"Stop philosophizing!" Grishutkin lost his temper. "Is it possible you're still hesitating? Why, that's cynicism!"

For a long while he tried to persuade the doctor; he spoke angrily, he implored, he even went down on his knees. He ended with a loud curse, spat, and flung himself on his bed. A quarter of an hour later he jumped up and waked the doctor.

"Listen! You positively refuse to go to her?" he asked severely.

"But what should I go for? What a restless man you are, Agey Alexeich! It's torture to drive to an autopsy with you!"

"Then, damn you, *I'll* go to her! I'm no worse than a jurist or an old woman of a doctor. *I'll* go!"

He dressed rapidly and went to the door.

The doctor looked at him inquiringly, as if not understanding what he was about, then jumped up.

"This is a joke, I assume," he said, barring Grishutkin's way.

"I have no time to talk to you. . . . Let me pass!"

"No, I'm not going to let you pass, Agey Alexeich. Go to sleep. . . . You're drunk."

"By what right, medico, do you bar my way?"

"By the right of a man whose duty it is to protect a lady.

Agey Alexeich, come to your senses, what do you want to do? You're an old man! You're sixty-seven!"

"I—an old man?" Grishutkin took offense. "What scoundrel told you that I'm an old man?"

"You've had a drop too much, Agey Alexeich, and you're excited. It's wrong! Don't forget that you're a human being, not an animal! It's all right for an animal to obey its instincts, but you are the crown of creation, Agey Alexeich!"

The crown of creation grew purple and thrust his hands into his pockets.

"For the last time I ask you: will you let me pass, or not?" he suddenly screamed in a piercing voice, as though he were shouting at the driver on the country road. "You blackguard!"

But at once he was taken aback by his own shout, and moved away from the door to the window. Drunk as he was, he now felt ashamed of his outburst, which must have awakened everyone in the house. After a pause, the doctor went over to him and touched him on the shoulder. The doctor's eyes were wet, his cheeks ablaze.

"Agey Alexeich," he said in a trembling voice, "after your sharp words, after you called me a blackguard, in defiance of all the proprieties, we cannot, you will agree, remain under the same roof. You've insulted me frightfully. . . . Let's assume that I'm to blame, but . . . what am I to blame for? A decent, high-minded lady, and all of a sudden you allow yourself such expressions. Excuse me, we are no longer friends."

"Excellent! I don't want such friends."

"I'm leaving immediately, I can no longer remain under the same roof with you and . . . I hope we never meet again."

"How will you travel?"

"I have my carriage and pair."

"What am I going to do? Come, do you want to go on behaving like a scoundrel? You brought me here, you are obliged to see that I get to my destination."

"I'll give you a lift, if you wish. Only at once . . . I'm leaving right now. I'm so upset that I cannot stay here another moment."

The two men dressed in silence and went out into the courtyard. They waked Mishka, got into the carriage and drove off.

"A cynic . . ." the magistrate kept muttering as they drove along. "If you don't know how to behave with decent women, then stay home, don't pay visits where there are women in the house. . . ."

It was difficult to understand whether he was reproving himself or the doctor. When the carriage halted before his house, he jumped out and, as he disappeared behind the gate, called out:

"We are no longer acquainted!"

Three days went by. The doctor, having made his rounds and come home, was lying on his couch, and, having nothing to do, was reading the list of Moscow and St. Petersburg doctors in the *Physicians' Almanac*, trying to choose the most beautiful and sonorous name. His mood was one of complete well-being, as unclouded and serene as an immaculately blue sky in which a lark hangs motionless, and that, because the previous night he had dreamed of a fire, which was an omen of happiness.

Suddenly he heard a sleigh (it had snowed in the night) stop in front of the house, and Grishutkin appeared on the threshold. This was an unexpected guest. The doctor sat up and looked at him in embarrassment and not without apprehension. The investigating magistrate coughed, dropped his eyes, and slowly moved toward the couch.

"I've come to apologize, Timofey Vasilich," he began. "I was rather rude to you and, I fear, even said something unpleasant. You will, of course, understand that I was in an agitated state at the time, because of the liqueur that I drank at that old blackguard's. Please forgive me."

The doctor jumped up and with tears in his eyes shook the hand that was stretched out to him.

"But, of course . . . Marya, tea!"

"No, let's not have tea. There's no time. Instead of tea, have some kvass served, if possible. We'll have some kvass and go to an autopsy."

"What autopsy?"

"But it's the same non-commissioned officer that we were going to open up, only we never got there."

The two men had some kvass and drove off to the autopsy.

"Of course, I apologize," the magistrate was saying, as they drove along. "I lost my temper then. Nevertheless, it hurt me, you know, that you didn't cuckold the district attorney, the blackguard."

As they were passing through Alimonovo, they noticed Yezhov's troika in front of the tavern.

"Yezhov is here!" said Grishutkin. "That's his team. Let's go in and have a word with him. We'll have a glass of seltzer and while we're at it have a look at the little barmaid. They have a famous barmaid here. Wow, what a woman! One of Nature's marvels!"

The travelers climbed out of the sleigh and entered the tavern. Yezhov and Tulpansky were sitting there, having tea with cranberry juice.

"Where are you bound for? Where do you come from?" Yezhov was amazed to see Grishutkin and the doctor.

"We keep going to an autopsy and somehow can't get there. We've gotten into a vicious circle. Where are you going?"

"We're on our way to the court session, old man."

"What, again! You were going to the court session the other day."

"The devil we were! The district attorney had a toothache and I was under the weather, too, all that time. What'll you have? Join us, thirty-three in a trice. Will it be vodka or beer? Give us both, ducky," he called out. "Ah, what a barmaid!"

"Yes, a famous barmaid!" the investigating magistrate agreed. "A prize barmaid! Wow, what a woman!"

Two hours later the doctor's Mishka emerged from the tavern and told the major general's coachman to unhitch the horses.

"That's the master's orders. They're playing cards," he said, and threw up his hands. "We're not going to get out of here till tomorrow. But look now, here's the chief of police coming! That means we'll be stuck here till the day after tomorrow."

The chief of police drove up to the tavern. Seeing Yezhov's team, he smiled with pleasure, and ran up the steps.

1884

the skit

Dinner was over. The cook was ordered to clear the table as quietly as possible and not to make a noise either with the dishes or her feet. The children were sent to play outside. Osip Fyodorych Klochkov, the host, a gaunt, consumptive man with sunken eyes and a sharp nose, pulled a manuscript out of his pocket and, clearing his throat in embarrassment, began to read a skit of his own composition.

The plot of his short skit was simple and there was nothing in it to offend the censor. Here it is. A government clerk by the name of Yasnosertsev runs onto the stage and announces to his wife that they are about to receive a visit from the ranking official in his department, no less a person than Councilor of State Kleshchov, who had taken a fancy to their daughter Liza. Follows a long monologue by Yasnosertsev on the pleasures of being the father-in-law of a general! "He's simply covered with stars . . . and there's red piping on his trousers, and you sit next to him and—nobody minds! As if you're really not the smallest cog in the whirligig of the universe!" Dreaming thus, the future father-in-law suddenly notices that there is a strong smell of fried goose in the flat. It is awkward to receive an important guest if there is an unpleasant odor in the rooms, and Yasnosertsev starts to bawl his wife out. The wife, exclaiming: "There's no pleasing you!" begins to howl. The future father-in-law tears his hair and commands his wife to stop crying, for superiors are not received with red eyes. "You fool, go wash your face, you brainless mummy." The wife goes into hysterics. The daughter declares that she cannot live with such quarrelsome parents, and gets dressed to leave the house. Things go from bad to worse. It ends with the important guest finding on the stage a doctor who is applying Garland's extract to the bruises on the husband's forehead, and a police officer, who is drawing up a report on the breach of the peace. That's all. The author also manages to bring on the scene Liza's fiancé, Gransky, a law school graduate, an "advanced" character, who talks about principles, and in the skit seems to exemplify the principle of virtue.

As Klochkov read, he kept glancing at the company out of the corner of his eye to see if they were laughing. To his satisfaction, the guests now and then crammed their fists into their mouths and exchanged looks.

"Well? What do you say?" Klochkov, having finished reading, appealed to his public. "How is it?"

In reply Mitrofan Nikolayevich Zamazurin, the eldest guest, with a fringe of white hair on a scalp as bald as the moon, rose and embraced Klochkov with tears in his eyes.

"Thank you, old man," he said. "That was a treat. You've described it all so well that you even brought tears to my eyes. . . . Let me embrace you once more."

"Excellent! Remarkable!" exclaimed Polumrakov, jumping up. "A genius, a real genius! You know what, brother? Resign from the service and take up writing! Write, write! It's wicked to hide your light under a bushel."

There were congratulations, transports, embraces. . . .
They sent for Russian champagne.

Klochkov turned crimson, lost his bearings, and in his
excitement began to ambulate about the table.

"I have felt this talent working in me for a long time!"
he said, coughing, and waving his arms. "Almost from
childhood . . . I write decently, I'm not without wit. . . .
I know the stage—I've taken part in amateur theatricals
for the past ten years. . . . What more do I need? If I do
a little work in this field, learn certain things—in what way
am I inferior to others?"

"Learn certain things, indeed!" said Zamazurin. "There
you're right. . . . Only here's what I'd say, old man. You
must excuse me, but I stand for the truth. The truth above
all else. You bring in Kleshchov, Councillor of State. . . .
That's not right, my dear fellow. Essentially, it's nothing,
and yet it's awkward, somehow, you know. You take a
general, and you—errh . . . Give it up, brother. Our own
chief may get angry, he may imagine that you have him
in mind. The old man may take offense. And so far he's
been very decent to us. Chuck it!"

"That's true," Klochkov grew troubled. "I'll have to
make a change. . . . I'll substitute 'your Honor' for 'your
Excellency' everywhere. Or else I'll just have no rank—
simply: Kleshchov."

"And here's another thing," Polumrakov observed. "Of
course, it's a trifle, but it, too, is out of the way . . . it hits
you in the face. . . . You have Gransky, the fiancé, tell
Liza that if her parents oppose their union, he'll marry her
anyway. Perhaps this is a small matter . . . perhaps parents
really are sometimes brutes, the way they tyrannize over
their children, but nowadays, how shall I put it? I'm afraid
you'll get it in the neck!"

"Yes, it's a bit strong," Zamazurin agreed. "You ought
to smooth over that passage somehow . . . And you

should cut out that speech about how pleasant it is to be your superior's father-in-law. Yes, it *is* pleasant, but you poke fun at it. It's no laughing matter, brother. Our chief, too, married a girl without money; does it mean that he did something wrong? Is that your opinion? Wouldn't it offend him? Well, suppose he goes to the theatre and sees this skit of yours . . . Will he like it? And remember, he backed you when both you and Salaleyev applied for a subsidy! 'He's a sick man,' he said, 'he needs money more than Salaleyev does.' Don't you see?"

"You were taking him off, weren't you? Admit it," Bulyagin said, winking at the author.

"Not at all!" protested Klochkov. "I wasn't thinking of anybody in particular, I swear!"

"Come, come—you can't fool us! We all know he chases after skirts. You've caught *that*. But you know what? Cut out that police officer. Better do without him. . . . And you don't want this Gransky, either. A hero, God knows what department he's in, and he talks so queerly. . . . It would be all right if you condemned him, but, on the contrary, you cotton to him. Maybe he is a decent sort, but the devil himself couldn't figure him out! You can imagine almost anything about him. . . ."

"And do you know who that Yasnosertsev is? It's the Yenakin in our office. Klochkov certainly had him in mind. A titular councillor, he and his wife are always fighting, there's a daughter, too. . . . That's him to the life. Thanks, friend! Serves the blackguard right! You've taken him down a peg!"

"True enough, but there's something else to be said about Yenakin," Zamazurin said, with a sigh. "A bad egg, a rascal, still, he always invites you to his house, he's godfather to your Nastya. . . . It's not right, Osip! Leave him out of it! It's my opinion you ought to give up this kind of business, by God. Before you know it there'll be talk: who, how, why? You'll only regret it!"

"That's so," Polumrakov chimed in. "It's tomfoolery, but this tomfoolery may cause trouble that it will take ten years to set right. It's a mistake to start all this, Osip. You're not the one to try to be a Gogol or a Krylov. They were, really, men of learning; but what education did you get? You're a worm, you're too small to be seen! A fly can crush you. Give it up, brother! If our chief finds out, then . . . Chuck it!"

"Tear it up!" whispered Bulyagin. "We won't tell anybody. If they ask us, we'll say that you read something to us, but that we didn't understand it."

"Why say anything? There's no need to talk," declared Zamazurin. "If they ask us, well, then . . . we're not going to lie. A man thinks of himself first. . . . That's how it is: you people do all kinds of mischief, and others have to pay for it! I get the worst of it. You're a sick man, no one will call you to account, but we won't be spared. I don't like it, by God!"

"Quiet, gentlemen! Someone's coming. . . . Put it away, Klochkov."

Klochkov, turning pale, quickly hid his manuscript, scratched the back of his head, and grew thoughtful.

"It's true," he sighed. "There'll be talk . . . all kinds of guesses. . . . Maybe there's something in my skit that we don't see but others will find there. . . . I'll tear it up. And you, friends, please . . . don't say anything to anybody."

The Russian champagne was brought in. The guests drank it, and dispersed.

1884

worse and worse

A lawyer by the name of Kalyakin was sitting with Gradusov, the choirmaster of the cathedral, in the latter's living room. Turning about in his fingers a summons from the justice of the peace addressed to the choirmaster, the lawyer was saying:

"You must admit, Dosifey Petrovich, you are guilty. I respect you, I appreciate your friendly attitude toward me. Nevertheless, I must say, though it hurts me, that you were in the wrong. Yes, sir, in the wrong. You insulted my client, Derevyashkin. . . . Tell me, why on earth did you insult him?"

"Who the devil insulted him?" burst out Gradusov, a tall old man with a low forehead that promised little, heavy eyebrows, and a brass medal in his lapel. "All I did was to talk morals to him, that's all! Fools must be taught! If you don't teach fools, they'll be all over the place."

"But, Dosifey Petrovich, it wasn't a lesson that you gave him. As he states in his petition, you addressed him as an inferior in public, and, what's worse, you called him an ass, a scoundrel, and so forth. . . . And once you even raised your hand, as if you were going to do him bodily injury."

"Well, why not thrash him if he deserves it? I don't understand."

"But realize that you have no right to do it!"

"I have no right? No, excuse me . . . that's a bit thick. Come off of it, and don't pull my leg! After they'd discharged him honorably from the archbishop's choir and kicked him out of there, he sang in my choir for ten years. I'm his benefactor, if you please. If he's sore because I threw him out of the choir, it's his own fault. I threw him out for philosophizing. And if you're a fool with no brains, then you sit in your corner and hold your tongue. . . . Hold your tongue, and listen to what intelligent people say. But he, the blockhead, he'd go out of his way to put his oar in. Here we're rehearsing or a mass is being sung, and he has to have something to say about Bismarck and about all kinds of Gladstones. Will you believe me, the blackguard has actually subscribed for a newspaper! And how many times I punched him in the jaw because of the Russo-Turkish War—that you can't even imagine! Here we have to get on with the singing and he leans over to the tenors and begins telling them how we blew up a Turkish ironclad with dynamite. Is that the way to act? Of course, it's nice that we won a victory. But that doesn't mean you stop singing. You can talk about these things after the mass is over. In one word: a swine."

"So you insulted him even before this?"

"Before this he didn't take offense. He felt that I was doing it for his own good, he understood why I did it. He knew that it is a sin to talk back to your elders and your benefactors, but when he became a clerk in the police station—why, then he got a swelled head and took leave of his senses. 'I'm no choir singer,' says he, 'I'm an official. I'm going to take an examination so as to get the rank of filing clerk.' 'Come,' says I, 'what a fool you are! You should cut down on your philosophizing and wipe your nose a little oftener, and that would be better than to be thinking about ranks. Rank isn't for the likes of you, you just look for humble pie. He wouldn't hear of it! Or take this very case—why is he dragging me into court? Isn't he the scum of the earth? I was sitting in Samopluyev's tavern, having tea with our churchwarden. The place was jammed, not a table to be had. . . . I looked round and there he was, with the other clerks, swilling beer. Dressed to kill, his snout in the air, shouting and waving his arms. . . . I kept my ears open—he was talking about the cholera epidemic. . . . Well, what can you do with a fellow like that? He was philosophizing! I kept mum, you know, I suffered. . . . Gab away, I thought, gab away. . . . The tongue has no bones. . . . Suddenly, as ill luck would have it, the machine started playing. He got worked up, the hoodlum, got to his feet and harangued his chums: 'Let's drink,' said he, 'to the prosperity of . . . ! I am a son of my fatherland,' said he, 'a born Slavophil! I'll shed my blood so it waves forever! Where's the enemy? Come on out! I'll take on whoever don't agree with me!' And he banged the table with his fist! That was more than I could stand. . . . I went up to him and said politely: 'Listen, Osip . . . If you don't understand anything, you swine, then you'd better shut up and don't hold forth. An educated man may air his opinions, but you should take a back seat. You're a louse, you're scum. . . .' For every word I said, he had ten. . . . And the fat was in the fire. Everything I said, of course, I said for his own good, but with him, it was his stupidity that was talking. . . . He took offense—and now he is haling me into court. . . ."

"Yes," said Kalyakin, sighing. "It's too bad. . . . Something trifling happens, and the devil knows what the results are. . . . You're a family man, well thought of, and here this lawsuit comes along, there's talk, gossip, possible arrest. . . . You must put an end to this business, Dosifey Petrovich. You have one way out, which suits Derevyash-kin, too. You will go to Samopluyev's tavern with me to-day at six o'clock, when the clerks and the actors and the others in whose presence you insulted him gather there, and you'll apologize to him. Then he will withdraw his petition. Understand? I hope you will agree to it. I'm speaking to you as a friend. . . . You insulted Derevyashkin, you shamed him, above all, you cast suspicion on his praiseworthy sentiments, you even . . . disparaged those sentiments. In these times, you know, that's not done. You must be more careful. Briefly, your remarks have been interpreted in a way that in these times, you know . . . It's now a quarter to six. Will you please come with me?"

Gradusov shook his head, but when Kalyakin vividly painted for him the interpretation placed on his words and the consequences which this interpretation could have, Gradusov took fright and consented.

"Now be sure and make your apology properly, in the right way," the lawyer instructed him, as they were walking toward the tavern. "Go up to him and address him politely, say: 'Excuse me, I withdraw my remarks,' and so on, and so forth."

On arriving at the tavern, Gradusov and Kalyakin found a whole crowd there. Merchants were present, and actors, petty officials, police clerks—all the 'rabble' that was in the habit of gathering there of evenings to have tea or beer. Sitting with the clerks was Derevyashkin himself, a fellow of uncertain age, with a shaven chin, big, unblinking eyes, a squashed nose, and hair so coarse that looking at it, you conceived the desire to clean your boots. His face was so tellingly built that a glance was sufficient to let you know that he was a drunkard, that he sang in a bass voice, that he was stupid, but not so stupid as to fail to consider himself very intelligent. Seeing the choirmaster, he half rose to his feet and twitched his whiskers like a cat. The crowd, apparently informed beforehand that there would be a public penance, pricked up its ears.

"Here, Mr. Gradusov has agreed," said Kalyakin, entering.

The choirmaster greeted a few people, blew his nose noisily, flushed, and went up to Derevyashkin.

"I apologize," he mumbled, without looking at him, and putting his handkerchief back in his pocket. "In the presence of everyone here, I take back my words."

"I accept your apology," Derevyashkin said in a bass voice, and glancing round triumphantly at the company, he sat down. "I'm satisfied. Mr. lawyer, please stop the proceedings."

"I apologize," Gradusov continued. "Forgive me . . . I don't like unpleasantnesses. You want me to address you formally—all right, I will. You want me to consider you intelligent—very well. I don't give a damn. I don't bear grudges, brother. Devil take you!"

"But, allow me, you were supposed to apologize to me, not swear at me."

"How else should I apologize? I have apologized! If I wasn't consistent about addressing you formally, that's just a slip of the tongue. I'm not to go down on my knees to you, am I? I apologize, and I even thank the Lord that you have enough sense to drop the case. I've no time to hang around the court. . . . In all my life I never yet went to law, I'm not going to law, and if you listen to your betters, excuse the expression, you'll take my advice and not go to law, either."

"Right you are! Won't you have a drink with me on the Peace of San Stephano?"

"I don't mind a drink. Only, Osip, you are a swine, brother. . . . I'm not swearing at you, it's just an expression. You're a swine, brother! Do you remember that time when you were grovelling before me, on your knees, after they kicked you out of the archbishop's choir? Eh? And you dare to hale your benefactor into court! You're a cur, a cur! And you're not ashamed? Gentlemen, I ask you, shouldn't this fellow be ashamed?"

"Allow me! But this is calling names again!"

"Who's calling names? I'm just talking, teaching you how to behave. . . . We've made up, and I'm telling you, for the last time, that I have no intention of swearing at you. . . . Catch me getting mixed up with you, you fiend, after you've tried to hale your benefactor into court! To hell with you! I don't even want to talk to you. And if I happened to call you a swine by accident just now, well, you really are a swine! . . . Instead of praying for your benefactor all your born days, because for ten years he fed you and taught you your notes, you file a stupid complaint against him and set a devil of a lawyer, a whole pack of them, on his trail!"

"Permit me, Dosifey Petrovich," put in Kalyakin, offended. "It was no devil who called on you: it was I. Please be a little more careful."

"Was I talking about you? You can call on me every day and welcome. But what astonishes me is that you, an educated man, a university graduate, instead of instructing this gander, you take his part! If I were you, I would send him to rot in prison! And besides, what are you angry about? I apologized, didn't I? What more do you want of me? I don't understand. Gentlemen, be my witnesses: I have apologized, and I have no intention of apologizing a second time to some idiot!"

"You're an idiot yourself," Osip brought out hoarsely, and struck his chest in an access of indignation.

"I'm an idiot? I! And you can say this to me?" Gradusov turned crimson and trembled. "You dared say it? Then take this! And the slap I just gave you, you scoundrel, isn't all: I'm going to take you to court. I'll show you what it means to insult a man. Gentlemen, be my witnesses. Officer, what's the matter with you, standing there just looking on? I'm being insulted and you don't lift a finger. You get your pay, but when it comes to keeping order, is it your business or not, eh? You think the law can't touch you?"

The police officer crossed over to Gradusov, and then the fun began.

A week later Gradusov was facing the justice of the peace, accused of having insulted Derevyashkin, the lawyer, and the police officer, the last as he was in the course of performing his official duties. At first he did not understand whether he was the plaintiff or the defendant, and when, finally, the justice sentenced him to a term of two months in jail, he smiled bitterly and muttered:

"H'mm, I was insulted and I am to do time! Queer . . . Your Honor, one must try a case according to law and not according to notions. Your dear mama, the late Varvara Sergeyevna, the Kingdom of Heaven be hers, would have had fellows like Osip flogged, and you back them up. What will be the result? You will acquit these rascals, another judge will acquit them. . . . With whom, then, can one lodge a complaint?"

"You may file an appeal within two weeks. . . . And please watch your tongue. You may go."

"Certainly . . . Everybody knows that nowadays you can't get along on just your salary," Gradusov brought out, with a meaningful wink. "Willy-nilly, if you want to eat, you put an innocent man into the cooler. That's how it is, and you can't blame a person . . ."

"What!"

"Nothing, sir. I was just, errh . . . I was talking about *haben Sie gewesen.* . . . You think that because you wear a gold chain you're above the law. Never mind, I'll show you up."

So now Gradusov was facing a charge of contempt of court. But the dean of the cathedral stepped in and somehow it was quashed.

When he appealed to the district court Gradusov was convinced that not only would he be acquitted, but that Osip would be clapped into jail. He clung to this conviction while the case was being tried. Standing before the justices, he behaved peaceably, with restraint, and said little. Only once, when the chairman invited him to sit down, he took offense and said:

"Is it written in the statute books that a choirmaster should sit next to one of his singers?"

When the court confirmed the verdict of the justice of the peace, he screwed up his eyes.

"What, sir? How's that, sir? he asked. "What do you mean, sir?"

"The district court has confirmed the verdict of the justice of the peace. If you're not satisfied, you may appeal to the senate."

"Yes, sir. My heartiest thanks, your Excellency, for this prompt and just verdict. Of course, one can't get along on just his salary nowadays. That I understand perfectly. But excuse me, we shall yet find a court that cannot be bribed."

I shall not repeat everything that Gradusov said to the district court. At present he is on trial again for contempt, but this time of a higher court, and he refuses to listen to friends who try to explain to him that he is to blame. He is convinced of his innocence and believes that, sooner or later, they will thank him for the abuses he has disclosed.

"There's nothing to be done with this fool," declared the dean, throwing up his arms, "he just doesn't understand."

1884

vint

One nasty autumn night Andrey Stepanovich Peresolin was being driven home from the theatre. As he rode along he meditated on the fact that theatres could be such useful institutions if only the plays produced there were of an improving nature. He was driving past the Provincial Administration building when he stopped his utilitarian meditations and directed his gaze to the windows of the building where, to use the language of poets and skippers, he was at the helm. Two windows in the secretaries' room were brightly lit.

"Can it be they're still busy with that report?" Peresolin wondered. "There are four of them there, and the fools haven't finished yet! Heaven help us, people may think I keep them working all night. I'll go and hurry them up. Stop, Gury!"

Peresolin climbed out of the carriage and walked toward the building. The front door was locked, but the back door had a broken latch and was open. Peresolin took advantage of this, and a moment later he was standing at the entrance to the secretaries' room. The door was ajar and Peresolin, looking in, was amazed at the sight that met his eyes. At the table, on which lay a pile of large sheets covered with figures and which was lit by a couple of lamps, sat four government clerks playing cards. Tense, immobile, their faces green with the reflection of the lampshades, they resembled the gnomes of the fairy tales or, God forbid, counterfeiters. . . . The game they were playing made them appear even more mysterious. To judge from their behavior and the card terms that they shouted from time to time, they were playing vint. To judge from everything else that Peresolin heard, however, they were occupied neither with vint nor any other card game. It was something unheard-of, weird, fantastic. Peresolin recognized the clerks to be Serafim Zvizdulin, Stepan Kulakevich, Yeremey Nedoyekhov and Ivan Pisulin.

"How are you leading, you Dutch devil?" Zvizdulin shouted angrily, glaring with exasperation at his partner opposite. "What kind of a lead is that? I had Dorofeyev, protected, in my hand, besides Shepelev and wife, and Yerlakov. You lead Kofeikin. And here we've lost two tricks! And you, you cabbage head, you should have led Pogankin!"

"What good would it have done?" his partner snapped. "Suppose I had led Pogankin—Ivan here has Peresolin in his hand."

"They're bandying my name about," Peresolin said to himself, shrugging his shoulders. "I can't make head or tail of it."

Pisulin dealt again, and the players continued:

"State Bank."

"Two Treasury."

"Got no ace."

"You haven't an ace? H'm! Two Provincial Administration. If I lose, then I lose, what the devil! Before, because I led Ministry of Education, I was cleaned out, and now I'll get into hot water with Provincial Administration. I don't give a damn."

"Small slam, thanks to my Ministry of Education!"

"I don't get it," whispered Peresolin.

"I lead State Councilor. Vanya, throw off a wee Titular Councilor or a Provincial Secretary."

"Why throw off a Titular? Anyway, we'll do something with Peresolin yet."

"We'll knock the stuffing out of Peresolin. We've got Rybnikov. You'll lose three tricks. Well, bring out Peresolin's missus: don't hide the bitch in your cuff."

"That's my wife they're talking about," thought Peresolin. "I don't get it."

Peresolin could not bear to remain in the dark any longer; he swung the door open and entered the room. If the Devil himself, with horns and tail, had materialized before the clerks, he wouldn't have astonished and terrified them as their Chief astonished and terrified them. If their colleague who had died the previous year had appeared there and said in a spectral voice: "Follow me, bless you, to the place prepared for rascals," and if he had breathed upon them the chill of the grave, they would not have blanched as they did when they recognized Peresolin. Fright gave Nedoyekhov a nosebleed. Kulakevich felt a drumming in his right ear, and his tie came loose of itself. The clerks threw down their cards, rose slowly, and after glancing at one another, fixed their gaze on the floor. For a moment silence reigned in the room.

"So that's the way you copy the report!" Peresolin began. "Now I understand why you like working on the report so much. What were you doing just now?"

"It was just for a minute or two, your Excellency," muttered Zvizdulin. "We were just looking at the cards . . . resting. . . ."

Peresolin approached the table and slowly shrugged his

shoulders. On the table lay not ordinary cards, but photographs of the usual size removed from their cardboard mats and pasted on playing cards. There were many such. Looking them over, Peresolin recognized himself, his wife, a number of his subordinates and acquaintances.

"It's absurd! How do you play?"

"We didn't invent this, your Excellency . . . God forbid! We just picked it up . . ."

"Explain it to me, Zvizdulin. How were you playing, anyway? I saw it all, and I heard how you topped me with Rybnikov. What are you fidgeting about, friend? I'm not going to eat you. Go ahead, tell me."

For a while Zvizdulin held back, in embarrassment and some fear. Finally, when Peresolin lost his temper, snorted and got red with impatience, he obeyed. Having collected the cards and shuffled them, he laid them out on the table and began his explanation:

"Each picture, your Excellency, just like a card, has its meaning . . . its value. . . . As in a regular pack, there are 52 cards and four suits. Treasury officials are hearts, Provincial Administration officials are clubs, those in the Ministry of Education are diamonds, and the employees of the State Bank are spades. Well, sir . . . Actual Councilors of State we count as aces, State Councilors as kings, their spouses as queens, Collegiate Councilors are jacks, Court Councilors are tens, and so on down. For instance, I, here's my card, I'm a three, since I am a Provincial Secretary."

"Well, think of that! That makes me an ace?"

"Ace of clubs. And her Excellency is queen of clubs."

"H'mm, that's original! Well, let's have a game. I'll see what it's like."

Peresolin took off his overcoat and, smiling skeptically, sat down at the table. At his behest, the clerks, too, sat down, and the game commenced.

When, at seven o'clock in the morning, Nazar, the porter, came in to sweep the secretaries' room, he was amazed. So striking was the picture he beheld when he entered with his mop that he still remembers it, even when he lies stupefied with drink. Peresolin, pale and sleepy-looking, his hair mussed, was standing in front of Nedoyek-hov, whom he had buttonholed, and was saying:

"Get it into your head that you couldn't lead Shepelev if you knew that in my hand I had myself, and the next three in the same suit. Zvizdulin had Rybnikov and wife, three high school teachers, and my wife; and Kulakevich had State Bank people and three small ones from the Provincial Administration. You should have led Kryshkin! You should have paid no attention to the fact that they led the Treasury. They're foxy."

"Your Excellency, I led a Titular Councilor because I thought that they had an Actual Councilor of State."

"Oh, my boy, that's no way to think! That's no game! Only shoemakers play that way. Consider: when Kulakevich led a Court Councilor you should have thrown off Ivan Ivanovich Grenlandsky, because you knew that he had Natalya Dmitryevna and two more in that suit, and Yegor Yegorych besides. You ruined everything! Here, I'll prove it to you. Sit down, gentlemen, we'll play another rubber."

And sending away the astounded Nazar, the company sat down and resumed the game.

1884

two of a kind

"You must by all means call on Baroness Scheppling (with two p's), *mes enfants*," my mother-in-law repeated for the tenth time, seeing my bride and me into a hackney coach. "The Baroness is an old friend of mine. . . . And while you're about it, go to see Madam Zherebchikov, the General's widow. She will be offended if you don't visit her."

We drove off to pay our post-nuptial calls. My wife's countenance, it seemed to me, took on an appropriate expression of solemnity, but my face fell and I was overcome with melancholy. . . . My wife and I differed in many particulars, but none caused me such torment as the dissimilarity between her connections, her friends, and mine. The list of her acquaintances was peppered with the wives of Colonels and Generals, such people as the Baroness Scheppling (with two p's), Count Derzai-Chertovshchinov, and a slew of aristocratic schoolmates, alumnae of the Institute for the Daughters of the Nobility. On my side there was nothing but solid common-herdishness: an uncle who was a retired warden, a female cousin who was a dressmaker, the petty officials who were my colleagues, all drunks and good-for-nothings, not one of them with a rank above that of a titular councilor, the merchant Plevkov, and such small potatoes. I was embarrassed. . . . To avoid disgrace, I should simply have omitted calling on these people, but not visiting them would have led to reproaches and a good deal of unpleasantness. I could perhaps skip my cousin, but a visit to my uncle and to Plevkov were unavoidable. From my uncle I had borrowed money for expenses incidental to the wedding, and to Plevkov I owed money for furniture.

"Darling, we are approaching my uncle Pupkin's house," I said to my bride in a tender tone, meant to soften her. "He comes of an old family of gentlefolk, and *his* uncle is a diocesan bishop. But he's quite a character and lives like a pig—I don't mean the bishop, it's my uncle I'm speaking of. I'm taking you there so that you can have a good laugh. . . . He's a terrible blockhead. . . ."

The hack stopped near a small house with three windows and rusty grey shutters. We got out of the carriage and rang the bell. There was the sound of loud barking and then a firm: "Shsh, you devil!" followed by yelping and a rumpus behind the door. This went on for quite a while; finally the door opened and we stepped into the entry. We were met by my youngest cousin, Masha, a little girl with a dirty nose, wearing a blouse of her mother's. I pretended not to recognize her and went over to the clothes tree. On it hung my uncle's foxfur-lined overcoat, a pair of trousers and a starched skirt. As I was taking off my galoshes, I peered timidly into the living room. There, at table sat my uncle in a dressing gown with slippers on his bare feet. My hope of not finding him at home was dashed. Screwing up his eyes and breathing noisily, he was taking orange peel out of a vodka decanter with a piece of wire. He had an air of anxious concentration as though he were inventing the telephone. We walked in. On seeing us, Pupkin was overcome with embarrassment, let the wire fall from his fingers, and grabbing the skirts of his dressing gown he shot out of the room.

"In a moment!" he called out.

"We've routed him . . ." I laughed, burning with shame and afraid to look at my wife. "Isn't he funny, Sonia? What a character! And look at this furniture! A three-legged table, a paralytic piano, a cuckoo clock . . . You'd imagine that not people were living here but antediluvian creatures."

"What's this a drawing of?" asked my wife, looking at a picture that was hanging between photographs.

"Oh, that's St. Seraphim feeding bears in the Sarov Monastery. And this is a portrait of the bishop when he was still the rector of a seminary. You see, he's wearing a decoration. Quite a respectable personage . . . I . . ." (I blew my nose).

But nothing distressed me as much as the odor. The place smelled of vodka, rotten oranges, coffee grounds and the turpentine that my uncle used to keep out moths, a sharp, sour blend. My cousin Mitya entered, a high school boy short for his age, with big ears that stuck out, and scraped his foot politely. He picked up the orange peel, removed a cushion from the couch, brushed the dust off the piano with his sleeve and left the room. Apparently he had been sent to "tidy things up."

"Here I am," my uncle said finally, buttoning his waistcoat as he came in. "Here I am. Delighted, I'm sure. Please sit down. Only don't sit on the couch, the back leg is broken. Sit down, Senya."

We sat down. A silence fell, during which Pupkin stroked his knee, and I tried not to look at my wife and felt embarrassed.

"M-myes," my uncle began, lighting a cigar (in the presence of guests he always smoked cigars). "So you're mar-

ried. . . . Well . . . On the one hand, it's a good thing
. . . A dear creature beside you, love, billings and coo-
ings . . . On the other hand, when children start coming,
there'll be weeping and gnashing of teeth. Boots for this
one, pants for that one, highschool tuition for a third . . .
Lord protect us! Half of mine were stillborn, thank God."

"How are you feeling?" I asked, in an attempt to change
the subject.

"Poorly, my boy. Just lately I spent the whole day in
bed. I had a pain in the chest, chills, fever. The wife said:
'Take quinine, and don't fret.' How can I help fretting?
In the morning I gave orders to have the snow removed
from the porch and nobody paid any attention. No one
lifted a finger. But I can't do it myself, I'm a weak, ailing
man, with piles moving round inside of me."

My embarrassment mounted, and I began to blow my
nose vociferously.

"Or maybe it's because of the baths," my uncle continued, looking pensively at the window. "Maybe. On
Thursday, you know, I went to the baths and I steamed
myself for three hours. Steam is apt to make piles worse.
. . . The doctors say that baths are not good for you. . . .
Madam, that isn't so. I've been taking steam baths since my
childhood, because my father owned public baths in Kiev.
I would steam myself all day long. Didn't have to pay a
kopeck."

I was ready to sink through the floor. I got up and stam-
meringly began to take leave.

"Leaving already?" said my uncle, astonished, and
clutched me by the sleeve. "Your aunt is coming directly.
We'll have a bite, it'll be potluck, but there's some corned
beef and fruit brandy. And Mitya just went out to get
some sausage. . . . What society airs you're putting on!
You're getting a swelled head, Senya. It's wrong. And you
didn't order the wedding dress from Glasha. My daughter,

Madam, is a dressmaker. . . . I know it was made by Madame Stepanide, but Stepanidka is not a patch on us. Besides, we would have charged less. . . ."

I don't remember how I took leave of uncle, how I got into the hack. I felt as though I had been spat upon, annihilated, and I expected momentarily to hear the contemptuous laugh of my wife, alumna of the Institute of the Daughters of the Nobility.

"And what boorishness awaits us at Plevkov's!" I thought, freezing with horror.. "If only we could get through with it quickly, devil take the lot of them!" As bad luck would have it, there wasn't one general among my acquaintances! I know a retired colonel, but he keeps a pothouse. How unfortunate I am!

"Sonechka," I turned to my wife and said in a tearful voice, "you must forgive me for having taken you to that pigsty just now. . . . I thought I would give you a chance to have a laugh, to observe queer types. . . . It isn't my fault that it turned out to be so vulgar, so vile . . . I apologize!"

I glanced timidly at my wife and what I saw exceeded my worst apprehensions. Her eyes were full of tears; her cheeks were burning, whether with shame or anger, I couldn't tell; her fingers were fitfully plucking at the fringe that bordered the carriage window. I felt flushed and started in my seat.

"I'm disgraced!" I thought, my arms and legs as heavy as lead. "But it isn't my fault, Sonia!" I wailed. "Isn't it silly of you! They're vulgar, coarse, yes, but see here: I didn't pick them out as relatives!"

"If you don't like your folks," she said, with a little sob and an imploring look, "then I don't know how you'll bear mine. . . . I was ashamed, and I couldn't bring myself to tell you . . . Honey, darling. . . . Baroness Scheppling will start telling you that Mama used to be her housekeeper, that Mama and I are ungrateful creatures, that we don't thank her for former favors, now that she's reduced to poverty. . . . But please don't believe her! The brazen baggage likes to tell lies. . . . I swear to you that every holiday we send her a head of sugar and a pound of tea!"

"But you're joking, Sonia!" I brought out, the lead vanishing from my limbs and a life-giving lightness filling my whole body. A head of sugar and a pound of tea for the Baroness! Heavens!"

"And when you meet General Zherebchikov's widow, don't laugh at her, darling. She's so unhappy! If she cries the whole time and talks idiotically, it's because she was robbed by Count Derzai-Chertovshchinov. She'll complain of her lot and try to borrow money from you; but don't . . . don't . . . give her any. It would be all right if she spent it on herself, but she'll only give it to the Count!"

"Darling . . . angel! . . ." I cried, hugging my wife in ecstasy. "Sugarplummikins! . . . but what a grand surprise! If you told me that your Baroness goes out walking in her birthday suit, you'd please me even more! Give me your little hand!"

And suddenly I was sorry that I had refused uncle's corned beef, that I hadn't tickled his paralytic piano, hadn't sipped some of that fruit brandy . . . But then I recalled that at Plevkov's they served good cognac and sucking pig with horseradish.

"To Plevkov's!" I shouted to the coachman at the top of my voice.

1885

drowning

a little scene

The quay of a wide, navigable river is bustling with the activity usual there on a summer afternoon. The loading and unloading of barges is in full swing. The air is thick with ceaseless cursing and the hissing of steamers. "Chrrrly-chrrrly" moan the windlasses. There is a heavy smell of smoked fish and pitch.

An agent of the Scribbler shipping firm is sitting at the very edge of the water, waiting for a consignor. He is approached by a stocky individual with a terribly ravaged, bloated face, who is dressed in a ragged jacket and patched striped trousers. He wears a faded cap with a broken visor and the mark left by a long since vanished badge. His tie has parted from his collar and rides up on his neck.

"My compliments, sir merchant!" the individual ejaculates hoarsely, with a military salute. "Evviva! How would you like to see a drowned man, your worship?"

"Where is your drowned man?" asks the agent.

"Actually, there is no drowned man, but I can impersonate him for you. A leap into the water and—and a drowning man perishes before your eyes. The tableau is

not tragic but ironical, in view of its comic features. . . .
Allow me to perform for you, sir merchant!"

"I'm no merchant."

"I regret my mistake. *Mille pardons* . . . Nowadays
merchants dress like everybody else, so that Noah himself
wouldn't be able to tell the clean from the unclean. But it's
all the better that you are a member of the educated classes.
. . . We shall understand each other. I, too, belong to the
gentry. I am the son of a commissioned officer, and at one
time I was accorded the rank of the fourteenth degree.*
. . . And so, milord, a master of arts is offering you his
services. . . . One leap into the water, and there is a
tableau before you."

"No, thank you."

"If considerations of a material nature trouble you, I
hasten to reassure you. . . . For you the fee will be a small
one. . . . Two rubles for drowning myself with my boots
on, one ruble—without them."

"Why the difference?"

"Because boots are the most expensive item of attire, and
the hardest to dry. Ergo, you will allow me to earn an
honest ruble?"

"No, I'm not a merchant, and I don't fancy such thrills."

"H'mm . . . I'm afraid that you are laboring under a
false impression. You seem to think that I'm offering you
something crude and vulgar, but I assure you, sir, it'll be
nothing but humorous and satirical. You will smile an extra
smile, and that's all. Isn't it funny to see a man fully dressed
battling with the waves? And besides, you will give me a
chance to earn an honest ruble."

"Instead of impersonating a drowning man, you ought to
do some useful work."

"Useful work . . . and what work would that be? No
one will give me employment in keeping with my station,

* The lowest degree in the bureaucratic hierarchy. *Ed.'s note.*

because I'm inclined to alcoholism, and further, for that you have to be able to pull wires. And a man of my rank cannot bring himself to accept manual labor."

"To hell with your rank."

"What do you mean: to hell with it?" the man says with a smirk, throwing back his head haughtily. "If a bird understands that it's a bird, how can a person of rank fail to understand what he is? I may be impoverished, yes, ragged, destitute, but I have my purr-rride—I'm proud of my birth!"

"Yet your pride does not prevent you from swimming around fully dressed."

"I blush! Your remark has its ingredient of bitter truth. One can see that you are a person of culture. But before casting a stone at a sinner, hear me out. True, there are many individuals among us who forget their dignity and allow ignorant merchants to plaster their heads with mustard, or who will smear themselves with soot in the public baths to masquerade as the devil, or even put on women's clothes and perform all sorts of indecencies: but me—you won't find me doing anything like that. No matter how much money a merchant offers me, I will not permit him to plaster my head with mustard or any other less ignoble substance. But I see nothing shameful in impersonating a drowning man. Water is a wet, clean object. Submersion will not soil you, quite the contrary: it cleanses you. Nor is medicine against it. However, if it doesn't suit you, I can reduce the fee. . . . So be it, I'll drown myself with my boots on for one ruble."

"No, I'm not interested."

"But why not, sir?"

"I don't care about it, that's all."

"You should see me gurgle and gasp in the water. There's no man the length of this river who drowns better than I do. If Messrs. the doctors could see the face I make when I'm dead, they'd give me a medal. Well, just for you I'll bring it down to sixty kopecks. You're the first customer, I'll do it for you cheap. I wouldn't perform even for three rubles if it were anybody else, but I see by your face that you are a kind gentleman. . . . The educated I charge less."

"Please leave me alone!"

"Just as you say. Freedom for the free, salvation for the saved. Only you're making a mistake. Another day you'll be ready to spend ten rubles, but you won't find a drowning man. . . ."

The individual sits down not far from the agent and, breathing heavily, begins to rummage in his pockets.

"Hmm . . . damn it . . ." he mumbles. "Where's my tobacco? I must have left it on the dock. . . . I got carried away arguing with an officer about politics, and I mislaid my cigarette case. There is a cabinet crisis in England now. People are queer! I wonder, could you let me have a cigarette, your Honor?"

The agent hands him a cigarette. At that moment a merchant, the consignor for whom the agent has been waiting, appears on the scene. The individual leaps to his feet, hides the cigarette in his hand and gives a military salute.

"My compliments, your Worship!" he brings out hoarsely. "Evviva!"

"Ah, it's you!" says the agent to the merchant. "You've kept me waiting quite a while. And this character here has been wearing me out. He keeps pestering me by offering to perform. For sixty kopecks he undertakes to impersonate a drowning man. . . ."

"Sixty kopecks? That's overcharging, brother," says the merchant, turning to the derelict. "Twenty-five kopecks is the outside price. Why, the other day thirty men acted out a whole shipwreck for us, and it didn't cost us more than a fiver, and you—you ask sixty kopecks! Well, I'll give you thirty kopecks!"

The individual puffs out his cheeks and smirks contemptuously.

"Thirty kopecks! . . . Nowadays you have to pay that much for a head of cabbage, and you want a drowned man for the same price. That won't do."

"Never mind, then. I have no time to bother with you."

"Well, all right, since you're the first customer. Only don't tell the other merchants that I've done it so cheaply."

The man takes off his boots and, lifting his chin, approaches the water with a frown and clumsily throws himself in. There is the thud of a heavy body falling into the water. Coming to the surface, he waves his arms absurdly, kicks his legs and tries to force an expression of panic. But, instead of showing panic, his face twitches with cold.

"Drown! Drown!" the merchant shouts. "You've done enough swimming—drown!"

The man blinks his eyes and, spreading his arms wide, sinks under the water. That's the end of the performance. Having "drowned," the individual climbs out of the water and, on receiving his thirty kopecks, walks off, wet and shivering with cold.

1885

the village elder

a little scene

In one of the dirty little taverns of the district town of N—— elder Shelma * is sitting at a table eating kasha that drips with fat, and after every three spoonfuls he gulps down a glass.

"Yes, my friend, peasant cases are hard to tackle," he says to the tavern keeper, his fingers under the table fumbling at his jacket as it keeps coming unbuttoned. "Yes, brother, peasant cases are such tricky business they'd stump even Bismarck. To handle them, you've got to have brains of a special kind, you've got to have the knack. Why do the peasants love me? Why do they stick to me like flies? Eh? And why do I eat kasha dripping with fat, while others in the law business eat their kasha dry? It's because I have brains, a talent, a gift."

Shelma empties a glass noisily and stretches his dirty neck importantly. Not only is this man's neck dirty. His hands, his ears, his shirt, his trousers, his napkin, everything about him is dirty.

* The word means "rascal." *Ed.'s note.*

"I'm not a man of learning. Why lie? I never took no degree. I'm not one of those wiseacres in a frock coat. But I can tell you without false modesty, brother, and without exadjuration, that you couldn't get another such jurist for a million. Of course, don't expect me to handle the Skopino case * for you, or the Sarah Becker case.† But give me anything in the peasant line, and no counsel for the defense, no public prosecutor will be able to stand up against me. So help me, I'm the only one who can settle peasant cases, and nobody else. You can be a Lomonosov or a Beethoven, but if you don't have my talent, leave those things alone. For instance, take the case of the Replovo Elder. You've heard about that case?"

"No, I haven't."

"It was a great case! A tricky one! Plevako ‡ would have muffed it, but I won it. Yes, sir! Now, not far from Moscow there is a bell foundry. In that foundry, my friend, the manager is nobody but our own Replovo peasant, Yevdokim Petrov. He has been on the job there for twenty years. Of course, according to his papers, he's a peasant, a bumpkin in bast shoes, but to look at his appearance—it's not a peasant's. In twenty years he's been licked into shape, got a polish on him. He wears broadcloth, rings on his fingers, a gold chain across the belly—keep your distance! Not like a peasant at all. It's simple, brother: fifteen hundred a year, food and lodging thrown in, the owner chumming with you—willy-nilly you'll climb to where the gentry are. And his physiog-mony too is . . . how should I put it?" (He empties a glass). "It's impressive. So you see, brother, this Yevdokim Petrov gets it into his head to pay a visit to his birthplace, that is to our village of Replovo. He's been going along year after year, and all at once he

* A celebrated bank failure in the eighties. *Ed's note.*
† A celebrated murder case, 1884-85. *Ed's note.*
‡ A famous Moscow lawyer. *Ed's note.*

gets a longing, so to speak. You have it good at a bell foundry, and a manager there, you'd think, has no call to get a longing. But, as the saying goes, the smoke from the native hearth smells sweet. Go to America, sit there up to your neck in hundred dollar bills, and still you'll have a longing for your home pothouse. So he, poor fellow, felt the same way. Well, brother, he got leave for a week from the owner and went off. Now he comes to Replovo. First off, he goes to see his own folks. 'Here I used to live,' says he. 'Here I herded my father's cattle. Here I slept,' and so forth. In a word, childhood recollections. And of course, not without puffing himself up a bit: 'Look at me, friends, I used to be a bumpkin like you, but by labor and sweat I rose in the world. I'm rich and I have a full stomach. So, work like I did.' The clodhoppers listened to him at first, and made much of him, and then they thought; 'That's all very fine, friend, but what good does it do us? You've been here a week and you haven't stood anybody a glass.' They sent the constable to see him.

" 'Yevdokim, hand over a hundred rubles.'

" 'What for?'

" 'Vodka for the village. . . . The peasants want to drink your health.'

"Now Yevdokim is an orderly, holy-minded man. He won't touch vodka, he don't smoke, and he hates to see anybody else do it.

" 'For vodka,' he says, 'I wouldn't give a copper.'

" 'What right have you to talk that way? Ain't you one of us?'

" 'Well, what if I am! I've paid my taxes to the village. I'm not in arrears. Why should I be milked?'

"That's how the trouble started. Yevdokim argues one way, the village argues another. The peasants get their dander up. You know what fools they are. There's no drumming sense into their heads. They wanted to celebrate, so even if you explained it to them in a dozen languages or fired off a cannon, they wouldn't understand anything. They've raised a thirst, and that's that. Besides, it's aggravating: here's a man come home, well-heeled—and to think you can't squeeze anything out of him! They start scheming how to get Yevdokim to cough up a hundred rubles. The peasants rack their brains and get nowhere. They hang around his cottage, and all they can do is threaten him: 'We'll show you! We'll make you sweat!' But he sits there and don't care a bean. 'I'm clear,' he thinks to himself, 'before God and before the law and before the village community, too. What have I got to be afraid of? I'm a free bird.' Good. It's plain to the peasants that they'll no more see his money than they'll see their own ears. And they start thinking up ways to pluck the feathers of this free bird for showing no respect. They've no wits of their own, so they send for me. I come to Replovo. 'Thus-and-so,' they say, 'he won't hand over any money. Think up some scheme, Denis Semyonych.' Well, brother, there's no thinking up any scheme. Everything's aboveboard, Yevdokim is within his rights. No district attorney could figure out how to turn the trick, even if he spent three years figuring. The devil himself would be in a fog."

Shelma empties a glass and winks an eye.

"But I thought up a trick," he sniggers. "Yes, sir! Guess what I thought up! You never will. Not on your life. 'Here's my advice, lads,' says I. 'Elect him to be your village Elder.' They got the idea straight off, and elected him. So listen! They present Yevdokim with the Elder's badge. He laughs. 'You're joking,' says he. 'I don't want to be your Elder.'

" 'But we want you!'

" 'I just don't want to! I'm leaving tomorrow!'

" 'Oh, no, you're not! You have no right to leave. The law says an Elder can't give up his office.'

" 'In that case,' says Yevdokim, 'I'm resigning my office.'

" 'You've no right to. An Elder has got to hold office not less than three years, and there's no putting him out of office except by court verdict!'

"My Yevdokim howls bloody murder. He rushes off like a lunatic to the district Chief. The Chief and his clerk show him the statutes.

" 'According to article so-and-so you can't resign your office till three years are up. Serve for three years, then you're free.'

" 'Three years! I can't stay away even for a month! Without me my boss is helpless! His losses are running into thousands! And aside from the foundry, I have a home there, a family!'

"And so on. A month passes. Yevdokim presses not a hundred rubles on the community, but three hundred: 'Only let me go, for Christ's sake!' The peasants would be glad to take the money, but there's nothing to do about it; it's too late. Yevdokim drives over to his Honor the Permanent Member of the Board.

" 'Thus-and-so, your Honor, due to family circumstances, I can't hold office. Let me off, for God's sake!'

" 'I haven't the right. There are no lawful causes for discharge. In the first place, you're not sick; and in the second, you've committed no felony. You've got to hold office.'

"I must tell you that over at the Board they think nothing of addressing us peasants familiarly. A district Chief or a village Elder is a somebody in the Empire, more important than any pen-pusher of a clerk, but he's spoken to as if he was a flunkey. Imagine how Yevdokim in his broadcloth feels about it. He pleads with the Permanent Member, in Christ's name.

" 'I have no right,' says the Permanent Member. 'If you don't believe me, ask the County Office. They'll tell you the same thing. Not only I, but the Governor himself can't let you off. The decision of a village assembly, if the form is in order, can't be annulled.'

"Yevdokim goes to the district Chief of Police, from the Chief of Police he goes to the Marshal of the Nobility. He drives all over the county, and everybody tells him the same thing: 'You've got to hold office, we have no right to let you off.' What's to be done? And from the foundry comes letter after letter, wire after wire. A relative of Yevdokim advises him to call me in. So—believe it or not, he doesn't send for me, but rushes over to my place. He comes in, and, without saying a word, thrusts a ten ruble bill into my hand. Meaning: you're my one hope.

" 'Well,' says I, 'for a hundred rubles, I'll arrange to have you let off.'

"I got the hundred, and I arranged it."

"How?" asks the tavern keeper.

"Guess! It was simple. There's a clue to the riddle in the law itself."

Shelma comes close to the tavern keeper and, chuckling, whispers in his ear.

"I advised him to commit larceny and go on trial. Well! Quite a trick, eh? You can imagine, friend, that he was taken aback. 'What do you mean—steal?' 'That's just what I mean,' says I. 'Here: steal my empty wallet, and you get six weeks in jail.' At first he balked: 'My good name,' and so forth. 'The devil!' says I, 'what do you want your good name for? Do they keep an official record of a peasant? You'll spend six weeks in jail, that'll be the end of it, but then you've committed your felony, and they'll take away your badge!'

"The man thought a bit, threw up his hands, and stole my wallet.

"He's done his stretch, and he names me in his prayers. So there you see, my dear friend, what it is to have brains! In the whole universe you won't find such tricky business as in peasant cases. And if anybody can handle them, it's me. Nobody can get an annulment, but me, I can. Yes, sir!"

Shelma calls for another bottle of vodka and begins another story—of how the Replovo peasants drank away a stand of corn that didn't belong to them.

1885

saintly simplicity

Father Savva Zhezlov, the aged prior of the Church of the Holy Trinity in the one-horse town of P——, had an unexpected guest: his son Alexander, a celebrated Moscow lawyer. It was some fifteen years since he had sent his only child off to the university, and he had not laid eyes on him since. On seeing him, the old man, widowed and lonely, turned white, trembled and could not move hand or foot. His joy was beyond measure, he was ravished.

On the first evening father and son were alone at dinner. The lawyer ate and drank, and chatted, not without emotion.

"You are well fixed here, it's nice!" he kept repeating enthusiastically, with fidgety movements of his body. "It's warm, it's cozy, and there is a kind of patriarchal smell about the place. By God, it's pleasant here!"

The old man was too excited to sit still. He kept getting up and walking around the table with his arms crossed behind his back. The old woman who cooked for him was hovering over the scene, and it was plain that he was eager to impress her with this big, gentlemanly son of his. Thinking that it would please his guest, he tried to give the conversation a "learned" turn.

"So, dear boy, there's no denying the facts. . . ." he said. "It has worked out just as my heart desired: you and I both labor in the field where education counts. You got your degree from the university, I graduated from the Kiev Seminary, yes, sir. . . . We have followed the same path, so to say. . . . We understand one another. . . . I must say though that I don't know what the seminaries are like nowadays. In my time they laid much stress on classical subjects, and they even taught us Hebrew. What is it like now?"

"I don't know. But your sterlet, dad, is first-rate. I'm full, but I must have another slice."

"Eat, eat! You must eat more, because your work is mental, not physical, h'm, not physical. . . . You are a university man, you work with your head. How long will your visit be?"

"I'm not here on a visit, dad. I've descended on you by chance, dad, as *deus ex machina*, in a manner of speaking. I've come here to defend your former mayor. . . . You probably know, the trial opens tomorrow."

"Is that so? You're in the legal profession, then? You're a jurist?"

"Yes, I'm a lawyer."

"So that's how it is. Well, may God prosper you. What rank do you have?"

"I'm sure I don't know, dad."

"Should I ask him how much he makes?" wondered Father Savva, "but he would perhaps find that indelicate. . . . To judge by his clothes and that gold watch of his, he must be getting more than a thousand."

There was a pause in the conversation.

"I didn't know you had such sterlet, or I would have come down to see you last year," said the son. "Last year

I was staying not far from here, in your provincial capital.
The towns around here are funny."

"Funny is right. . . . The towns are the limit!" Father
Savva agreed. "There's nothing to do about it. We're far
from the centers of culture—steeped in prejudice. Civilization hasn't reached us. . . ."

"That isn't it. . . . Just listen to what happened to me—
it's quite a story. I was staying in your provincial capital,
and I thought I'd go to the theatre. I went over to the box
office, but there they told me that there would be no performance. They hadn't sold a single ticket. 'What is your
entire take?' I asked the man. 'Three hundred rubles,' he
said. 'Well,' said I, 'tell them to put on the play—I'll be
good for the three hundred.' I handed over the money—out
of sheer boredom. But as I watched that thrilling drama,
I was more horribly bored than before. . . . Ha, ha . . ."

Father Savva looked skeptically at his son, glanced at the
cook, and laughed in his sleeve. . . .

"What a liar!" he thought. "But, Shurenka,* where did
you get these three hundred rubles?" he asked timidly.

"What do you mean? I had them in my pocket."

"H'm . . . Then—excuse the indelicate question—what's
your salary?"

"It's not a salary. . . . Some years I make thirty thousand, and some not even twenty. . . . It varies from year
to year."

"What a liar! Ho-ho-ho! How he lays it on!" thought
Father Savva, laughing boisterously and looking lovingly
at his son, whose face, after the abundant meal, looked
flushed and wore a sleepy expression. "Young people are
given to trifling with the truth. Ho-ho-ho . . . He's really
gone overboard—thirty thousand!"

"Hardly possible, Sashenka," † he said. "Excuse me, but—

---

* An affectionate diminutive of Alexander. *Ed.'s note.*
† Another affectionate diminutive of Alexander. *Ed.'s note.*

ho-ho-ho—that's going too far—thirty thousand! Why for
that money a man can build two big houses. . . ."

"You don't believe me?"

"Not that I don't believe you, son, but—how shall I put
it?—it's a bit too thick. . . . Ho-ho-ho . . . But if you
make all that money, what do you do with it?"

"I spend it, dad. . . . You see, dad, living is damn expensive in a place like Moscow. What costs one thousand here
will cost you five there. I keep a stable, I play cards . . .
sometimes I go on a spree."

"Well, perhaps . . . But you should be saving money!"

"I can't. . . . Save money—I'm not made that way."
The lawyer sighed. "I just can't help myself. Last year I
bought a house in the Polyanka district. Cost me sixty thousand. All the same, I thought, it would be something for
my old age! Well, what do you think? Within two months
I had to mortgage it. I mortgaged it, and the money flew
out of the window! Some of it I lost at the card tables,
some I drank up."

"Ho—ho—ho! What a liar!" the old man beamed. "It's a
treat to listen to him!"

"I'm not making it up, dad."

"But how can a man gamble away or drink up a house?"

"You can drink up not only a house, but the whole
globe. Tomorrow I'll bleed your mayor for five thousand,
but I'm ready to wager they'll be gone before I get back to
Moscow. It's written in the planets."

"Written in the stars, you mean," Father Savva corrected
his son, with a little cough and a dignified look at the cook.
"Excuse me, Shurenka, but I doubt what you say. What
do they pay you all that money for?"

"My wits . . ."

"H'm . . . Perhaps they do pay you three thousand, but
thirty thousand . . . and those houses you talk of buying,
forgive me but . . . I can't believe it. However, don't let

us quarrel about it. Now tell me, what's it like in Moscow?
It's jolly, I suppose? You have a lot of friends?"

"A great many. All Moscow knows me."

"Ho—ho—ho! What a liar! Ho—ho! Marvels, my boy,
marvels, no end to them!"

Father and son kept on talking thus for a long time.
Among other things, the lawyer described a trip of his to
Nizhny-Novgorod, mentioned his marriage to a girl with a
dowry of forty thousand and his divorce which cost him
ten thousand. The old man listened greedily, struck his
hands together in amazement and laughed boisterously.

"What a liar! Ho-ho-ho! I didn't know, Shurenka, that
you were such a master at telling tall tales. Ho-ho-ho! Mind
you, I don't hold it against you. It's a treat to listen to you.
Do go on!"

"Oh, I've chatted long enough," the lawyer concluded,
getting up from the table. "The trial starts tomorrow, and
I haven't gone over the papers yet. Good night!"

Having seen his son off to his room—he had surrendered
his own bedroom to him—Father Savva gave himself up to
transports.

"Well, what do you say? Did you get a good look at
him?" he whispered to the cook. "There you have it. . . .
A graduate of the university, a man of culture, *émancipé*,
but he didn't disdain to look in on the old man. He had put
him out of his mind, and then suddenly he remembered him.
Yes, he did remember him. Let me pay some attention to
the old fellow, he thought to himself. Ho-ho-ho! A good
son! A kindhearted son! And, did you notice? He treated
me as his equal. . . . He sees in me an educated man, one
of his own sort. He understands things. It's a pity we didn't
invite the deacon, he ought to have had a look at him."

Having opened his heart to the old woman, Father Savva
tiptoed over to his bedroom and peered through the keyhole. The lawyer lay on the bed fully dressed, smoking a

cigar and reading a bulky manuscript. Near him, on a small table was a bottle of wine, which Father Savva had not seen before.

"I'll only be a minute. . . . Just to see that you're all right," mumbled the old man as he entered the room. "Are you comfortable? Is it a soft bed? Why don't you take your things off?"

The lawyer muttered something indistinct and frowned. Father Savva sat down at the foot of the bed and looked thoughtful.

"That's how it is . . ." he began after a pause. "I keep thinking about all the things you said. On the one hand, I am grateful to you for cheering up the old man; on the other hand, as your father and . . . a man of education, I can't be silent, I can't refrain from a remark. I realize that you were joking at dinner, but, as you know, both religion and science condemn lying even in jest. Hem . . . I have a cough. Hem . . . Forgive me, I speak as your father. Where did you get this wine, my boy?"

"I brought it with me. Want some? It's good stuff, eight rubles a bottle."

"Eight rubles? What a liar!" Father Savva struck his hands together in amazement. "Ho-ho-ho! What's it made of that you pay eight rubles for it? Ho-ho-ho! Why, I'll buy you the best wine ever for one ruble. Ho-ho-ho!"

"Well, make yourself scarce, old man. You're interfering with my work. . . . Out with you!"

The old man left the room, chuckling and striking his hands together, and quietly closed the door behind him.

At midnight, having given the cook the order for next day's dinner and having said his prayers, Father Savva once more looked into his son's room. The lawyer kept on reading, smoking and drinking.

"Time to turn in . . . take off your things and put out the light . . ." said the old man, who carried with him into the room the odor of incense and the smell of snuffed-out candles. "It's twelve o'clock. . . . That's the second bottle, isn't it? Oho!"

"I've got to drink, dad. . . . Without a stimulant I can't work."

Father Savva sat down on the bed and began:

"It's this way . . . M'yes . . . I don't know how long I'll last, and whether I'll see you again, so I might as well tell you this now . . . You see . . . In the forty years since I was ordained I've saved up fifteen hundred rubles for you. When I'm gone they're yours, but . . ."

Father Savva blew his nose solemnly and went on:

"But don't squander them, hold on to them. . . . And I beg you, after my death send cousin Varenka a hundred rubles. Also, if you don't begrudge it, send twenty to Zinaida. They are orphans."

"Send them the whole fifteen hundred. I don't need the money, dad. . . ."

"You mean it?"

"Of course . . . I'll run through it anyhow."

"H'm . . . It took me a long time to save it up, you know," said Father Savva, offended. "I put it away copper by copper . . ."

"All right, I'll keep the money under glass, as a sign of paternal love, but since I don't need it . . . Fifteen hundred—pah!"

"Well, suit yourself . . . If I had known, I wouldn't have saved it up, taken such care of it—well, good night!"

Father Savva made the sign of the cross over his son and went out of the room. He was somewhat mortified. . . . His son's callous, indifferent attitude toward his savings of a lifetime had taken him aback. But his mortification and discomfiture soon vanished. . . . The old man was again drawn to have a chat with his son, to engage in another "learned" conversation with him, to recall the past, but he didn't dare disturb the busy lawyer. He kept walking back and forth through the dark rooms, kept thinking to himself, and finally went into the anteroom to have a look at his son's fur coat. In an access of paternal rapture he clasped the coat in both arms, and all at once he was hugging it, kissing it, signing it with the cross, as though it were not a fur coat but his son himself, the university man. . . . Sleep was out of the question.

1885

hydrophobia

(A true story)

This narrative was first published in the issue of a Peters-burg daily for March 17, 1886 (O. S.). A later version of it, entitled "The Wolf," has recently come to light. Chekhov apparently prepared for it, though he did not include it in, the edition of his collected works issued in 1899-1901. He made some minor changes in the wording, deleted two short passages, and completely altered the end-ing. This is bracketed in the text below, as are the deleted sentences, and the original ending is followed by the one that Chekhov wrote after a lapse of some fifteen years.

Nilov, a thickset, robust man, known throughout the province in which his estate was located for his extraordi-nary physical strength, was returning from a hunting trip with Kuprianov, an examining magistrate, and they dropped in on old man Maxim at the mill. Nilov's manor was only two versts away, but they were so tired that they did not want to walk any farther and decided to make a long halt at the mill. The decision was all the more sensible since tea and sugar were usually available at Maxim's, and the huntsmen themselves were provided with a decent supply of vodka, cognac and all kinds of edibles.

Having satisfied their hunger and thirst, they fell to talking.

"What's the news, grandfather?" Nilov asked Maxim.

"The news?" the old man grinned. "The news is that I'm about to ask your Honor to lend me a gun."

"What do you want a gun for?"

"What do I want it for? Well, maybe I don't really need it. I just said it because I wanted to talk big. . . . The truth is I don't see well enough to shoot. A mad wolf has turned up, deuce knows where from. He's been hanging around the neighborhood for two days. . . . Last night he killed a colt and two dogs near the village, and this morning at dawn I went out and there he sat, damn him, under a willow, pawing at his snout. I shouted at him "Shoo!" but he kept eyeing me, as if the devil was in him. I pitched a stone at him, and he snarled, his eyes shone like candles, and he made for the aspen grove. . . . I was scared stiff."

"What the hell . . ." the magistrate muttered. "A mad wolf at large in the district, and here we've been trotting about . . ."

"Well, what of it?" said Nilov. "We have guns."

"You can't use a shotgun on a wolf."

"Why shoot? The butt will serve."

And Nilov proceeded to contend that there was nothing easier than to kill a wolf with the butt of a gun. He told the story of how with one blow of an ordinary walking stick he had killed a huge mad dog that had attacked him.

"It's easy for you to argue like that," the magistrate sighed, looking enviously at Nilov's broad shoulders. "You've the strength of ten, thank heaven. You can kill a dog with your little finger, let alone a cane. But an ordinary mortal will be bitten by a dog five times before he has a chance to raise the stick and choose the spot to hit. An unpleasant affair . . . There's nothing more agonizing and horrible than hydrophobia. The first time I saw someone afflicted by it, I walked around like a man who had lost his mind, and I loathed all dogs and dog fanciers. In the first place, the suddenness of the thing is terrible. Here is a man, healthy, at ease, thinking of nothing, and suddenly—bam! out of a clear sky he's bitten by a mad dog! At once he is possessed by the appalling thought that he is irrevocably lost, that he is beyond hope. Then you can imagine the anguished, oppressive waiting for the onset of the disease, the dread that doesn't leave the victim for a single moment. And then comes the disease itself. The worst of it is that hydrophobia is incurable. Once you've contracted it, you're lost. In medicine, as far as I know, there's not even a hint of the possibility of a cure."

"But in our village they do cure it, master!" said Maxim. "Miron will get anybody well.'

"Nonsense . . ." Nilov sighed. "It's nothing but talk, all this about Miron. Last summer Styopka was bitten by a mad dog, and no Mirons helped. . . . They made him swallow all kinds of stuff, but in the end the sickness got him. No, Granddaddy, there is no help for it. If I were bitten by a mad dog, I would blow my brains out."

The frightening stories about hydrophobia had their effect. Gradually a hush fell, and the huntsmen sipped their tea in silence. Involuntarily each began to think of the fatal dependence of man's life and happiness on accidents and trifles, seemingly negligible, not worth a straw, as the saying goes. They became dull and depressed.

After tea Nilov stretched himself and got to his feet. He wanted a breath of fresh air. He stepped out of doors, and after a stroll near the cornbins opened a wicket and walked toward the dam. It was long past twilight and already dark. Quiet and deep slumber were wafted from the river.

The dam, flooded with moonlight, showed not a bit of shade; on it, in the middle, the neck of a broken bottle glittered like a star. The two wheels of the mill, half-hidden in the shadow of an ample willow, looked angry, despondent . . .

Nilov drew a deep breath and gazed at the river. Nothing budged. The water and the banks were asleep, even the fish did not splash. Suddenly it seemed to Nilov that on the farther bank, above the osier bushes, something resembling a shadow rolled by like a black ball. He screwed up his eyes. The shadow vanished, but soon reappeared again, rolling in a zigzag fashion toward the dam.

"The wolf!" flashed through Nilov's mind.

But he had barely conceived the thought that he must run back into the mill, when the black ball was already rolling along the dam, not straight toward Nilov, but in zigzags.

"If I run, he'll attack me from behind," Nilov reflected, his scalp turning cold. "My God, I haven't even a stick! Well, I'll stand up to him and . . . I'll choke him!"

And Nilov started carefully watching the wolf's movements and noting what his appearance suggested. The wolf ran along the edge of the dam. Now he was almost upon Nilov.

"He'll pass me by," Nilov thought, without taking his eyes off the animal.

But at that moment the wolf, without looking at the man, and reluctantly, as it were, uttered a plaintive, hoarse cry, turned his snout toward him and stopped short. He seemed to deliberate: attack or not?

"To punch his head," thought Nilov, "to stun him. . . ."

Nilov was so dazed that he did not know who had started the struggle: he or the wolf. The only thing he was conscious of was that a peculiarly dreadful critical moment had come when it was imperative for him to concentrate all his strength in his right hand and seize the wolf by the scruff of the neck. Then something extraordinary, incredible, occurred that seemed to Nilov to be happening in a dream. The wolf growled plaintively and jerked his neck out of Nilov's grip with such force that the cold, moist fold of his skin started slipping from Nilov's fingers. Trying to free his neck, the wolf reared on his hind legs. Then with his left hand Nilov firmly seized the beast's right foreleg where it joined the body, and then quickly letting go of the wolf's neck and grasping the left foreleg with his right hand, he lifted the wolf off the ground. All this was the matter of a moment. To prevent the wolf from biting his hands and to make it impossible for him to turn his head, Nilov thrust his two thumbs like spurs into the animal's neck at the collarbone. The wolf leaned his paws against Nilov's shoulders and, having thus obtained a support, tried with terrible force to shake himself free. He could not bite Nilov's hands or forearms, and he was prevented by the thumbs that pressed on his neck and hurt him badly from reaching the man's face or shoulders with his fangs.

"It's bad!" thought Nilov, pulling his head away from the snout as far as possible. "His saliva got on my lip. So I'm lost all the same, even if by a miracle I should get rid of him."

"Help!" he shouted, "Maxim, help!"

Nilov and the wolf, their heads at the same level, looked into each other's eyes. The wolf's fangs clicked, he sputtered and growled hoarsely. His hind legs, seeking a foothold, pawed Nilov's knees. The moon was reflected in the animal's eyes; there was nothing like anger in them; they were tearful and looked human. [What did the sick animal feel? All of Nilov's strength, muscular and nervous, was concentrated in his hands. He did not think, he felt little, and his entire effort was to keep his hold.

The least details of the dreadful pictures painted by his companion were vividly before him, but briefly. The present was so appalling that he could not think either of the past or the future.]

"Help!" Nilov shouted again. "Maxim!"

But those at the mill did not hear him. Instinctively he felt that shouting might reduce his strength, and so did not raise his voice.

"I'll back up," he decided. "And when I reach the gate, I'll shout."

He began moving backwards, but he had not gone very far when he felt that his right arm was weakening and beginning to swell. And suddenly he heard his own heart-rending scream and felt a sharp pain in his right shoulder and warm wetness on his arm and chest. Then he became aware of Maxim's voice and of the expression of horror on the magistrate's face.

He let go of his enemy only when they forcibly unclasped his fingers and made it clear to him that the beast was dead. Stunned by what he had endured, feeling the blood on his thighs and in his right boot, close to fainting, he returned to the mill.

The light, the sight of the samovar and the bottles brought him to himself and reminded him of the terrors he had just gone through and of the danger that was just beginning for him. Pale, wide-eyed, his head wet, he dropped down on the sacks and wearily let his arms fall. The investigating magistrate and Maxim undressed him and busied themselves with the wound. It was quite deep. The wolf had torn the skin on the shoulder and lacerated even the muscles.

"Why didn't you pitch him into the river?" asked the

magistrate, pale and indignant, as he tried to stop the bleeding. "Why didn't you pitch him into the river?"

"I didn't have the sense! My God, I didn't have the
sense!"

The magistrate started to comfort and reassure Nilov,
but having just described hydrophobia in colors so dark,
he realized that all such talk was inappropriate and felt it
best to hold his peace. Having then dressed the wound
somehow, he sent Maxim to the manor to fetch horses, but
Nilov would not wait and went home on foot.

Early in the morning, pale and haggard with pain and a
sleepless night, his hair uncombed, he drove to the mill.

"Grandfather," he said, turning to Maxim, "take me to
Miron! Hurry up! Come on, get into my carriage!"

Maxim, who was also pale and had not slept all night,
grew embarrassed, glanced about him several times and
whispered:

"You needn't go to Miron, master; I, too, excuse me,
know how to treat people."

"Very well, only please hurry!"

And Nilov stamped his feet with impatience. The old
man placed him so that he faced east, mumbled something,
and handed him a mug from which he made him drink some
disgusting lukewarm liquid tasting of wormwood.

"Yet Styopka died . . ." muttered Nilov. "Let's say that
the country people have certain remedies, but . . . but
why did Styopka die? Take me to Miron anyhow!"

What now fell to Nilov's lot is a story in itself. As the
ghost of an unrepentant sinner is said to do, he began
wandering, dismal and restless, from place to place, seeking
momentary relief. The little confidence he had had in Miron
having been dissipated by his visit, he drove to the hospital
to see Dr. Ovchinnikov. There he was given belladonna
pills and the advice to go to bed. He promptly got fresh

horses and, without paying attention to the terrible pain in his arm, drove to consult the doctors in town.

Several days later, after dusk, he rushed into Ovchinnikov's office and dropped onto the sofa.

"Doctor!" he began, choking and wiping the sweat from his pale, haggard face with his sleeve. "Grigory Ivanych! Do what you please with me, but I can't go on like this any longer! Either treat me, or poison me, but don't leave me like this! For God's sake! I'm losing my mind!"

"You must go to bed," said Ovchinnikov.

"Oh, blast this going to bed! I ask you in plain language: What shall I do? You're a physician and you must help me! I suffer torture. Every moment I imagine that I'm getting hydrophobia. I can't sleep, I can't eat, I can't go about my business! I carry a revolver in my pocket. Every minute I'm ready to blow my brains out with it! Grigory Ivanych, help me, for God's sake! What shall I do? I have an idea: perhaps I should consult a specialist?"

"Why not? Do."

"Listen, what about printing a notice announcing a reward of fifty thousand for a cure? What do you think? But before the notice is printed, I can get hydrophobia ten times. I'm ready to part with all I have. Cure me, and I'll give you fifty thousand! But do something for me! I can't understand this revolting indifference! Get it into your head that nowadays I envy every fly. . . . I'm miserable! My family is miserable!"

Nilov's shoulders shook and he began sobbing.

"See here," Ovchinnikov said. "I don't quite understand your distress. What are you crying about? Why exaggerate the danger? Your chances of not contracting the disease are very good. In the first place, out of a hundred who are bitten only thirty get hydrophobia. Besides, and this is very important, the wolf bit you through your clothing, therefore the poison must have stayed in the cloth. And even if the poison did get into the wound, it probably flowed out with the blood, since you lost a lot of blood. I am not at all anxious about hydrophobia, what worries me is your wound. With your negligence you may easily get erysipelas or something like it."

"You think so? Are you saying this just to reassure me, or do you really mean it?"

"Word of honor, I mean it. Here, take this, read it for yourself!"

Ovchinnikov pulled a volume from the shelf and, skipping the more terrifying passages, read Nilov the chapter on rabies.

"So you're worried for no good reason," he said, when he was done reading. "Add to all this that neither you nor I know if the wolf was really rabid."

"M'mmyes . . ." Nilov assented, smiling. "Of course, now I understand. So all this is nonsense!"

"Of course, nonsense."

"Well, thank you, old man . . ." Nilov laughed, rubbing his hands cheerfully. "How wonderful it is to have your knowledge of things. Now, my dear fellow, I'm completely reassured. [Here's something for your services . . . five hundred . . . Come, come, don't make a fuss . . . I'm so happy now that I'd give you a thousand, if I had the money on me . . . Let's have a drink!"

Nilov had dinner with the doctor and drove away completely at ease. But the following day he was again running to doctors and quacks. Fear of solitude was now added to his other troubles. He moved in on the doctor and did not stop pestering him night and day.

The hands of a watch move imperceptibly. But if you are attentive, you may be able to observe the movement of the minute hand. Thus, the doctor, with Nilov forced on his attention, was able to observe how a robust individual was losing weight, getting gray, an enlightened man falling prey to mysticism.

Nilov did not contract rabies. A month passed, another, a third, and gradually he began coming to himself. A year went by, and he would have forgotten the incident with the wolf, if his premature gray hair and wrinkles had not reminded him of it.

Man has a weak memory. The other day Maxim was bitten by a mad dog. Without hesitation the doctor went to see Nilov.

"We are sending Maxim to Pasteur," he said to him. "We are taking up a collection. Will you make a contribution?"

"Oh, with pleasure!" said Nilov, left the room and on returning, handed the doctor *ten* rubles.]

The ending that Chekhov substituted for the bracketed passage beginning with the sentence: "Here's something for your services . . ."

"I'm satisfied, in fact, I'm overjoyed, by God! Word of honor, I'm overjoyed."

Nilov embraced Ovchinnikov and kissed him three times. Then he gave vent to an outburst of boyish high spirits, to which good-natured, physically strong people are inclined. He seized a horseshoe from the table and tried to straighten it, but grown weak with joy and the pain in his shoulder, he was helpless. He confined himself to putting his left arm around the doctor's hips, lifting him bodily, and carrying him on his shoulder from the study into the dining room. He was in a state of such exhilaration when he left Ovchinnikov that it seemed even the teardrops sparkling in his broad black beard were rejoicing with him. Walking down the steps, he laughed resonantly and shook the handrail of the porch with such force that one banister jumped out, and Ovchinnikov, seeing him off, felt the entire porch tremble under his feet.

"What strength!" thought Ovchinnikov, looking with emotion at his broad back. "What a capital fellow!"

Once in his carriage, Nilov started telling the story of how he had fought the wolf on the dam—rehearsing it from the beginning and in great detail.

"That was sport!" he wound up, laughing gaily. "That will be something to remember in my old age. Whip up the horses, Trishka!"

other people's misfortune

It was not later than six o'clock in the morning when Stepan Kovalyov, a young man fresh from law school, got into a carriage with his bride, and they were soon rolling along a country road. Neither he nor his young wife had ever risen so early, and the magnificence of the still summer morning struck them as something out of a fairy tale. The earth, clothed in green, sprinkled with diamond dew, seemed beautiful and happy. The sunlight lay in bright patches on the forest, shimmered on the sparkling river, and there was a freshness in the extraordinarily transparent azure air that made it seem as if all of God's world had just emerged from a bath, and so was refreshed and invigorated.

For the Kovalyovs, as they admitted afterwards, this was the happiest morning of their honeymoon, and indeed of their whole life together. They chatted without stopping, laughed boisterously for no reason, and carried on in such an unrestrained fashion that in the end they were ashamed before the coachman.

Happiness was smiling upon their present and upon their future as well: they were on their way to buy an estate—

a small "romantic nook," for which they had been planning since their wedding day. The future held out the brightest prospect for them both. He had visions of a zemstvo post, scientific farming, all the labors and pleasures associated with country life, of which he had heard and read so much; she was captivated by purely romantic aspects: excursions on the lake, dark alleys, fragrant nights. . . .

What with the laughter and the talk, they did not notice that they had covered the eighteen versts to the estate of aulic councilor Mikhailov that they were going to look over. There was a stream just below the hill on which the house stood, almost hidden by a birch grove. The red roof was barely visible through the thick foliage, and the clayey slope was studded with saplings.

"Not a bad view!" said Kovalyov, as they were fording the watercourse. "A house on a hill, a stream at the foot of it! Devilishly nice! But, Verochka, these stairs aren't any good . . . they spoil the view, they are ugly. . . . If we buy the estate, we must certainly replace them with a cast-iron flight of stairs."

Verochka too liked the view. Shaking with vivacious laughter, she ran up the steps, her husband after her, and the two of them, breathless, disheveled, walked into the grove. The first person they caught sight of at the house was a big, hairy peasant, sleepy and sullen. He sat on the porch, cleaning a child's boot.

"Is Mr. Mikhailov in?" Kovalyov asked him. "Go tell him that people who want to buy the estate have come to look at it."

The peasant stared at the Kovalyov couple with vacant amazement and trudged off slowly, not to the mansion, but to the kitchen, which was a structure apart from the house. Immediately faces appeared in the kitchen windows, one more sleepy and astonished than the other.

"Buyers have arrived!" the whisper was heard. "Lord, it's your will. Mikhalkovo's being sold. Look, what a young couple!"

A dog barked somewhere, and there was a shriek like that of a cat when her tail is stepped on. The alarm of the servants soon infected the chickens, the geese, the turkeys that had been wandering about. Presently a fellow who looked like a flunkey emerged from the kitchen; he screwed up his eyes at the Kovalyovs and, putting on his jacket as he went, ran toward the house. All this excitement seemed ridiculous to the Kovalyovs and they could hardly keep from laughing.

"What funny faces!" said Kovalyov, exchanging glances with his wife. "They look at us as if we were savages."

Finally, there emerged from the house a little man with a shaven, wizened face and tousled hair. He scraped his feet, which were thrust into torn, embroidered slippers, as he bowed, smiled sourly, and stared at the unbidden guests.

"Mr. Mikhailov?" Kovalyov began, raising his hat. "Permit me to introduce myself. . . . My wife and I read the notice of the Land Bank to the effect that your estate is for sale, and we have come to look it over. Perhaps we'll buy it. . . . Be so good as to show it to us."

Mikhailov became embarrassed, produced another forced smile, and blinked his eyes. In his confusion he mussed up his hair even more, and his shaven face assumed such a ludicrously sheepish and stunned expression that Kovalyov and his Verochka exchanged glances again and could not suppress smiles.

"Pleased to meet you . . ." he mumbled. "I'm at your service. . . . Did you have a long trip?"

"We're coming from Konkovo. We have a summer cottage there."

"So . . . a summer cottage . . . Wonderful! Excuse us,

excuse us! We've just gotten up, and we haven't quite tidied the place."

Mikhailov, smiling sourly and rubbing his hands, led the visitors to the back of the house. Kovalyov put on his glasses and with the air of a knowledgeable tourist seeing the sights began to examine the estate. He started with the house. It was a stone structure built in a heavy, old-fashioned style, with armorial bearings, lions, and peeling plaster. The roof was badly in need of a coat of paint, the windowpanes were iridescent with age, grass was growing in the cracks between the steps. Everything was dilapidated and unkempt, but the prospective buyers liked the house on the whole. It had a poetic, modest, good-natured air, like an aged maiden aunt. In front, a few steps from the main entrance, a pond sparkled in the sun. Two ducks and a toy boat were floating on it. The pond was surrounded by birches of uniform height and thickness.

"Aha, you have a pond, too!" said Kovalyov, narrowing his eyes in the sun. "That's nice. Are there crucian in it?"

"Yes, sir . . . There used to be carp there, too, but when we stopped cleaning the pond, all the carp died."

"Too bad," said Kovalyov, in a professorial manner. "A pond should be cleaned as often as possible, all the more so that the silt and water plants are excellent fertilizer for the fields. You know what, Vera? When we buy this estate, we'll build a summer house on piles in the pond with a bridge. I saw a summer house like that at Prince Afontov's place."

"We can have tea in the summer house," Verochka murmured sweetly.

"Of course . . . And what is that tower with a spire?"

"That's a guest house," Mikhailov replied.

"It looks out of place, somehow. We'll pull it down. Generally speaking, a good deal will have to be torn down here. A great deal!"

Suddenly a woman's weeping was distinctly heard. The Kovalyovs looked toward the house, but at that very moment one of the windows banged and two large tear-stained eyes flashed briefly behind the iridescent panes. Apparently, the woman who was crying grew ashamed of her tears, and, shutting the window, hid behind the curtain.

"Won't you look at the garden and the outbuildings?" Mikhailov started talking rapidly, wrinkling his lined face more noticeably and more sourly than ever. "Let's go . . . The most important thing, you know, is not the house, but . . . the grounds, and the rest. . . ."

The Kovalyovs went to look at the stables and the outbuildings. The newly-fledged lawyer walked around each building, looked at it, sniffed at it and made a show of his knowledge of agronomy. He inquired about the acreage of the estate, the number of head of cattle, scolded Russia for the destruction of her forests, reproved Mikhailov for the large amount of manure he wasted, and so forth. He talked away and from time to time glanced at his Verochka, and she kept her loving eyes riveted on him and was thinking: "How clever this man of mine is!"

During the inspection of the barn, the sound of crying was heard again.

"Please tell me, who is that crying?" asked Verochka.

Mikhailov waved his hand and turned aside.

"Strange," murmured Verochka, when the sobs turned into ceaseless hysterical weeping. "It's as though someone were being beaten or murdered."

"It's my wife, the Lord help her," said Mikhailov.

"But why is she crying?"

"A weak woman, Madam. She cannot bear to see her homestead sold."

"Why are you selling it, then?" asked Verochka.

"We're not selling it, it's the bank. . . ."

"Strange, why do you allow it?"

Mikhailov cast an astonished glance at Verochka's pink face and shrugged his shoulders.

"We must pay interest on the mortgage," he said. "Twenty-one hundred rubles every year. And where are we to get it? And that makes her cry. Women are weak, you know. It grieves her to lose her home, she is sorry for me, for the children . . . and she is ashamed before the servants. Near the pond you were pleased to observe," he said, turning to Kovalyov, "that this had to be torn down, that should be built, and for her it's like a knife in her heart."

Passing the house on the way back, Vera saw in the window the close-cropped head of a high school boy and two little girls—obviously Mikhailov's children. What did they think about, looking at the purchasers? Verochka seemed to understand their thoughts. . . . When she got into the carriage to drive back, the fresh morning and the dreams of a romantic nook had lost all charm for her.

"This is all very disagreeable!" she said to her husband. "Really, why not give them the twenty-one hundred? Let them live on their estate."

"How clever you are!" Kovalyov laughed. "Of course, I'm sorry for them, but it's their own fault. Who forced them to mortgage the estate? Why have they neglected it so? We really oughtn't to be sorry for them. If one were to work this estate intelligently, introduce scientific farming . . . raise livestock, one could make a very good thing of it here . . . But these wasters—they've done nothing. . . . He is probably a drunkard and a gambler—did you see his mug?—and she is a woman of fashion and a spendthrift. I know those characters!"

"How do you know them, Styopa?"

"I know! He complains that he can't pay the interest on the mortgage. How is it that he can't scrape two thousand together? If you were to introduce scientific farming . . .

use fertilizer and raise livestock . . . if you take account of the climatic and economic conditions, you can make a living on a couple of acres!"

Styopa kept chatting all the way to the house; his wife listened to him and believed every word he said, but her former mood had vanished. She could not stop thinking of Mikhailov's forced smile and the two eyes big with tears of which she had caught a glimpse.

When, later on, jaunty Styopa attended the auction and purchased the estate with her dowry, she was distressed. . . . Her imagination did not stop picturing Mikhailov and his family getting into a carriage and leaving their old home with tears. And the gloomier and more touching the pictures that her imagination painted, the jauntier Styopa became. With the utmost aplomb he talked about scientific farming, ordered books and periodicals on agronomy, made fun of Mikhailov. His agricultural planning always ended in the boldest, most shameful bragging. . . .

"You'll see," he would say. "I am no Mikhailov, I'll show you how to farm. Yes!"

When the Kovalyovs moved to deserted Mikhalkovo, the first thing that Verochka noticed was a few intimate traces left behind by the former occupants: a program of lessons written in a childish hand, a headless doll, a pencilled scribble on the wall: "Natasha is a fool," a titmouse coming for its customary crumbs, and the like. There was much repainting and repapering to be done, there was much to be torn down, in order to erase the memory of other people's misfortune.

1886

women make trouble

a little scene

It is between six and seven o'clock in the morning. Popikov, deputy examining magistrate at N., a market town, is sleeping the sweet sleep of one who in addition to his salary gets an allowance for his lodgings and for transportation. He hasn't yet acquired a bed, and he sleeps on court records. Stillness. Out of doors, too, not a sound. But now in the entry, behind the door, something is scraping and rustling, as if a pig had come into the entry and were scratching its back against the jamb. After a while the door opens with a plaintive squeak and then shuts. A few minutes later the door opens again and with such a pained squeak that Popikov starts and opens his eyes.

"Who is there?" he asks, looking at the door with alarm.

A spiderlike object appears in the doorway—a large shaggy head with beetling eyebrows and a thick matted beard.

"Does the Judge live here?" the head wheezes.

"He does. What do you want?"

"Go tell him Ivan Filaretov is here. There was a summons to come."

"But why did you come so early? The summons is for eleven o'clock."

"And what time is it now?"

"It's not seven yet."

"H'm . . . Not seven yet . . . We got no clock, your Honor. So you'll be the judge?"

"That's right. . . . Well, be off, wait outside. . . . I'm still sleeping. . . ."

"Sleep, sleep . . . I'll wait. That can be done."

Filaretov's head vanishes. Popikov rolls over on the other side, closes his eyes, but sleep does not return. After continuing to lie there about half an hour, he stretches zestfully and smokes a cigarette. Then, to drag out the time, he slowly sips three glasses of milk, one after another.

"He's waked me up, the rascal!" he grumbles. "I'll have to tell the landlady to lock the door at night. Well, what can I do at this unearthly hour? Devil take him . . . I'll question him now, instead of waiting till later."

Popikov thrusts his feet into his slippers and, still in his pyjamas, throws a cape over his shoulders. Yawning so that his jaws ache, he sits down at the desk.

"Come in!" he shouts.

The door squeaks again, and Ivan Filaretov appears on the threshold. Popikov opens the folder entitled: "The case of reservist Alexey Andreyev Drykhunov accused of committing assault and battery against his wife Marfa," takes pen in hand and starts setting forth the preliminaries to the testimony in the bold hand fancied by the legal profession.

"Move up closer," he says, making a scratchy noise on the paper with his pen. "Answer my questions. You are Ivan Filaretov, peasant of the village of Dunkino, Pustyrev County, age forty-two?"

"Yes."

"Occupation?"

"It's a herdsman I am. Look out for the village livestock."

"Have you ever been brought to court?"

"Yes, I have. . . ."

"What for, and when?"

"Before Easter three of us from our county were summoned to be jurymen. . . ."

"That's not being brought to court."

"There's no knowing what's what! Anyhow they kept
us nearly five days. . . ."

The investigating judge draws his cape together and says,
in somewhat lower tones:

"You have been summoned as a witness in the case of
reservist Alexey Drykhunov accused of having committed
assault and battery against his wife. I warn you that you
must say nothing but the truth and that all you say here
you will have to confirm under oath at the trial. What do
you know about the case?"

"What about the money allowed for getting here, your
Honor?" Filaretov mumbles. "I've driven twenty-two
versts, the horse don't belong to me, I'll have to pay for
it. . . ."

"We'll talk about the allowance later."

"Why later? They say the allowance must be claimed at
the court, or else you don't get it."

"I haven't any time to talk about the allowance," the
judge says angrily. "Tell just what happened. How did
Drykhunov beat up his wife?"

"What can I tell you?" Filaretov sighs, raising his beetling
eyebrows. "It's very simple, a fight there was, no denying
it! It was this way. Here I'm driving the cows to water, and
I see some ducks swimming in the pond. . . . Are they
the master's ducks or the peasants'? Christ knows. Only
the boy Grishka, my helper, he picks up a stone and starts
throwing. 'Why do you throw stones?' I ask. 'You can do

a mischief,' I says. 'You'll hit one of them ducks, and you'll kill it.'"

Filaretov sighs and lifts his eyes to the ceiling. Then he goes on.

"Even a human being can be killed, but a duck is a weak creature, you can do it in with a stick. . . . I talk to him, but Grishka, he pays no attention. . . . Of course, just a boy, no sense, not in his head. . . . 'Why don't you mind my words?' I says to him. 'I'll pull your ears for you! You fool you!'"

"All this is irrelevant," says the magistrate. "Confine yourself to what has to do with the case."

"Yes, sir . . . So here I am trying to get him by the ear, when suddenly Drykhunov turns up out of nowhere. He's walking along the shore with the factory lads, and he waves his arms. His mug is all swollen, and it's red, his eyes start out of his head, and he's swaying from side to side. . . . He's drunk, damn his hide! People are still at matins, but he's already pickled himself proper, and he makes the devil happy. He sees me going for the boy's ear, and he raises hell: 'You mustn't pull the ears of a Christian soul!' says he. 'Mind your own business, or you'll get it in the neck!' I says to him polite-like, decent, as God would have it. 'Be on your way,' I says, 'you souse you!' He gets mad, comes up to me, and as hard as he can, your Honor, bang on the back of my neck! What for? What's the occasion? 'Are you a justice of the peace,' I asks, 'that you've a perfect right to strike me?' and he says: 'Well, well, Vanyukha, don't take no offense, I pasted you one in friendship, for fun. I got illumination,' says he. 'I know who I am,' says he; 'I'm the biggest man around here . . .' says he, 'My wages at the factory are no less than twenty rubles, and leave out the director, there's nobody over me. . . . I spit on all the others!' says he. 'And what a lot of all kinds of people have got killed, no end of 'em!' says he. 'Let's

go and have a spot!' says he. 'No,' says I, 'I don't want to
drink with you. . . . People are still at matins, and you—
guzzle!' And now all the other fellows as was with him
crowd around me, like so many dogs, and keep yapping:
'Come on, come!' I just couldn't go against the whole lot
of them, your Honor. I didn't want no drink, and then
. . . damn their hides!"

"Where did you go, then?"

"We have only one place," Filaretov sighs. "We went to
the inn, the one Abram Moyseich keeps. We go there
every time. A bad place, deuce take it! Sure, you know it.
. . . When you drive on the highway to Dunkino, on the
right there's the place that belongs to his honor, Severin
Frantzych, and further to the right there's Plakhtovo, and
in between there's that same inn. Sure, friend, you know
Severin Frantzych?"

"Come to the point. Don't forget that you're addressing
a judge."

"Oh, of course, your Honor! Don't I understand it? But
listen to what happened next. . . . We come to Abramka's
place. . . . 'Set 'em up!' says he, 'it's on me!' "

"Who says that?"

"This fellow . . . Drykhunov, that is! 'You so-and-so,'
he shouts, 'set 'em up or I'll stave in the barrel! I got illumination!' Well, we downed a glass, waited a while and had
another, and this way in about an hour we knocked off, if
memory don't fail me, eight glasses apiece! What do I care?
I drink, I don't worry: it's not my money! Treat me to a
thousand glasses! I'm not to blame, your Honor! Ask
Abram Moyseich."

"What happened next?"

"Nothing happened next. It's true, while we were drinking, there was a fight, but afterwards everything was fine
and decent."

"But who was fighting?"

"You know who. . . . 'I got illumination!' he shouts. He shouts and he starts socking everybody in the jaw. He sure let himself go. He hit me and Abramka and the fellows. . . . He hands you a glass, lets you empty it, and then hits you with all his might. 'Drink,' says he, 'and feel my fist! I spit on the lot of you!' "

"And did he beat his wife?"

"You mean Marfa? Yes, she got it in the neck too. Just as our blood was up, Marfa steps into the pot house. 'Come home,' she says, 'brother Stepan is here! You've had enough vodka, you robber!' And he, without saying a bad word, gives her a mean wallop!"

"What for?"

"Just like that, for nothing. . . . 'Let her take it in,' says he. 'I get twenty rubles,' says he. And she a weak woman, skinny, she took and flopped and even rolled up her eyes. She started complaining of her lot and calling on God, but he was at it again. . . . He kept giving her what for, and there was no end to it!"

"Why didn't you come to her defense? A man crazed by vodka is murdering a woman, and you don't lift a finger!"

"And why should we lift a finger? It's his wife, he's giving her a lesson . . . When two are at it, a third should keep out . . . Abramka wanted to stop him, he didn't want him to carry on in the place, so he hit him. Then Abramka's man went for him. . . . He got hold of him, lifted him up and threw him down on the floor. Then the other one straddled him and started pummeling his back. . . . We pulled him out from under him by the legs."

"Whom?"

"It's plain who . . . Who he straddled . . ."

"Who was that?"

"Why, the man I'm talking about."

"Ugh! Talk sense, you fool! Answer my questions, and don't go on babbling to no purpose!"

"I'm telling you the whole thing, your Honor, plain . . . just as it happened, I swear to God. Drykhunov did give his woman a lesson, that's the truth. . . . I'll say it again under oath."

The judge listens, selects some passages from Filaretov's long, incoherent speech, and his pen scratches away. He does a good deal of crossing out.

"I'm not to blame at all . . ." Filaretov mutters. "Ask anybody, your Honor. And the woman isn't worth driving to court for."

After he has had the record of his testimony read to him, the witness stares stupidly at the judge for a while, then sighs.

"Women make trouble!" he brings out hoarsely. "And the allowance, your Honor, will you pay it yourself, or will you give me a paper?"

1886

the lodger

Brykovich, a young man already bald, had at one time worked in a law office, but now he had thrown up his job and was supported by his well-to-do spouse, owner of the lodging-house that bore the sign: "Tunis."

Late one night he rushed out of his apartment into the corridor, banging the door behind him with all his might. "Oh, the vicious, brainless, stupid creature!" he muttered, clenching his fists. "The devil hitched me up with her! Ugh! That big-mouthed witch—only a cannon could roar louder!"

Brykovich was choking with indignation and anger, and if, while he was pacing the long corridor of "Tunis," he had come upon some fragile object or a sleepy houseman, he would have been delighted to make free with his hands in order to vent his wrath. He wanted to shout, to curse, to stamp his feet . . . And Fate, as though aware of his mood and wishing to accommodate him, put in his way Khalyavkin, a musician who occupied No. 31 and was habitually behind with his rent. Khalyavkin was standing before his door and, swaying noticeably, was poking at the

keyhole with his key. He was groaning and sending someone to hell, but the key refused to obey him and go where
it was supposed to. With one hand he poked unsteadily at
the keyhole, with the other he clutched a violin case.
Brykovich swooped down on him like a hawk and shouted
angrily:

"Ah, so it's you! See here, my dear sir, when are you going to come across with the rent? You're two weeks behind, my dear sir! I'll cut off your heat! I'll evict you, my
dear sir, devil take it!"

"You're in my . . . way . . ." the musician drawled
quietly. "Au . . . revoir!"

"Shame on you, Mr. Khalyavkin!" Brykovich went on.
"You get a hundred and twenty rubles a month, and you
could pay promptly! It's not right, my dear sir! It's out-
rageous!"

Finally the lock clicked and the door opened.

"Yes, sir, it's dishonest!" Brykovich continued, following the musician into his room. "I warn you, if you don't
pay up tomorrow, I won't wait to take you to court. I'll
show you! And please don't throw lighted matches on the
floor, you'll start a fire here! I'm not going to keep people
in my lodging house who aren't abstainers."

Khalyavkin looked at Brykovich with his merry, drunk-
en eyes and grinned.

"I'm co-completely at a losh as to why you're getting
excited. . . ." he mumbled, lighting a cigarette and burning his fingers. "I don't undershtand! Les's say that I don't
p-pay my rent; yes, I don't, but how does it concern you,
please tell me? What b-business is that of yours? You don't
pay any rent either, but I don't badger you, do I? You
don't pay, well, God bless you, you don't have to!"

"What do you mean"

"Jusht that. . . . You're not the b-boss here, but your
most esteemed s-spouse. . . . You're as much of a lodger

here as the resht. You don't own the house, so why do you trouble yourself? Follow my example: I don't trouble myself, do I? You aren't paying a kopeck for your lodging—well? Don't pay—you don't have to. I don't trouble myself a bit."

"I don't understand you, my dear sir!" muttered Brykovich, and assumed the attitude of a man who has been insulted and is ready to defend his honor at the drop of a hat.

"I apologize, though! I've forgotten that you got the house as your marriage settlement. . . . I apologize again! Although, to look at the matter from an ethical point of view," Khalyavkin continued, swaying as he stood, "you shtill don't have to get excited. . . . The house you got for nothing . . . for a song. . . . To take a broad view of the matter, it's just as much yours as mine. . . . Why have you appro-priated it? Because you occupy the post of a husband? What of it? It isn't at all difficult to be a husband. My dear fellow, bring me a gross of wives, and I'll be the husband to all of 'em—free for nothing! It'd be a favor!"

The musician's drunken babbling seemed to cut Brykovich to the quick. He flushed, and for a long time was at a loss as to what to say. Then he jumped at Khalyavkin and, looking daggers, struck the table violently with his fist.

"How dare you say this to me" he hissed. "How dare you?"

"Allow me . . ." Khalyavkin muttered, recoiling. "That's fortissimo. I don't know why you're offended, I . . . I didn't mean to insult you, but . . . to praise you. If a lady who owned such a lodging house came my way, then I . . . I'd open my arms to it!"

"But . . . but how dare you insult me?" Brykovich cried out, and again banged the table with his fist.

"I don't know what to make of it!" Khalyavkin shrugged

his shoulders, no longer smiling. "Of course, I'm drunk . . . maybe I did insult you. . . . In that case, forgive me, I'm sorry. Papa darling, forgive the first violin! I shertainly didn't want to insult you."

"That was cynical, what you said before. . . ." Brykovich brought out, somewhat mollified by Khalyavkin's apologetic tone. "There are things that people don't talk about this way. . . ."

"Well, well, never again . . . Never again, papa darling! Your hand!"

"All the more so that I have given you no cause. . . ." Brykovich continued in an offended tone, now completely mollified, but still not giving the musician his hand. "I've done nothing to injure you."

"Really I shouldn't have . . . touched on that delicate subject. . . . I blurted it out because I'm drunk and foolish. . . . Forgive me, papa darling! I'm really a beast! I'll douse my head with cold water, and I'll sober up."

"As it is, life is loathsome, disgusting, and now you come along with your insults!" said Brykovich, agitatedly pacing the room. "No one sees the truth, and everyone has his own stupid notions and makes no bones about coming out with them. I can just imagine what's said behind people's backs in this house! I can just imagine! True, I'm in the wrong: it was silly of me to come down on you at midnight on account of money. I'm wrong, but . . . one ought to be forbearing, enter into my situation, but you . . . you make filthy insinuations to my face!"

"Sweetheart, but I'm drunk! I repent, and it hurts me! Word of honor, it hurts me! And, papa darling, I'll pay up! As soon as I get my salary—that'll be on the first—I'll pay up! So it's peashe and good will? Bravo! Ah, my dear fellow, I love educated people! I myself studied at the c-conserv—devil take it, I can't get my tongue around it . . ."

The musician grew tearful, caught Brykovich by the

sleeve as he was pacing the room, and implanted a kiss on his cheek.

"Ah, my dear fellow, I'm as drunk as an owl, but 1 see everything clearly enough. Papa darling, have the houseman bring in a samovar for the first violin. You've a law here that after eleven o'clock one is not to lounge in the corridor or ashk for a samovar, but after the theatre I'm dying for a glass of tea!"

Brykovich rang for the houseman.

"Timofey," he said when the servant appeared, "bring a samovar for Mr. Khalyavkin."

"Not allowed, sir!" Timofey boomed in a bass voice. "Madam has given orders not to serve samovars after eleven o'clock."

"I'm giving you the order!" shouted Brykovich, turning pale.

"No use giving orders, if we ain't allowed . . ." the houseman grumbled, as he left the room. "If it ain't allowed, it can't be done. What's the use?"

Brykovich bit his lip, and turned toward the window.

"What a situation!" Khalyavkin sighed. "M-yes, words are useless. . . . Well, you don't have to be ashamed in front of me, I see everything clearly . . . I see through a man. I know the psychology of it. Well, if tea can't be had, there is nothing for it but to drink vodka. Let's have some vodka, eh?"

Khalyavkin took a bottle of vodka from the window sill, and some sausage too, and made himself comfortable on the couch, prepared to eat and drink. Brykovich looked at the drunk and listened to his endless babble. Perhaps because, at the sight of the musician's shaggy head, the pint of vodka and the cheap sausage, he recalled his own recent past when he had been poor but a free man, his face assumed a yet darker expression, and suddenly he wanted a drink. He went over to the table, downed a glass, and cleared his throat.

"It's a dog's life," he said, and shook his head. "Disgusting! You've just insulted me, the houseman has insulted me . . . and so it goes on, without an end. And why? Essentially, just so, for no reason. . . ."

After the third glass, Brykovich sat down on the couch and grew meditative, his head in his hands, then he sighed sadly and said:

"I've made a mistake! Oh, what a mistake! I sold my youth, my career, my principles—and now life is taking revenge. And what a cruel revenge!"

Because of the vodka and the unhappy thoughts, he turned very pale and, indeed, even seemed to have grown thin. Several times he clutched his head in desperation and moaned: "Oh, what a life, if you only knew!"

"Own up, tell me on your honor," he said, peering intently at Khalyavkin's face, "tell me on your honor, what . . . what do people think of me here? What do the students living here say? You must have heard them talking, I'm sure. . . ."

"Yes, I have. . . ."

"Well?"

"They don't say anything, they just . . . despise you."

The new-made friends talked no more. They parted only at dawn, when the servants had already started to get the stoves going.

"Don't you pay her . . . anything. . . ." Brykovich muttered, as he was leaving. "Don't you pay her a kopeck! Let her . . ."

Khalyavkin collapsed on the couch, and, putting his head on his violin case, began snoring noisily.

The following midnight they met again.

Brykovich, having tasted the sweetness of amicable libations, doesn't let a single night go by without them, and if he doesn't find Khalyavkin at home, he drops in on another lodger, to whom he complains of his lot, and he drinks, drinks, and complains again—and so it goes, night after night.

1886

boa constrictor and rabbit

Pyotr Semyonych, a played-out, bald-headed individual in a velvet dressing gown with crimson tassels, stroked his fluffy side whiskers and went on:

And here, *mon cher*, is, if you please, another method. It is the subtlest, cleverest and most venomous of them all, and the one most dangerous to husbands. Only psychologists and connoisseurs of the feminine heart can apply it. In using it the *conditio sine qua non* is patience, patience, and patience. It won't suit anyone who doesn't know how to wait and persist. According to this method, if you're trying to seduce a man's wife, you should keep as far away from her as possible. As soon as you begin to find her attractive, you stop visiting her, you meet her as seldom as possible, and that for a moment only, and you deprive yourself of the pleasure of talking to her. You act on her at a distance. It's all a matter of a kind of hypnosis. She must not see you but feel you, just as a rabbit feels the gaze of the boa constrictor. You hypnotize her not with your eyes, but with the poison of your tongue, and, what is more, the best channel is the husband himself.

For example, I am in love with N.N. and I want to win her. Somewhere, in a club or at the theatre, I run into her husband.

"And how is your spouse?" I asked him casually. "A charming woman, let me tell you! I like her immensely! Immensely, devil take it!"

"Hm . . . What is it about her that fascinates you so?" asks the gratified husband.

"She's a most charming, exquisite creature; she can rouse a stone and make it fall in love with her! But you husbands are such prosaic people. It's only during the honeymoon that you appreciate your wives. Don't you see that your wife is an ideal woman? Recognize it, and be glad that Fate gave you a wife like that! Such women are badly needed in this day and generation, just that sort!"

"What is it about her that you find so unusual?" the husband inquires.

"Why, she is a beauty, full of grace and life, candid, poetical, sincere, and at the same time enigmatic! Such women, once they fall in love with you, love you deeply, ardently. . . ."

And more of the same thing. That very night the husband, going to bed, will be sure to say to his wife: "I saw Pyotr Semyonych today. He spoke most enthusiastically about you. He was enraptured. According to him, you're a beauty, and you're graceful and enigmatic . . . and you are capable of loving in some extraordinary way. He certainly had a lot to say about you . . . Ha-ha . . ."

After that, still without seeing *her*, I seek out her spouse.

"By the way, old man . . ." I say to him, "yesterday a painter I know came to see me. Some prince or other had given him an order to paint the head of a typical Russian beauty. He gets two thousand for it. He asked me to look out for a model for him. I wanted to suggest that he turn to your wife, but couldn't bring myself to do it. But your wife would be just the type! That lovely head of hers! It's a damn shame that such a wonderful model escapes the artist's eye! A damn shame!"

No husband would be so lacking in gallantry as not to repeat this to his wife. In the morning the wife spends a long time before her mirror and thinks: "Where did he get the idea that I have a typically Russian face?"

After that, every time she looks in the mirror she thinks of me. Meanwhile, my accidental meetings with her husband continue. After one of them the husband comes home and starts staring at his wife's face.

"Why are you looking at me like that?" she asks.

"Well, that queer character, Pyotr Semyonych, has discovered that one of your eyes is darker than the other. For the life of me, I can't see it!"

The wife is before the mirror again. She scrutinizes herself for a long time and reflects: "Yes, the left eye does seem somewhat darker than the right . . . No, it's the right eye that seems darker than the left . . . But maybe it just seemed so to him!"

After the eighth or ninth encounter the husband says to the wife:

"I saw Pyotr Semyonych at the theatre. He apologizes for not coming to see you: he has no time. Says that he's awfully busy. It seems to me that he hasn't come to see us in about four months. I scolded him for it, but he excused himself, saying that he wouldn't visit us until he had finished a certain piece of work."

"But when does he expect to be through with it?" asks the wife.

"He says not before a year or two. And what kind of work can that trifler be doing, devil take him! He's a queer one, by Jove! He kept on badgering me like a madman:

'Why doesn't your wife go on the stage? With such an attractive appearance, such intelligence, and sensitiveness, it is a sin for her to be just a housewife. She ought to give up everything,' says he, 'and go where her inner voice summons her. Ordinary demands don't exist for such women. Natures like that should not be bound by time and space.'"

Of course, the wife has only the vaguest idea of what all this highfalutin talk means, but she melts, she is breathless with rapture.

"What nonsense!" she says, pretending indifference. "And what else did he say?"

"'If I weren't so busy,' says he, 'I'd take her away from you.' 'Well,' I say, 'take her, I'm not going to fight a duel over her.' 'You don't understand her!' he shouts. 'It is essential to understand her! She's an exceptional creature,' he says, 'strong, seeking a way out! It's a pity that I'm not Turgenev,' he says, 'or I'd put her in a novel.' Ha-ha . . . He's hipped on you! 'Well,' I say to myself, 'if you were to live with her two or three years, brother, you'd sing another tune. . . .' A queer fellow!"

The poor wife ends by being consumed with the passionate desire to meet me. I am the only person who has understood her, and there is so much that she can say to me alone! But I stubbornly persist in not calling on her and in keeping out of her way. She hasn't seen me in a long time, but my tormentingly sweet poison is working on her. The husband, yawning, transmits my remarks, and it seems to her that she hears my voice, that she sees my shining eyes.

The psychological moment arrives. One evening the husband comes home and says: "I've just met Pyotr Semyonych. He's dull, blue, down in the mouth."

"Why? What's the matter with him?"

"I can't make out. Complains that he's depressed. 'I'm lonely,' he says; 'I've no relatives, no friends,' he says, 'not a soul who could understand me and with whom I could really commune. No one understands me,' he says, 'and I desire one thing only: death . . .' "

"How foolish!" says the wife, but in her heart she thinks: "The poor darling! I understand him perfectly! I am lonely, too, no one understands me, except him; who but I can appreciate his state of mind?"

"Yes, a queer fellow . . ." the husband goes on. 'What with my depression,' he says, 'I can't stay home, I spend the night walking in the public gardens.' "

The wife is in a fever. She is dying to go to the public gardens and see, if only with one eye, the man who has been able to understand her, and is now so depressed. Who knows? If she were to speak to him, if she were to say two or three words of comfort to him, perhaps he would feel better. If she were to tell him that he had a friend who understood him and valued him, perhaps he would be resurrected.

"But this is impossible . . . absurd," she says to herself. "I mustn't even think of it! I may fall in love with him if I don't look out, and that would be stupid and ridiculous."

When her husband is asleep, she raises her fevered head, puts a finger to her lips, and reflects: what would happen if she risked leaving the house, now? Afterwards she could invent a story that she had run down to the druggist, to the dentist. "I'll go," she decides.

Her plan is ready: she will leave the house by the back door, and take a cab to the public gardens; once there, she will walk past him, glance at him, and then return home. Thus she will compromise neither herself nor her husband.

She dresses, quietly leaves the house, and hastens to the public gardens. The place is dark, deserted. The bare trees are asleep. There's not a soul to be seen. But then she glimpses a silhouette. It must be the man. Shivering all over, beside herself, she slowly moves toward me . . . and I toward her. For a moment we stand still and peer into each other's eyes. Another moment passes in silence and . . . the rabbit drops helplessly into the boa constrictor's jaws.

1887

an unpleasantness

Grigory Ivanovich Ovchinnikov, a zemstvo doctor, was a nervous man of about thirty-five, in poor health. He was known to his colleagues by his short papers on medical statistics and for his keen interest in so-called "problems of daily life." One morning he was making the rounds of the wards in the hospital of which he was in charge, followed, as usual, by his feldscher [medical assistant], Mikhail Zakharych, an elderly man with a fleshy face, greasy hair plastered down over his scalp, and one earring.

No sooner did the doctor start his rounds than one trifling circumstance began to seem very suspicious to him: the feldscher's waistcoat was creased and was continually riding up, in spite of the fact that he kept pulling at it and straightening it. His shirt, too, was mussed and rumpled; there was white fluff on his long, black jacket, on his trousers, and even on his tie. Obviously, the feldscher had slept in his clothes all night, and, to judge by his expression as he pulled at his waistcoat and straightened his tie, he felt uncomfortable in his clothes.

The doctor looked at him closely and grasped the situation. The feldscher was steady on his feet, he answered questions coherently, but the dull and sullen expression of his face, his lustreless eyes, his jerking neck and trembling hands, his disordered clothes, above all, the strenuous efforts he was making to conceal his condition—all pointed to the fact that he had just tumbled out of bed, that he had not had enough sleep, and that he had not got over the effects of the previous night's drinking-bout. . . . He was in the grip of an excruciating hangover and apparently very much displeased with himself.

The doctor, who disliked the feldscher, and had his reasons for it, felt a strong desire to say to him: "I see you're drunk!" All at once he was overcome by a disgust for the waistcoat, the long jacket, the ring in the fleshy ear, but he controlled his irritation and said gently and politely, as usual:

"Did Gerasim get his milk?"

"Yes, sir . . ." Makhail Zakharych replied, also in a mild tone.

As the doctor talked to Gerasim, he glanced at the temperature chart and was overcome by a new access of loathing. He checked himself, but lost control and asked rudely, choking on the words:

"Why isn't the temperature noted?"

"But it is, sir!" said Mikhail Zakharych quietly; then, glancing at the chart and discovering that the temperature had indeed not been noted, he shrugged his shoulders with an air of confusion and mumbled:

"I don't know, sir, Nadezhda Osipovna must have . . ."

"Last night's temperature wasn't noted, either!" the doctor went on. "All you do is get drunk, damn you! Even now you're as drunk as a cobbler! Where is Nadezhda Osipovna?"

Nadezhda Osipovna, the midwife, was not in the ward, although it was her duty to be present at the dressings every morning. The doctor looked around, and it seemed to him that the ward had not been tidied up, that everything was at sixes and sevens, that nothing had been done that should have been done and that everything was messy, crumpled, covered with fluff, like the feldscher's loathsome waistcoat, and he was filled with a desire to tear off his white apron, to rant, to throw everything up, to send it to the devil and get out. But he mastered himself and continued his rounds.

After Gerasim came a patient who had inflammation of the cellular tissue of the entire right arm. He needed a dressing. The doctor sat down on a stool in front of him and busied himself with the arm.

"Last night they must have had a gay time at a birthday celebration . . ." he thought to himself, slowly removing the bandage. "Wait, I'll show you a birthday! Although, what can I do? I can do nothing."

He felt an abscess on the red, swollen arm, and said:

"A scalpel!"

Mikhail Zakharych, who was at pains to prove that he was steady on his pins and as fit as a fiddle, dashed from where he was standing and quickly handed over a scalpel.

"Not this! A new one," said the doctor.

The assistant walked mincingly across to the stool on which stood the box with supplies and instruments and began hastily rummaging in it. He kept on whispering to the nurses, noisily moving the box about on the stool, and twice he dropped something. Meanwhile, the doctor sat there, waiting, and felt a physical sense of irritation at the whispering and the other noise.

"Well?" he demanded. "You must have left them downstairs. . . ."

The feldscher ran up to him and handed him two scalpels, and in doing so carelessly breathed in the doctor's face.

"Not these," the doctor snapped irritably. "I told you

plainly: give me a new one. Never mind, go and get some sleep; you reek like a pothouse. You can't be trusted."

"What other kind of knives do you want?" asked the feldscher, in a tone of irritation and with a lazy shrug of his shoulders.

He was annoyed with himself and ashamed because all the patients and nurses were staring at him, and to hide the fact that he was ashamed, he forced a smirk and repeated:

"What other kind of knives do you want?"

The doctor felt tears rising to his eyes and was conscious of a tremor in his fingers. He made another effort to control himself and brought out in a shaking voice:

"Go and sleep it out! I don't want to talk to a drunk. . . ."

"You can call me to account only for cause," said the assistant, "and if I've had a drop, well, nobody has the right to throw it up to me. I'm on duty, ain't I? What more do you want? I'm on duty, ain't I?"

The doctor leapt to his feet and, without realizing what he was doing, swung his fist and hit the feldscher with all his might. He did not understand why he had done it, but he felt great pleasure because the blow landed smack in the feldscher's face, and that solid citizen, a family man, a churchgoer, substantial, self-respecting, staggered, bounced like a ball and sat down on a stool. The doctor had a passionate urge to hit out again, but when he saw the pale, alarmed faces of the nurses clustered about that hateful countenance, his pleasure died away, he waved his hand in a gesture of desperation and ran out of the ward.

In the courtyard he encountered Nadezhda Osipovna, an unmarried woman about twenty-seven years old, with a sallow complexion and her hair loose over her shoulders, who was on her way to the hospital. The skirt of her pink cotton dress was narrow, and so she walked mincingly. Her dress rustled, she jerked her shoulders in time with her steps and tossed her head as if she were mentally humming a gay tune.

"Aha, the siren!" the doctor said to himself, recalling that in the hospital they called the midwife a siren to tease her. And he took pleasure in the thought that he was about to give a piece of his mind to this mincing, self-infatuated, would-be dressy creature.

"Where on earth have you been?" he exclaimed, as they approached each other. "Why aren't you in the hospital? The temperatures haven't been recorded, everything's at sixes and sevens, the feldscher is drunk, you sleep till noon! . . . You'd better look for another position! You're fired!"

Having reached his apartment, the doctor tore off his white apron and the towel which served him as a belt, angrily tossed both of them into a corner, and began pacing the room.

"God, what people, what people!" he groaned. "They're no help, they just get in the way of the work! I haven't the strength to go on! I can't do it. I'm getting out."

His heart was pounding, he was trembling all over, and he felt like bursting into tears. He tried to quiet himself with the thought that he had been in the right, and that it was a good thing that he had struck the feldscher. In the first place, reflected the doctor, it was abominable that the hospital should have engaged a man not on his own merits but owing to the intercession of his aunt, who was employed as a nursemaid by the chairman of the zemstvo board. It was disgusting to see how this influential nanny, when she drove to the hospital for treatment, behaved as though she were at home and refused to wait her turn. The feldscher was badly trained, knew very little, and did not understand what he had learned. He drank, was insolent, untidy, accepted bribes from the patients, and secretly sold the medicines supplied free by the zemstvo. Moreover, everyone knew that he practiced medicine on the quiet, and treated young men from the town for unmentionable diseases, using remedies of his own concoction. It would not have been so bad if he had simply been a quack, of whom there were plenty, but no—he was a quack who believed in himself, a quack who was furtively in revolt. Behind the doctor's back he cupped and bled dispensary patients, he assisted at operations without having washed his hands, he always examined wounds with a dirty probe. All this was sufficient to show how profoundly and completely he despised the doctors' medicine with its rules and regulations.

When at last his fingers were steady again, the doctor sat down at his desk and wrote a letter to the chairman of the board:

Esteemed Lev Trofimovich!

If on receipt of this note your board does not discharge feldscher Mikhail Zakharych Smirnovsky, and will not grant me the right to choose my feldscher, I shall regretfully be forced to resign as physician of the N. hospital and request you to secure someone to succeed me. Please remember me to Lubov Fyodorovna and to Yus.

Respectfully,

G. Ovchinnikov.

Having reread this letter, the doctor decided that it was too short and not sufficiently formal. Besides, the mention of Lubov Fyodorovna and of Yus (the nickname of the chairman's younger son) was hardly appropriate in a business letter dealing with an official matter.

"The devil, why bring in Yus?" the doctor said to himself, tore the letter to bits, and started thinking of another. "Dear Sir," he began. Through the open window he could see a flock of ducks with their young. Waddling and stumbling, they were hurrying down the road, apparently on their way to the pond. One duckling picked up a piece of gut that was lying on the ground, tried to swallow it,

choked on it and raised an alarmed squeaking. Another
duckling ran up, pulled the gut out of its beak and choked
on the thing too. . . . At some distance from the fence, in
the lacy shadow cast on the grass by the young lindens,
the cook Darya was wandering about, picking sorrel for
a vegetable soup. . . . Voices were heard. . . . Zot, the
coachman, with a bridle in his hand, and Manuilo, the hospital attendant, wearing a dirty apron, were standing by
the shed, chatting and laughing.

"They are talking about my having struck the feldscher . . ." thought the doctor. "Before the day is over the
whole district will know about this scandal. . . . And so:
'Dear Sir! If your board does not discharge . . .'"

The doctor knew very well that under no circumstance
would the board dismiss him rather than the feldscher,
that it would let every feldscher in the whole district go,
rather than lose such an excellent man as Doctor Ovchinnikov. Certainly, as soon as Lev Trofimovich got the letter
he would drive up in his troika and commence: "What's
this that you've taken into your head, old man? My dear
fellow! What is it? In Christ's name! Why? What's the
matter? Where is he? Fetch the blackguard here! He must
be fired! Out with him, by all means! There mustn't be a
sign of the fellow here tomorrow!" Then he and the doctor would have dinner, and after dinner he would stretch
out on his back on this raspberry-colored couch, cover his
face with a newspaper and begin to snore; after a good
sleep he would have tea, and then drive the doctor over to
his own place for the night. And the upshot of it all would
be that the feldscher would remain in the hospital and the
doctor would not resign.

But at heart the doctor wanted an altogether different
dénouement. His wish was that the feldscher's old aunt
should be triumphant, that the board, in spite of his eight
years of continuous service, should accept his resignation

without a word of protest and, indeed, even with pleasure. He dreamed of how he would leave the hospital, to which he had got accustomed, how he would write a letter to the editor of *The Physician*, how his colleagues would tender him an address of sympathy. . . .

The siren appeared on the road. With a mincing gait and a swish of her dress, she walked over to the window and said:

"Grigory Ivanovich, will you be receiving the patients yourself or do you want us to receive them without you?"

Her eyes were saying: "You lost your temper, but now you have calmed down and you're ashamed of yourself; I am magnanimous, however, and don't notice it."

"I'll come right away," said the doctor.

He put on his apron, belted it with the towel, and went to the hospital.

"It wasn't right that I ran out after I struck him," he thought on the way. "It looked as though I were abashed or frightened. . . . I acted like a schoolboy. . . . It was all wrong!"

It seemed to him that when he entered the ward, the patients would look at him with embarrassment and that he, too, would be discomfited. But when he entered, the patients lay quietly in their beds and scarcely paid any attention to him. The face of the consumptive Gerasim expressed complete indifference and seemed to say: "You were put out with him and you gave him a dressing down. That's as it should be, brother."

The doctor opened two abscesses on the arm and bandaged it. Then he went to the women's ward, where he performed an operation on a peasant woman's eye. The siren was continually at his side and assisted him as though nothing had happened and everything were all right. Then came the turn of the ambulatory patients. In the doctor's small examining room the window was wide open. If you sat down on the window-sill and leaned over slightly, you could see the young grass two or three feet below. There had been a heavy thunderstorm the previous evening, and the grass looked somewhat trampled and glossy. The path which ran just beyond the window and led to the ravine looked washed clean, and the pieces of broken medicine bottles and jars scattered on both sides of it also looked washed, sparkling in the sun and sending out dazzling beams. Farther on, beyond the path, young firs garmented in luxuriant green, pressed close to one another; behind them loomed birches, their trunks white as paper, and through the foliage of the birches that trembled slightly in the breeze, you could see the blue, bottomless sky. When you looked out of the window, there were starlings hopping on the path, turning their foolish beaks in the direction of the window and debating with themselves: to get scared or not? Deciding to get scared, one by one they darted toward the treetops with a gay chirp, as if poking fun at the doctor who didn't know how to fly. . . .

The heavy smell of iodoform could not drown out the freshness and fragrance of the spring day. It was good to breathe!

"Anna Spiridonova!" the doctor called.

A young peasant woman in a red dress entered the examining room and turned to the icon, murmuring a prayer.

"What hurts you?" asked the doctor.

The woman glanced distrustfully at the door through which she had just entered and at the other door which led to the drug dispensary, came closer to the doctor, and whispered:

"No children!"

"Who hasn't registered yet?" the siren shouted from the dispensary. "Report here."

"He is a beast," the doctor thought to himself as he examined the patient, "just because he made me strike him. I never in my life struck anyone before."

Anna Spiridonova left. Next came an old man who had a venereal disease, then a peasant woman with three children, all suffering from scabies, and things began to hum. There was no sign of the feldscher. Behind the door in the drug dispensary, the siren was making gay little noises, swishing her dress and clinking the bottles. Now and then she came into the examining room, to help with an operation or to fetch a prescription, and all with an air as though everything were as it should be.

"She's glad that I struck him," reflected the doctor, listening to the midwife's voice. "She and the feldscher were like cat and dog, and it will be a red letter day for her if he's discharged. I think the nurses are glad, too. . . . How disgusting!"

When he was at his busiest, he began to feel as though the midwife and the nurses, and the very patients, had purposely assumed an indifferent and even a cheerful expression. It was as though they understood that he was ashamed and pained, but out of delicacy they pretended not to. And he, wishing to show them that he was not ashamed, shouted roughly:

"Hey, you there! Shut the door, it's drafty!"

But he was ashamed, and ill at ease. Having examined forty-five patients, he took his time leaving the hospital.

The midwife had already been to her quarters. A crimson kerchief round her shoulders, a cigarette between her teeth and a flower in her loose hair, she was hurrying off, either on a case or to visit friends. Patients sat on the porch and warmed themselves in the sun. The starlings were still making a racket and chasing beetles. The doctor looked about and reflected that among these untroubled existences of even tenor only two lives, his and the feldscher's, stuck out and were worthless, like two damaged piano keys. The feldscher must surely have gone to bed to sleep it off, but was probably unable to fall asleep because he knew that he was in a bad way, that he had been insulted and had lost his job. His position was excruciating. As for the doctor, who had never struck anyone, he felt as though he had lost his chastity. He no longer blamed the feldscher and exonerated himself, he was only perplexed: how had it happened that he, a decent fellow who had never struck even a dog, could have hit a man? Once in his lodging, he went to his study and lay down on the couch with his face to the back of it, and reflected thus:

"He is a wicked man, he does the patients no good; he's been with me three years now and I'm just fed up; still, what I did was inexcusable. I took advantage of the fact that I was the stronger of the two. He is my subordinate, he was at fault, and, besides, he was drunk; I'm his superior, I was in the right and I was sober. And so I was the stronger. In the second place, I struck him in front of people who look up to me, and so I set them an abominable example."

The doctor was called to dinner. He had scarcely tasted the soup when he left the table and went to lie down again.

"What should I do then?" he continued communing with himself. "As soon as possible he must be given satisfaction. . . . But how? As a hard-headed man, he probably thinks that a duel is stupid, or it doesn't mean anything to him. If I were to apologize to him in that very ward in front of the nurses and the patients, the apology would satisfy me but not him; being a horrid fellow, he would interpret my apology as cowardice, as fear that he would lodge a complaint against me with the authorities. Besides, the apology would just be the end of discipline in the hospital. Shall I offer him money? No, that is immoral and smacks of bribery. Or shall I put the problem up to our immediate superiors, that is, to the board? They could reprimand me or discharge me. But they won't. Besides, it's awkward to get the board mixed up in the intimate affairs of the hospital, and anyway the board has no legal right to deal with these things."

About three hours after dinner the doctor went down to the pond for a swim, and as he walked he was thinking to himself:

"And shouldn't I do what everyone does under such circumstances? Let him sue me. I am unquestionably guilty, I'll put up no defense, and the judge will send me to jail. In this way the injured party will receive satisfaction, and those who look up to me will see that I was in the wrong."

The idea appealed to him. He was pleased, and decided that the problem was settled and that there could be no happier solution.

"Well, that's fine!" he thought, getting into the water and watching the shoals of small golden crucians that were scurrying away from him. "Let him sue me. That will be all the easier for him because he's no longer on the job, and after this scandal one of us obviously must leave the hospital. . . ."

In the evening the doctor ordered his gig, intending to drive over to the captain's to play vint. As he stood in his study, in his coat and hat, putting on his gloves and ready to leave, the outer door opened creakingly and someone noiselessly entered the anteroom.

"Who's there?" the doctor called out.

"It's me, sir . . ." a muffled voice answered.

The doctor felt his heart begin to pound and he was chilled through with shame and a kind of incomprehensible fear. Mikhail Zakharych (it was he) coughed softly, and timidly entered the study. After a pause, he said in a muffled, guilty tone of voice:

"Forgive me, Grigory Ivanovich!"

The doctor was taken aback and didn't know what to

say. He realized that the feldscher had come to abase himself and apologize, not out of Christian humility, nor in order to heap coals of fire on the man who had insulted him, but simply for a sordid reason: "I'll force myself to apologize, and perhaps they won't fire me and take the bread out of my mouth. . . ." What could be more degrading?

"Forgive me . . ." repeated the feldscher.

"Listen," began the doctor, without looking at him, and still not knowing what to say. "Listen . . . I insulted you and . . . I must suffer for it, that is, I must give you satisfaction. . . . You're not the man to fight a duel. . . . Nor am I, for that matter. I insulted you and you . . . can lodge a complaint against me with the justice of the peace, and I'll take my punishment. . . . But the two of us can't stay in the same place. . . . One of us, you or I, must go! ('My God! I'm saying just the wrong thing!' the doctor was horrified. 'How stupid, how stupid!') In a word, sue me! But we can't go on working together! . . . It's either you or I! Lodge your complaint tomorrow!"

The feldscher looked at the doctor with a frown, and the frankest contempt flared up in his dark, turbid eyes. He had always thought that the doctor was an impractical, capricious, puerile fellow, and now he despised him for his nervousness, for his incomprehensible, jerky way of speaking.

"I will bring suit," he said, with a look of sullen hatred.

"Well, do!"

"You think I won't sue you? I won't? I will. . . . You've no right to use your fists on me. You ought to be ashamed of yourself! Only drunken peasants fight, and you're an educated man. . . ."

Suddenly the doctor's chest tightened with hatred, and in a voice that did not sound like his own he shouted:

"Get out!"

The feldscher reluctantly took a step or two (he looked

as though he wanted to say something further), then walked into the anteroom and stood there, thinking. Having apparently made up his mind, he resolutely went out.

"How stupid, how stupid!" the doctor muttered, when the feldscher was gone. "How stupid and vulgar all this is!"

He felt that his behavior toward the man had been puerile, and he already realized that all his notions about the lawsuit were foolish, that they did not solve the problem but only complicated it.

"How stupid!" he repeated to himself, as he sat in his gig and later while he was playing vint at the captain's. "Is it possible that I am so badly educated and know life so little that I can't solve this simple problem? What shall I do?"

The next morning the doctor saw the feldscher's wife step into a carriage and reflected: "She must be going to his aunt's. Let her!"

The hospital managed to get along without a feldscher. It was necessary to notify the board, but the doctor was still unable to decide what form his letter should take. Now, it seemed to him, the tenor of the letter should be: "I request you to discharge the feldscher, although I am to blame, not he." For a decent person it was almost impossible to make this statement in a way which would not be stupid and shameful.

Two or three days later the doctor was informed that the feldscher had complained to Lev Trofimovich. The chairman hadn't let him say a word, had stamped his feet and chased him out, shouting: "I know you! Get out! I won't listen to you!" From there the feldscher had gone to the office of the zemstvo and filed a report, in which he did not mention the slap in the face and asked nothing for himself, but informed the board that in his presence the doctor had several times commented unfavorably on the board and its chairman, that he treated patients in a manner contrary to accepted rules, that he was neglectful about making the prescribed rounds of his district, etc., etc. On learning of this, the doctor laughed, and thought: "What a fool!" And he felt shame and pity for the man who was behaving so foolishly; the more stupid things a man does in his defence, the weaker and more helpless he obviously is.

Exactly a week later the doctor received a summons from the justice of the peace.

"This is altogether absurd," he thought as he signed the necessary paper. "You couldn't conceive anything stupider."

As he was on his way to the court on a windless morning under an overcast sky, what he felt was not shame, but annoyance and disgust. He was vexed with himself, with the feldscher, with the situation.

"I'll up and say in court: 'To the devil with the lot of you!'" he raged inwardly. "'You're all asses and you understand nothing!'"

When he reached the building in which court was to be held, he saw in the doorway three of his nurses who had been called as witnesses, and the siren as well. In her impatience she was shifting her weight from one foot to the other, and she even blushed with pleasure when she beheld the principal character in the impending trial. The doctor, furious, was about to swoop down on them like a hawk and stun them by saying: "Who permitted you to leave the hospital? Be good enough to get back to your posts right away!" But he controlled himself and, pretending calmness, made his way through the crowd of peasants to the courtroom. The chamber was empty, and the justice's chain hung on the back of his armchair. The doctor went into the clerk's cubbyhole. There he saw a thin-faced young man wearing a cotton jacket with bulging pockets—it was the clerk—and the feldscher. He was sitting at a desk and, having nothing better to do, was paging a law journal. At the doctor's entrance the clerk rose, the feldscher looked abashed and rose also.

"Alexander Arkhipovich isn't here yet?" asked the doctor, embarrassed.

"Not yet, sir. He's in his own apartments," the clerk answered.

The court was located on the justice's estate, in one of the wings of his large house. The doctor left the court and walked unhurriedly toward the justice's apartments. He found Alexander Arkhipovich in the dining-room, where a samovar was steaming. The justice, with his coat off and not even a waistcoat, his shirt open, so that his chest was bare, was standing at the table and, holding the teakettle with both hands, was pouring himself a tumbler of tea black as coffee. When he saw his visitor, he quietly drew another tumbler toward himself, filled it, and, without greeting the doctor, asked:

"With or without sugar?"

Long ago the justice of the peace had been in the cavalry, but now because for many years he had held elective offices he had the rank of Actual Councilor of State. Yet he had not discarded his army uniform or his military habits. He had long moustaches, the kind fancied by chiefs of police, wore trousers with piping, and all his gestures and words breathed military grace. He spoke with his head slightly thrown back, and garnishing his speech with the juicy, dignified "m'yeses" of a general, he swayed his shoulders and rolled his eyes. When he greeted you or gave you a light, he scraped his feet, and when he walked, he clinked his spurs as gently and cautiously as if every sound they made caused him intolerable pain. Having seated the doctor at table and provided him with tea, he stroked his broad chest and his stomach, heaved a deep sigh, and said:

"M'yes. . . . Would you perhaps have some vodka and a bite to eat . . . m'yes?"

"No, thank you, I'm not hungry."

Both felt that they could not avoid the subject of the scandal at the hospital, and both felt awkward. The doctor was silent. The justice, with a graceful movement of the hand, caught an insect which had bit him on his chest, examined it carefully and let it go. Then he drew a deep sigh, looked up at the doctor, and, speaking deliberately, asked:

"Listen, why don't you send him packing?"

The doctor caught a note of sympathy in his voice; he was suddenly sorry for himself, and he felt tired and jaded by the disagreeable experiences he had endured in the course of the preceding week. His face showed that he had finally reached the end of his patience. He rose from the table, frowning irritably and shrugging his shoulders, and said:

"Send him packing! Good Lord, the logic of you people! It's astonishing, your logic! Don't you know that I can't send him packing? You sit here and think that I'm boss at the hospital and can do what I please! It's astonishing, your logic! Can I send the feldscher packing, if his aunt is employed as a nursemaid by Lev Trofimovich, and if Lev Trofimovich wants such gossips and flunkies as this Zakharych? What can I do if the zemstvo people wipe the floor with us physicians, if they hinder us at every step? To hell with them, I don't want to work for them, that's all! I don't want to!"

"Well, well, well, old man. . . . You're making a mountain out of a molehill, you know. . . ."

"The marshal of the nobility goes out of his way to prove that we're all nihilists, he spies on us and treats us as his clerks. What right has he to come to the hospital in my absence and question the nurses and patients? Isn't it insulting? And this crazy Semyon Alexeich of yours, who does his own plowing and doesn't believe in medicine because he is as strong as an ox and eats like one, calls us parasites

out loud and to our faces and begrudges us our salaries.
Devil take him! I work day and night, I get no rest, I'm
needed here more than all these psychopaths, bigots, reformers, and all the other clowns taken together! I've made
myself sick with work, and what I get instead of gratitude
is to have my salary thrown in my teeth! Many·thanks!
And everybody thinks he's entitled to stick his nose into
what's none of his business, to teach me, to discipline me!
At one meeting this Kamchatsky, a member of your board,
reprimanded the physicians for wasting potassium iodide,
and advised us to be careful in using cocaine! What does he
know about it, I ask you? How's he concerned? Why
doesn't he teach you how you run your court?"

"But he's a cad, my dear fellow, he's a bounder. . . .
You mustn't pay any attention to him. . . ."

"A cad, a bounder, and yet you've elected this character
to the board and you allow him to stick his nose everywhere! You smile! According to you, these are trifles, baga-
telles, but get it into your head that there are so many of
these trifles that they make up my whole life, the way
grains of sand make a mountain! I can't stand it any longer!
I haven't the strength, Alexander Arkhipovich! A little
more, and I'll not only use my fists on people, I'll draw a
gun on them! Get it into your head, my nerves aren't made
of iron. I'm a human being like you. . . ."

Tears came to the doctor's eyes, and his voice quavered;
he turned aside and looked out of the window. Silence fell.

"M'yes, my dear fellow . . ." mumbled the justice
thoughtfully. "On the other hand, to take a cold-blooded
view . . ." (the justice caught a mosquito and, screwing
his eyes tight, examined it carefully, crushed it and threw
it into the slop-basin). "You see, there's no reason why he
should be sent packing. Send him packing, and he'll be
replaced by someone just like him or worse. You can try
out a hundred men, and you won't find one you want to

keep. . . . They're all no good." The justice stroked his armpits and then slowly lit a cigarette. "We must put up with it, bad as it is. Let me tell you that right now honest, sober, reliable workers can be found only among the intellectuals and the peasants, that is at the poles of society and only there. You can find a thoroughly honest physician, let's say, an excellent teacher, an honest plowman or a blacksmith, but the people in between, so to speak, those who no longer belong to the masses and who haven't yet become part of the intelligentsia, are an unreliable element. It's very hard to find an honest and sober feldscher, a clerk, a salesman, and so forth. Exceedingly hard! I've been in the courts since God knows when, and in all these years I've never had an honest, sober clerk, although I've tried out no end of them in my time. They are people who have no discipline, let alone principles, so to speak. . . ."

"Why is he talking this way?" thought the doctor. "Neither of us is saying what ought to be said."

"Here is a trick my own clerk played on me only last Friday," the justice continued. "In the evening he got together with some drunks, the devil knows who, and all night long they were boozing in my chambers. How do you like that? I've nothing against drinking. Devil take you, drink, but why bring utter strangers into my chambers? Judge for yourself: how long would it take to steal some document, say, a promissory note, from the files? And what do you think? After that orgy I spent two days checking up to see if anything was missing. . . . Well, what are you going to do about this wretch? Send him packing? Very well. . . . And what's the guarantee that the next one won't be worse?"

"Besides, how can you send a man packing?" asked the doctor. "It's easy to say it. How can I fire him and take the bread out of his mouth, when I know that he is a family man and has nothing? Where would he go with his family?"

"Devil take it, I'm saying the wrong thing!" he thought to himself, and it seemed odd to him that he could not fix his mind on some one definite idea or sentiment. "It's because I'm shallow and don't know how to think," he reflected.

"The man in-between, as you called him, is unreliable," he went on. "We send him packing, scold him, slap him in the face, but we also ought to enter into his situation. He is neither a peasant nor a master, neither fish, flesh, nor fowl. His past is bleak, at present he has twenty-five rubles a month, a hungry family and a job in which he's not his own master. The future holds the same twenty-five rubles and the same dependent position, even if he holds on to his job for a hundred years. He has neither education nor property; he has no time to read or to go to church; he doesn't profit by our example, because we don't let him get close enough to us. So he goes on living like that, day in, day out, till he dies, without hoping for anything better, underfed, always afraid that any day he may be evicted from the quarters the Government provides him with, and that his children won't have a roof over their heads. Under such circumstances, how is a man to keep from drinking, from stealing? Under such conditions, how can he have principles?"

"So here we are, solving social problems!" the doctor thought to himself. "And, my God, how awkwardly! And what's all this for?"

The sound of bells was heard. Someone drove into the yard and halted before the wing in which the court chambers were located and then went on and stopped at the porch of the big house.

"Himself is here," said the justice, glancing out of the window. "Well, you'll get it in the neck!"

"Please, let's be done with it, and fast," the doctor pleaded. "If possible, take my case out of turn. I've no time, by Jove!"

"All right, all right. . . . Only, I don't know, old man, if the case is within my jurisdiction. Your relations with the assistant were, so to speak, official, and, besides, you smacked him while he was on duty. But I don't know for certain. Let's ask Lev Trofimovich."

Hurried steps were heard, and heavy breathing, and Lev Trofimovich, chairman of the board, a white-haired, bald-headed old man with a long beard and red eyelids, appeared in the doorway.

"Greetings!" he brought out, panting.

"Ouf! My dears! Tell them to bring me some kvass, judge! I can't stand it. . . ."

He sank into an armchair, but immediately jumped up, trotted over to the doctor and, staring at him angrily, said in a squeaking tenor:

"Many, many thanks to you, Grigory Ivanovich! You've done me a great favor, thank you! I won't forget it to my dying day, amen! Friends don't act like that! Say what you will, it's not decent of you. Why didn't you let me know? What do you think I am? Whom do you take me for? Am I your enemy or an utter stranger to you? Am I your enemy? Have I ever refused you anything? Eh?"

Staring hard and twiddling his fingers, the chairman drank his kvass, wiped his lips hurriedly, and continued:

"Thank you very, very kindly! Why didn't you let me know? If you had had any feeling for me, you would have driven up and talked to me as a friend: 'Lev Trofimovich, my dear fellow, the facts are so-and-so. . . . This is what happened, and so on and so forth . . .' Before you could turn round, I would have arranged everything, and there would have been no scandal. . . . That fool has gone completely crazy, he wanders through the district, concocts stories and gossips with the women, and you, it's really shameful, if you'll excuse my saying so, you've started the devil knows what kind of a row, you've got that fool to sue you! It's shameful! Just shameful! Everybody asks me: What's the matter? What happened? How did it happen? And I, the chairman, know nothing of what's going on. You have no need of me! Many, many thanks, Grigory Ivanovich!"

The chairman made him such a low bow that he turned crimson, then he went over to the window and called:

"Zhigalov, ask Mikhail Zakharych to come up here! Tell him to come up at once! It isn't right, my dear sir!" he said, walking away from the window. "Even my wife has taken offense, and you know how much she likes you. The trouble with you, gentlemen, is that you rely too much on reason! Everything has to be logical with you, you drag in principles, and worry about all the fine points, and as a result all you do is get things balled up!"

"And with you everything has to be illogical, and what is the result?" asked the doctor.

"What's the result? The result is that if I hadn't come here just now, you'd have disgraced yourself, and us, too. . . . It's your luck that I came!"

The feldscher entered and stopped on the threshold. The chairman took up such a position that he was half turned away from the feldscher, put his hands in his pockets, cleared his throat, and said:

"Apologize to the doctor at once!"

The doctor flushed and ran into another room.

"You see, the doctor doesn't want to accept your apology!" the chairman went on. "He wants you to show that you're sorry not in words, but in deeds. Do you give your word of honor that from now on you will follow his orders and lead a sober life?"

"I do," the assistant brought out sullenly, in a deep voice.

"Watch out, then! And Heaven help you, if you don't!

I'll fire you before you can say knife. If anything happens, don't come begging for mercy. . . . Now, go on home. . . ."

For the feldscher, who had already accepted his misfortune, such a turn of events was a breath-taking surprise. So much so that he grew pale with joy. He wanted to say something, put out his hand, but could not bring out a word, smiled stupidly and left.

"That's that!" said the chairman. "And there's no need for any trial."

He drew a sigh of relief, and with an air of having just accomplished something difficult and important, he looked closely at the samovar and the glasses, rubbed his hands, and said:

"Blessed are the peacemakers. . . . Pour out a glass for me, Sasha. But wait, have them bring me a bite. . . . And, well, some vodka."

"Gentlemen, this is absurd!" said the doctor, as he entered the dining-room, still flushed, and wringing his hands. "This . . . this is a comedy! It's vile! I can't bear it! It's better to have twenty trials than to settle matters in this farcical fashion. No, I can't stand it!"

"What do you want, then?" the chairman snapped at him. "Shall we fire him? Very well, I'll fire him."

"No, not that. I don't know what I want, but to take such an attitude towards life, gentlemen. . . . Oh, my God! It's torture!"

The doctor started to bustle about nervously, looking for his hat, and failing to find it, sank into an armchair, exhausted.

"It's vile!" he repeated.

"My dear fellow," the justice muttered, "to some extent I fail to understand you, so to speak. . . . You're the one who is at fault in this affair, aren't you? To go about at the end of the nineteenth century, biffing people on the

jaw, that is, you will agree, not quite . . . so to speak.
. . . He's a scoundrel, bu-u-ut, you will agree, you acted
heedlessly, too."

"Of course!" the chairman chimed in.

Vodka and hors d'oeuvres were served.

Before taking his leave the doctor emptied a glass of
vodka and ate a radish. As he was returning to the hospital,
a mist, such as veils the grass on autumn mornings, was
beclouding his thoughts.

"Can it be," he reflected, "that after all that was said and
thought and suffered during the past week, the end should
be something so absurd and vulgar? How stupid! How
stupid!"

He was ashamed of having involved strangers in his personal problem, ashamed of the things he had said to these
people, ashamed of having drunk vodka out of a habit of
idle drinking and idle living, ashamed of his blunt, shallow
mind.

Back in the hospital, he immediately started making the
rounds of the wards. The feldscher followed him, stepping
softly, like a cat, and answering questions gently. The
feldscher, the siren, the nurses, all pretended that nothing
had occurred and that everything was as it should be. The
doctor himself made every effort to appear indifferent. He
issued orders, fumed, cracked jokes with the patients, but
in his brain a thought kept stirring:

"Stupid, stupid, stupid . . ."

1888

a fragment

Having retired from the service, Actual State Councilor Kozerogov bought himself a modest property and settled down in the country. Here, in imitation partly of Cincinnatus, partly of the distinguished professor of natural history, Kaigorodov, he toiled in the sweat of his face and noted in his diary his observations of Nature. After his death the diary, together with his other effects. by his testament came into the possession of his housekeeper, Marfa Yevlampievna. As everyone knows, that estimable old soul tore down the manor house and on its site erected a wonderful eating-house which was licensed to serve spirituous liquors. In this tavern there was a "better" room set aside for traveling landowners and functionaries, and there the diary of the deceased lay on a table for the convenience of such guests as might be in need of paper. I chanced to get hold of one sheet. Apparently it related to the very beginning of the agricultural activities of the deceased and contained the following entries:

"March 3. The spring migration of birds has started: yesterday I saw sparrows. I greet you, feathered children of the south! In your sweet warbling I seem to hear the wish: 'Be happy, your Excellency!'

"March 14. Today I asked Marfa Yevlampievna; 'Why does the cock crow so often?' She replied: 'Because he has a throat.' My retort was: 'I too have a throat, yet I do not crow!' How many mysteries does Nature harbor! During my service in St. Petersburg I ate turkey more than once, but live turkeys I saw only yesterday. A very remarkable bird.

"March 22. The local police officer called. For a long time we discussed virtue—I sitting down, he standing up. Among other things, he asked me: 'Would you wish, your Excellency, to be young again?' To this I replied: 'No, I would not wish it, for, were I young, I would not have my present high rank.' He saw eye to eye with me, and drove off visibly moved.

"April 16. With my own hands I dug up two beds in the kitchen garden and planted buckwheat grits in them. I said nothing about it to anyone, in order to have a surprise for my Marfa Yevlampievna, to whom I owe so many happy moments of my life. Yesterday at tea she complained bitterly of her corpulence, saying that already her increasing girth was preventing her from passing through the doorway of the storeroom. I observed to her in reply: 'On the contrary, darling, the fullness of your figure is an adornment to you and serves to dispose me toward you even more favorably.' She blushed, and I arose and embraced her, placing both arms around her, for with one arm alone you cannot embrace her.

"May 28. An old man, seeing me at the riverside near the women's bathing huts, asked me why I was sitting there. My answer was: 'I am staying to see to it that young men don't come and loiter here.' To this the old man replied: 'Let us see to it together.' Having said this, he sat down beside me, and we began to talk of virtue."

1892

peasants

The first nine chapters of this story form a tale complete in itself. It originally appeared in the issue of a Moscow monthly for April, 1897, and has long been available in more than one English rendering. Half a dozen years ago two chapters of an unfinished sequel, previously unknown, were published in the definitive edition of Chekhov's works. A translation of the entire narrative is given here, the last two chapters appearing in English for the first time.

Nikolay Chikildeyev, a waiter in the Moscow hotel, Slavyansky Bazar, had been taken ill. His legs went numb and his gait became unsteady, so that one day, as he was going along the corridor, carrying an order of ham and peas on a tray, he stumbled and fell. He had to give up his job. Whatever money he and his wife had had they had spent on doctors and medicines; they had nothing left to live on; idleness weighed heavily upon him and he decided to go back to the village from which he had come. It was easier to be ill at home, and it was cheaper living there; and not for nothing is it said there is help in the walls of home.

666666

666666666

He arrived in his native Zhukovo towards evening. In his childhood the house in which he was born figured as a bright, cosy, comfortable place. But now, entering the log cabin, he was positively frightened: it was so dark and crowded and squalid. His wife Olga and his daughter Sasha, who had come with him, stared in bewilderment at the big dirty stove, which occupied almost half the room and was black with soot and flies. What a lot of flies! The stove was lopsided, the logs in the walls sloped, and it looked as though the cabin were about to collapse. In the corner, near the icons, bottle labels and scraps of newspaper were pasted on the walls instead of pictures. The poverty, the poverty! None of the grown-ups was at home; all were at work, reaping. On the stove sat a white-headed girl of eight, unwashed, apathetic; she did not even look up at the newcomers. Below, a white cat was rubbing itself against the oven fork.

"Pussy, pussy!" Sasha called to it coaxingly. "Pussy!"

"It can't hear," said the little girl; "it's gone deaf."

"Why?"

"Oh, it was hit."

Nikolay and Olga realized at first glance what life was like here, but said nothing to each other; silently they put down their bundles, and silently went out into the village street. Their cabin was the third from the end and seemed the poorest and oldest-looking; the second was not much better; but the last one had an iron roof and curtains at the windows. That cottage stood apart, and was not enclosed; it was a tavern. The cabins were all in a single row, and the entire little village—quiet and pensive, with willows, elders, and mountain ash peeping out from the court yards—had a pleasant look.

Behind the peasant homesteads the ground sloped down to the river, steeply and precipitously, so that huge boulders jutted out here and there through the clay. On the steep slope paths wound among the stones and pits dug by the potters; pieces of broken pottery, brown and red, lay about in heaps, and below stretched a broad, level, bright-green meadow, already mowed, over which the peasants' cattle were now wandering. The river, two thirds of a mile from the village, ran, twisting and turning, between beautiful wooded banks. Beyond it was another broad meadow, a herd of cattle, long files of white geese; then, just as on the hither side, there was a steep rise, and at the top of it, on a ridge, a village with a church that had five domes, and, at a little distance, a manor house.

"It's nice here!" said Olga, crossing herself at the sight of the church. "Lord, what space!"

Just at that moment the bells began ringing for vespers (it was Saturday evening). Two little girls, down below, who were carrying a pail of water, looked round at the church to listen to the chimes.

"About this time they are serving the dinners at the Slavyansky Bazar," said Nikolay dreamily.

Sitting on the edge of the ravine, Nikolay and Olga watched the sunset, and saw the golden and crimson sky reflected in the river, in the church windows, and in the very air, which was soft and still and inexpressibly pure, as it never was in Moscow. And when the sun had set, the herds went past, bleating and bellowing; geese flew across from the other side of the river, and then all was hushed; the soft light faded from the air, and dusk began its rapid descent.

Meanwhile Nikolay's father and mother, two gaunt, bent, toothless old people, of the same height, had returned. The daughters-in-law, Marya and Fyokla, who had been working on the estate across the river, came home, too. Marya, the wife of Nikolay's brother Kiryak, had six children, and Fyokla, the wife of his brother Denis, who was in the army, had two; and when Nikolay, stepping into the

THE UNKNOWN CHEKHOV   166

cabin, saw the whole family, all those bodies big and little
stirring on the sleeping platforms, in the cradles and in all
the corners, and when he saw the greed with which his old
father and the women ate the black bread, dipping it in
water, it was borne in upon him that he had made a mistake
in coming here, sick, penniless, and with a family, too—a
mistake!

"And where is brother Kiryak?" he asked when they
had greeted each other.

"He works as a watchman for a merchant," answered his
father; "he stays there in the woods. He ain't a bad worker
but he's too fond of the drink."

"He's no breadwinner," said the old woman tearfully.
"Our men are a poor lot; they bring nothing into the house,
but take plenty out. Kiryak drinks, and the old man too
knows his way to the tavern—it's no use hiding the sin. The
wrath of the Queen of Heaven is on us."

On account of the guests they heated the samovar. The
tea smelt of fish; the sugar was gray and had been nibbled;
cockroaches ran about over the bread and the crockery.
It was disgusting to drink, and the conversation was disgusting, too—about nothing but poverty and sickness. And
before they had emptied their first cups there came a loud,
long-drawn-out, drunken shout from the courtyard:

"Ma-arya!"

"Looks like Kiryak's coming," said the old man. "Talk
of the devil . . ."

Silence fell. And after a little while, the shout sounded
again, coarse and long-drawn-out, as though it came from
under the ground:

"Ma-arya!"

Marya, the elder daughter-in-law, turned pale and huddled against the stove, and it was odd to see the look of
terror on the face of this strong, broad-shouldered, homely
woman. Her daughter, the apathetic-looking little girl who

had been sitting on the stove, suddenly broke into loud weeping.

"What are you bawling for, you pest?" Fyokla, a handsome woman, also strong and broad-shouldered, shouted at her. "He won't kill her, no fear!"

From the old man Nikolay learned that Marya was afraid to live in the woods with Kiryak, and that whenever he was drunk he came for her, raised Cain, and beat her mercilessly.

"Ma-arya!" the shout sounded at the very door.

"Help me, for Christ's sake, good people," stammered Marya, breathing as though she were being plunged into icy water. "Help me, good people . . ."

All the children in the cabin began crying and, affected by their example, Sasha too started to cry. A drunken cough was heard, and a tall, black-bearded peasant wearing a winter cap came into the cabin, and because his face could not be seen in the dim light of the little lamp, he looked terrifying. It was Kiryak. Going up to his wife, he swung his arm and punched her in the face; stunned by the blow, she did not utter a sound, but sank down, and her nose instantly began bleeding.

"What a shame! What a shame!" muttered the old man, clambering up onto the stove. "Before guests, too! What a sin!"

The old woman sat silent, hunched, lost in thought; Fyokla rocked the cradle.

Evidently aware of inspiring terror, and pleased by it, Kiryak seized Marya by the arm, dragged her toward the door, and growled like a beast in order to seem still more terrible; but at that moment he suddenly caught sight of the guests and halted.

"Oh, they have come . . ." he said, letting go of his wife; "my own brother with his family . . ."

Staggering, and opening his blood-shot, drunken eyes wide, he muttered a prayer before the icon and went on:

"My dear brother and his family, come to the parental home . . . from Moscow, I mean. The ancient capital city of Moscow, I mean, mother of cities . . . Excuse me."

He sank down on the bench near the samovar and began to drink tea, sipping it loudly from the saucer amid general silence. . . . He had a dozen cups, then lay down on the bench and began to snore.

They started going to bed. Nikolay, being ill, was to sleep on the stove with the old man; Sasha lay down on the floor, while Olga went into the shed with the other women.

"Now, now, dearie," she said, lying down on the hay beside Marya; "tears won't help. Bear your cross, that's all. It says in Scripture: 'Whosoever shall smite thee on thy right cheek, turn to him the other also.' . . . Now, now, dearie."

Then, speaking under her breath in a singsong manner, she told them about Moscow, about her life, how she had been a chambermaid in furnished rooms.

"And in Moscow the houses are big, made of stone," she said; "and there are many, many churches, forty times forty, dearie; and in the houses they're all gentry, so good-looking and so proper!"

Marya said that not only had she never been to Moscow, but had not even been in their own district town; she could neither read nor write, and knew no prayers, not even "Our Father." Both she and Fyokla, her sister-in-law, who was sitting a little way off listening, were exceedingly backward and dull-witted. They both disliked their husbands; Marya was afraid of Kiryak, and whenever he stayed with her she shook with fear and always got a headache from the fumes of vodka and tobacco of which he reeked. And in response to the question whether she did not miss her husband, Fyokla replied sourly:

"Deuce take him!"

They talked a while and then grew silent.

It was cool, and a cock was crowing at the top of his voice near the shed, interfering with sleep. When the bluish morning light was already showing through every crack, Fyokla got up quietly and went out, and then they heard her hurry off somewhere, her bare feet thumping as she ran.

II

Olga went to church and took Marya with her. As they went down the path towards the meadow, both were cheerful. Olga liked the open country, and Marya felt that in her sister-in-law she had found someone near and dear to her. The sun was rising. Low over the meadow hovered a drowsy hawk; the river looked dull; wisps of mist were floating here and there, but on the farther shore a streak of light already lay across the hill; the church was shining, and in the garden attached to the manor the rooks were cawing frantically.

"The old man ain't bad," Marya said, "but Granny is strict, and is free with her hand. Our own flour lasted till Carnival, but now we buy it at the tavern; so she's cross; she says we eat too much."

"Now, now, dearie! Bear your cross, that's all. It's written: 'Come unto me, all ye that labor and are heavy laden.' "

Olga spoke sedately, in a singsong, and her gait was that of a pilgrim woman, rapid and fidgety. Every day she read the Gospel, read it aloud like a deacon; a great deal of it she did not understand, but the sacred phrases moved her to tears, and such words as "behold" and "whosoever" she pronounced with a sweet faintness at her heart. She believed in God, in the Holy Virgin, in the saints; she believed that it was wrong to harm anyone—whether simple folk, or Germans, or gypsies, or Jews—and that misfortune awaited even those who did not pity animals. She believed that this was written in the Scriptures; and so when she pronounced words from Holy Writ, even though she did not understand them, her face softened with emotion, grew compassionate and radiant.

"Where do you come from?" Marya asked her.

"I am from the province of Vladimir. But I was taken to Moscow long ago, when I was eight years old."

They reached the river. On the other side a woman stood at the water's edge, taking off her clothes.

"That's our Fyokla," said Marya, recognizing her. "She's been across the river to the manor yard. She's been with the hired men. She's a hussy and foul-mouthed—she is that!"

Black-browed Fyokla, her hair undone, still young and with the firm flesh of a girl, jumped off the bank and began thrashing the water with her feet, sending waves in all directions.

"A hussy—she is that!" repeated Marya.

The river was spanned by a rickety little bridge of logs, and below in the clean, clear water shoals of broad-headed chub were swimming. The dew was glistening on the green shrubs that were mirrored in the water. Then the air grew warmer; it was pleasant. What a glorious morning it was! And how glorious life would probably be in this world, were it not for want, horrible, inescapable want, from which you cannot hide anywhere! Only to look round at the village was to remember all that had happened the day before, and the spell of the happiness that they thought they felt around them vanished instantly.

They went into the church. Marya stood in the entrance and did not dare to go farther. Nor did she dare to sit down either, though they only began ringing for Mass after eight o'clock. She remained standing the whole time.

While the gospel was being read the crowd suddenly parted to make way for the landowner's family. Two young ladies in white frocks and wide-brimmed hats walked in, and with them was a chubby, rosy boy in a sailor suit. Their appearance moved Olga; she concluded at first glance that they were decent, elegant, cultivated people. But Marya glared at them from under her brows, sullenly, dejectedly, as though they were not human beings but monsters who might crush her if she did not move aside.

And every time the deacon intoned in his bass voice, she imagined that she heard the cry, "Ma-arya!" and she shuddered.

III

The arrival of the guests became known in the village, and directly after Mass a great many people assembled in the cabin. The Leonychevs and the Matveichevs and the Ilyichovs came to make inquiries about relatives of theirs who had situations in Moscow. All the lads of Zhukovo who could read and write were packed off to Moscow and hired out as bellboys or waiters (just as the lads from the village on the other side of the river were all apprenticed to bakers), and this had been the custom from the days of serfdom, long ago, when a certain Luka Ivanych, a peasant from Zhukovo, now a legendary figure, who had been a bartender in one of the Moscow clubs, would take none but his fellow villagers into his service, and these in turn, as they got up in the world, sent for their kinsfolk and found jobs for them in taverns and restaurants; and from that time on the village of Zhukovo was known throughout the countryside round about as Flunkeyville or Toadytown. Nikolay had been taken to Moscow when he was eleven, and gotten a situation by Ivan Makarych, a Matveichev, who was then an attendant at the Hermitage garden restaurant. And now, addressing the Matveichevs, Nikolay said unctuously:

"Ivan Makarych is my benefactor, and I am bound to pray for him day and night, because it was he who set me on the right path."

"God bless you!" a tall old woman, the sister of Ivan

Markarych, said tearfully, "and not a word have we heard about him, the dear man."

"Last winter he was in service at Omon's, and there was a rumor that this season he was somewhere out of town, in a garden restaurant. . . . He has aged! Why, it used to be that he would bring home as much as ten rubles a day in the summertime, but now things are very quiet everywhere. It's hard on the old man."

The women and the old crones looked at Nikolay's feet, shod in felt boots, and at his pale face, and said mournfully:

"You're no breadwinner, Nikolay Osipych; you're no breadwinner! No, indeed!"

And they all fondled Sasha. She was going on eleven, but she was small and very thin, and she looked no more than seven. Among the other little girls, with their sunburnt faces and roughly cropped hair, and their long, faded shifts, she, with her pallor, her big dark eyes and the red ribbon in her hair, looked droll, as though she were some little wild thing that had been caught in the fields and brought into the cabin.

"She can read, too," said Olga, looking tenderly at her daughter and showing her off. "Read a little, child!" she said, taking the Gospels from the corner. "You read, and the good Christian folk will listen."

It was an old, heavy volume in a leather binding with dog-eared edges, and it gave off a smell as though monks had come into the house. Sasha raised her eyebrows and began in a loud singsong:

" 'And when they were departed, behold, the angel of the Lord appeareth to Joseph in a dream, saying, Arise, and take the young child and his mother . . .' "

" 'The young child and his mother,' " Olga repeated, and flushed all over with emotion.

" 'And flee into Egypt, and be thou there until I bring

thee word: for Herod will seek the young child, to destroy him . . .' "

At these words Olga could not contain herself and burst into tears. Affected by her example, Marya began to whimper, and then Ivan Makarych's sister followed suit. The old man coughed, and bustled about looking for a present for his granddaughter, but finding nothing, gave it up with a wave of his hand. And when the reading was over, the neighbors dispersed to their homes, deeply moved and very much pleased with Olga and Sasha.

Because of the holiday, the family stayed home all day. The old woman, whom her husband, her daughters-in-law, her grandchildren, all alike called Granny, always tried to do everything herself; she lit the stove and heated the samovar with her own hands, even carried the midday meal to the men in the fields, and then complained that she was worn out with work. And all the time she fretted for fear that someone should eat a bite too much or that her husband and daughters-in-law should sit idle. Now she would hear the tavern-keeper's geese making for her kitchen garden by the back way, and she would run out of the cabin with a long stick and spend half an hour screaming beside her cabbages, which were as meager and flabby as herself; again she would imagine that a crow was after her chickens and would rush at it with loud words of abuse. She was cross and full of complaints from morning till night, and often raised such a hubbub that passersby stopped in the street.

She treated the old man roughly, calling him a lazybones and a plague. He was a shiftless, undependable man, and perhaps if she had not been prodding him continually he would not have worked at all, but would just have sat on the stove and talked. He told his son at great length about certain enemies of his, complained of the injuries he suffered

every day at the hands of the neighbors, and it was tedious
to listen to him.

"Yes," he would hold forth, with his arms akimbo, "yes
. . . A week after the Exaltation of the Cross I sold my
hay at thirty kopecks a pood, of my own free will. . . .
Yes, well and good . . . So you see I was taking the hay
in the morning of my own free will; I wasn't doing no one
no harm. In an unlucky hour I see the village elder, Antip
Sedelnikov, coming out of the tavern. 'Where are you taking it, you so-and-so?' says he, and fetches me a box on
the ear."

Kiryak had a terrible hangover and was ashamed to face
his brother.

"What vodka will do! Oh, my God!" he muttered, as he
shook his throbbing head. "For Christ's sake, forgive me,
dear brother and sister; I'm not happy about it myself."

Because it was a holiday, they bought a herring at the
tavern and made a soup of the herring head. At midday
they sat down to have tea and went on drinking it until
they were all perspiring: they looked actually swollen with
tea; and then they attacked the soup, all helping themselves
out of one pot. The herring itself Granny hid away.

In the evening a potter was firing pots on the slope.
Down below in the meadow the girls got up a round dance
and sang songs. Someone played an accordion. On the other
side of the river, too, one kiln was going, and the girls sang
songs, and in the distance the singing sounded soft and
melodious. In and about the tavern the peasants were making a racket. They sang with drunken voices, discordantly,
and swore at one another so filthily that Olga could only
shudder and repeat: "Oh, holy saints!"

What amazed her was that the swearing was incessant,
and that the old men who were near their end were the
loudest and most persistent in using this foul language. And
the girls and children listened to the swearing without turn-

ing a hair; it was evident that they had been used to it from their cradles.

It got to be past midnight. The fire in the kilns on both sides of the river died down, but in the meadow below and in the tavern the merrymaking continued. The old man and Kiryak, both drunk, walking arm in arm, their shoulders jostling, went up to the shed where Olga and Marya were lying.

"Let her be," the old man pleaded; "let her be. . . . She's a harmless woman. . . . It's a sin. . . ."

"Ma-arya!" shouted Kiryak.

"Let her be. . . . It's a sin. . . . She's not a bad woman."

Both stood there for a minute and then went on.

"I lo-ove the flowers of the fi-ield," the old man burst forth in a high, piercing tenor. "I lo-ove to pick them in the meadows!"

Then he spat, swore filthily, and went into the cabin.

IV

Granny stationed Sasha near her kitchen garden and ordered her to see to it that the geese did not get in. It was a hot August day. The tavern-keeper's geese could get into the kitchen garden by the back way, but at the moment they were seriously engaged: they were picking up oats near the tavern, peacefully chatting together, and only the gander craned his neck as though to see if the old woman were not coming with a stick. Other geese from down below might have trespassed, but they were now feeding far away on the other side of the river, stretching across the meadow in a long white garland. Sasha stood about a while, grew bored, and, seeing that the geese were not coming, went up to the brink of the slope.

There she saw Marya's eldest daughter, Motka, who was standing motionless on a huge boulder, staring at the church. Marya had been brought to bed thirteen times, but she had only six living children, all girls, not one boy, and the eldest was eight. Motka, barefoot and wearing a long shift, was standing in the full sunshine; the sun was blazing down right on her head, but she did not notice it, and seemed as though turned to stone. Sasha stood beside her and said, looking at the church:

"God lives in the church. People have lamps and candles, but God has little green and red and blue icon-lamps like weeny eyes. At night God walks about the church, and with Him the Holy Mother of God and Saint Nicholas—clump, clump, clump they go! And the watchman is scared, so scared! Now, now, dearie," she added, imitating her mother. "And when the end of the world comes, all the churches will fly up to heaven."

"With the be-elfri-ies?" Motka asked in a deep voice, drawling the syllables.

"With the belfries. And when the end of the world comes, the good people will go to Paradise, but the wicked will burn in fire eternal and unquenchable, dearie. To my mama and to Marya, too, God will say: 'You never harmed anyone, and so you go to the right, to Paradise'; but to Kiryak and Granny He will say: 'You go to the left, into the fire.' And the ones who ate forbidden food on fast days will be sent into the fire, too."

She looked up at the sky, opening her eyes wide, and said:

"Look at the sky and don't blink, and you will see angels."

Motka began looking at the sky, too, and a minute passed in silence.

"Do you see them?" asked Sasha.

"I don't," said Motka in her deep voice.

"But I do. Little angels are flying about the sky and go flap, flap with their little wings like midges."

Motka thought for a while, with her eyes on the ground, and asked:

"Will Granny burn?"

"She will, dearie."

From the boulder down to the very bottom there was a smooth, gentle slope, covered with soft green grass, which one longed to touch with one's hands or to lie upon.

Sasha lay down and rolled to the bottom. Motka, with a grave, stern face, and breathing heavily, followed suit, and as she did so, her shift rolled up to her shoulders.

"What fun!" said Sasha, delighted.

They walked up to the top to roll down again, but just then they heard the familiar, shrill voice. Oh, how awful it was! Granny, toothless, bony, hunched, her short gray hair flying in the wind, was driving the geese out of the kitchen garden with a long stick, screaming.

"They have trampled all the cabbages, the cursed creatures! May you croak, you thrice accursed plagues! Why don't the devil take you!"

She saw the little girls, threw down the stick, picked up a switch, and, seizing Sasha by the neck with her fingers, dry and hard as spikes, began whipping her. Sasha cried with pain and fear, while the gander, waddling and craning his neck, went up to the old woman and hissed something, and when he went back to his flock all the geese greeted him approvingly with a "Ga-ga-ga!" Then Granny proceeded to whip Motka, and so Motka's shift was rolled up again. In despair and crying loudly, Sasha went to the cabin to complain. Motka followed her; she, too, was crying, but on a deeper note, without wiping her tears, and her face as wet as though it had been dipped in water.

"Holy Fathers!" cried Olga, dismayed, as the two came into the cabin. "Queen of Heaven!"

Sasha began telling her story, when Granny walked in

with shrill cries and abuse; then Fyokla got angry, and there was a hubbub in the house.

"Never mind, never mind!" Olga, pale and distressed, tried to comfort the children, stroking Sasha's head. "She's your grandmother; it's a sin to be cross with her. Never mind, child."

Nikolay, who was already worn out by the continual clamor, the hunger, the sickening fumes from the stove, the stench, who already hated and despised the poverty, who was ashamed of his father and mother before his wife and daughter, swung his legs off the stove and said to his mother in an irritable, tearful voice:

"You shouldn't beat her! You have no right to beat her!"

"You're ready to croak there on the stove, you loafer!" Fyokla snapped at him spitefully. "The devil has brought you here, you spongers!"

Sasha and Motka and all the little girls in the household huddled into a corner on top of the stove behind Nikolay's back, and from there listened to all this in silence and terror, and one could hear the beating of their little hearts. When there is someone in a family who has long been ill, and hopelessly ill, there come terrible moments when all those close to him timidly, secretly, at the bottom of their hearts wish for his death, and only the children fear the death of someone close to them and always feel horrified at the thought of it. And now the little girls, with bated breath and a mournful look on their faces, stared at Nikolay and thought that he would soon die; and they wanted to cry and to say something friendly and compassionate to him.

He was pressing close to Olga, as though seeking her protection, and saying to her softly in a shaking voice:

"Olga dear, I can't bear it here any longer. I haven't the strength. For Christ's sake, for the sake of God in heaven, write to your sister, Klavdia Abramovna. Let her sell and pawn everything she has; let her send us the money, and we'll go away from here. Oh, Lord," he went on with anguish, "to have one peep at Moscow! To see mother Moscow, if only in my dreams!"

And when evening came and it was dark in the cabin, it got so dismal that it was hard to bring out a word. Granny, cross as ever, soaked some crusts of rye bread in a cup and was a whole hour sucking at them. Marya, having milked the cow, brought in a pail of milk and set it on a bench; then Granny poured it from the pail into jugs slowly and deliberately, evidently pleased that it was now the Fast of Assumption, so that no one would drink milk and all of it would be left untouched. And she only poured out just a little into a saucer for Fyokla's baby. When she and Marya carried the jugs down to the cellar, Motka suddenly came to life, slipped down from the stove, and going to the bench where the wooden cup full of crusts was standing, splashed some milk from the saucer into it.

Granny, coming back into the cabin, attacked her soaked crusts again, while Sasha and Motka sat on the stove, staring at her, and were glad that she had taken forbidden food and now was sure to go to hell. They were comforted and lay down to sleep, and as she dozed off, Sasha pictured the Last Judgment to herself: a fire was burning in a stove something like a potter's kiln, and the Evil One, with horns like a cow's and black all over, was driving Granny into the fire with a long stick, just as Granny herself had driven the geese.

v

On the Feast of Assumption, after ten o'clock at night, the girls and boys who were making merry down in the meadow suddenly began to scream and shout, and ran in the direction of the village; and those who were sitting up on the brink of the slope at first could not make out what was the matter.

"Fire! Fire!" desperate shouts sounded from below. "The place is on fire!"

Those who were sitting above looked back, and a terrible and extraordinary spectacle presented itself to them. From the thatched roof of one of the last cabins in the village rose a pillar of flame, seven feet high, which coiled and scattered sparks in all directions as though it were a fountain playing. And all at once the whole roof burst into bright flame, and the crackling of the fire was heard.

The moonlight was dimmed, and now the whole village was enveloped in a quivering red glow: black shadows moved over the ground, there was a smell of burning, and those who ran up from below were all gasping and trembling so that they could not speak; they jostled each other, fell down, and, unaccustomed to the bright light, could hardly see and did not recognize each other. It was terrifying. What was particularly frightening was that pigeons were flying in the smoke above the flames, and that in the tavern, where they did not yet know of the fire, people were still singing and playing the accordion as though nothing were wrong.

"Uncle Semyon's place is on fire," someone shouted in a loud, coarse voice.

Marya was rushing about near her cabin, weeping and wringing her hands, her teeth chattering, though the fire was a long way off, at the other end of the village. Nikolay came out in felt boots, the children ran about in their little shifts. Near the village policeman's cabin an iron sheet was struck. Boom, boom, boom! floated through the air, and this rapid, incessant sound sent a pang to the heart and chilled one to the bone. The old women stood about, holding the icons. Sheep, calves, cows were driven out of the courtyards into the street; chests, sheepskins, tubs were carried out. A black stallion that was kept apart from the drove of horses because he kicked and injured them was set free and ran back and forth through the village once or twice, neighing and pawing the ground, then suddenly stopped short near a cart and started kicking it with his hind legs.

The bells in the church on the other side of the river began ringing.

Near the burning cabin it was very hot and so bright that every blade of grass on the ground was distinctly visible. On one of the chests that they had managed to carry out sat Semyon, a carrot-haired peasant with a long nose, wearing a jacket and a cap pulled down over his ears; his wife was lying face down, unconscious and moaning. A little old man of eighty with a big beard, who looked like a gnome, a stranger to the village, but apparently connected in some way with the fire, walked about near it, bareheaded, with a white bundle in his arms. The flames were reflected on his bald spot. The village elder, Antip Sedelnikov, as swarthy and black-haired as a gypsy, went up to the cabin with an axe and hacked out the windows one after another —no one knew why—and then began chopping up the porch.

"Women, water!" he shouted. "Bring the engine! Shake a leg!"

The peasants who had just been carousing in the tavern were dragging up the engine. They were all drunk; they kept stumbling and falling down, and all had a helpless expression and tears in their eyes.

"Girls, water!" shouted the elder, who was drunk, too. "Shake a leg, girls!"

The women and the girls ran downhill to a spring, and hauled pails and tubs of water up the hill, and, after pouring it into the engine, ran down again. Olga and Marya and Sasha and Motka, too, all carried water. The women and the boys pumped the water; the hose hissed, and the elder, directing it now at the door, now at the windows, held back the stream with his finger, which made it hiss yet more sharply.

"He's a topnotcher, Antip is!" voices shouted approvingly. "Keep it up!"

Antip dove into the burning cabin and shouted from within.

"Pump! Lend a hand, good Orthodox folk, on the occasion of such a terrible accident!"

The peasants stood round in a crowd, doing nothing and staring at the fire. No one knew what to do, no one knew how to do anything, and there were stacks of grain and hay, piles of faggots, and sheds all about. Kiryak and old Osip, his father, both tipsy, stood there, too. And, as though to justify his inaction, old Osip said to the woman lying on the ground:

"Why carry on so, friend? The cabin's insured—why worry?"

Semyon, addressing himself now to one person, now to another, kept telling how the fire had started.

"That same old man, the one with the bundle, a house-serf of General Zhukov's. . . . He was cook at our general's, God rest his soul! He came over this evening: 'Let me stay the night,' says he. . . . Well, we had a glass, to be sure. . . . The wife got busy with the samovar—we were going to give the old man some tea, and in an unlucky hour she set the samovar in the entry. And the sparks from the chimney blew straight up to the thatch. Well, that's how it was. We were nearly burnt up ourselves. And the old man's cap got burnt; it's a shame!"

And the sheet of iron was struck tirelessly, and the bells of the church on the other side of the river kept ringing. Ruddy with the glow, and breathless, Olga, looking with horror at the red sheep and at the pink pigeons flying through the smoke, kept running down the slope and up again. It seemed to her that the ringing had entered her soul like a sharp thorn, that the fire would never be over, that Sasha was lost. . . . And when the ceiling of the cabin fell in with a crash, the thought that now the whole village was sure to burn down made her faint, and she could no longer go on carrying water, but sat down on the brink of the slope, setting the buckets near her; beside her and below her, the peasant women sat wailing as though at a wake.

Then, from the village across the river, came men in two carts, bringing a fire engine with them. A very young student, his white tunic wide open, rode up on horseback. There was the sound of axes. A ladder was placed against the burning frame of the house, and five men ran up it at once, led by the student, who was red in the face and shouted in a harsh, hoarse voice, and in the tone of one who was used to putting out fires. They pulled the house to pieces, a log at a time; they took apart the stable and the wattled fence, and removed the nearby stack of hay.

"Don't let them smash things!" cried stern voices in the crowd. "Don't let them."

Kiryak made his way to the cabin with a resolute air, as though he meant to prevent the newcomers from smashing things, but one of the workmen turned him round and hit him on the neck. There was the sound of laughter, the workman struck him again, Kiryak fell and crawled back into the crowd on all fours.

Two pretty girls in hats, probably the student's sisters, came from the other side of the river. They stood at a distance, looking at the fire. The logs that had been pulled away were no longer burning, but were smoking badly; the student who was working the hose, turned the stream first on the logs, then on the peasants, then on the women who were hauling the water.

"Georges!" the girls called to him reproachfully and anxiously, "Georges!"

The fire was over. And only when the crowd began to disperse they noticed that day was breaking, that all were pale and rather dark in the face, as people always appear in the early morning when the last stars are fading. As they separated, the peasants laughed and cracked jokes about General Zhukov's cook and his cap which had been burnt; they already wanted to turn the fire into a jest, and even seemed sorry that it had been put out so soon.

"You were good at putting out the fire, sir!" said Olga to the student. "You ought to come to us in Moscow: there we have a fire 'most every day."

"Why, do you come from Moscow?" asked one of the young ladies.

"Yes, miss. My husband was employed at the Slavyansky Bazar. And this is my daughter," she said, pointing to Sasha, who was chilly and huddled up to her. "She is a Moscow girl, too."

The two young ladies said something in French to the student and he gave Sasha a twenty-kopeck piece.

Old Osip noticed this, and a gleam of hope came into his face.

"We must thank God, your honor, there was no wind," he said, addressing the student, "or else we should have been all burnt out in no time. Your honor, kind gentlefolk," he added, with embarrassment in a lower tone, "the dawn's chilly . . . something to warm a man . . . half a bottle to your honor's health."

He was given nothing, and clearing his throat, he shuffled off towards home. Afterwards Olga stood on the edge of the slope and watched the two carts fording the river and the gentlefolk walking across the meadow; a carriage was waiting for them on the other side of the river. Going into the cabin, she said to her husband with enthusiasm:

"Such kind people! And so good-looking! The young ladies were like cherubs!"

"May they burst!" Fyokla, who was sleepy, said spitefully.

VI

Marya thought herself unhappy, and often said that she longed to die; Fyokla, on the contrary, found everything in this life to her taste: the poverty, the filth, the incessant cursing. She ate whatever was given her indiscriminately; slept anywhere and on whatever came to hand. She would empty the slops just at the porch, would splash them out from the doorsill, and then walk barefoot through the puddle. And from the very first day she conceived a hatred for Olga and Nikolay just because they did not like this life.

"I'll see what you'll eat here, you Moscow gentry!" she would say maliciously. "I'll see!"

One morning at the beginning of September Fyokla, vigorous, good-looking, and rosy from the cold, brought up two pails of water from down below on a yoke; Marya and Olga were just then sitting at the table, having tea.

"Enjoy your tea!" said Fyokla sarcastically. "The fine ladies!" she added, setting down the pails. "They've gotten into the habit of tea every day. You'd better look out you don't swell up with your tea-drinking," she went on, looking at Olga with hatred. "She's come by her fat mug in Moscow, the tub of lard!"

She swung the yoke and hit Olga a blow on the shoulder, so that the two sisters-in-law could only strike their hands together and say:

"Oh, holy saints!"

Then Fyokla went down to the river to wash the clothes, swearing all the time so loudly that she could be heard in the house.

The day passed and then came the long autumn evening. They wound silk in the cabin; everyone did it except Fyokla; she had gone across the river. They got the silk from a factory nearby, and the whole family working together earned a mere trifle, some twenty kopecks a week.

"Under the masters things were better," said the old man as he wound silk. "You worked and ate and slept, everything in its turn. At dinner you had *shchi* [cabbage soup] and *kasha* [cooked cereal], and at supper the same again. Cucumbers and cabbage galore: you could eat to your heart's content, as much as you liked. And there was more strictness. Everyone knew his place."

The cabin was lighted by a single little lamp, which burned dimly and smoked. When someone stood in front of the lamp and a large shadow fell across the window, one noticed the bright moonlight. Speaking unhurriedly, old Osip related how people used to live before Emancipation; how in these very parts, where life was now so poverty-stricken and dreary, they used to hunt with harriers, greyhounds, and specially trained stalkers, and the peasants who were employed as beaters got vodka; how caravans loaded with slaughtered fowls were sent to Moscow for the young masters; how the serfs that were bad were beaten with rods or sent off to the Tver estate, while those who were good were rewarded. And Granny, too, had something to tell. She remembered everything, absolutely everything. She told about her mistress, a kind, God-fearing woman, whose husband was a boozer and a rake, and all of whose daughters made wretched marriages: one married a drunkard, another a commoner, a third eloped (Granny herself, a young girl at the time, had helped with the elopement), and they had all three soon died of grief, as did their mother. And remembering all this, Granny shed a tear.

Suddenly someone knocked at the door, and they all started.

"Uncle Osip, put me up for the night."

The little bald old man, General Zhukov's cook, the very one whose cap had been burnt, walked in. He sat down and listened. Then he, too, began to reminisce and tell stories. Nikolay, sitting on the stove with his legs hanging down, listened and asked questions about the dishes that were prepared for the gentry in the old days. They talked about chops, cutlets, various soups and sauces, and the cook, who remembered everything very well, mentioned dishes that are no longer prepared; there was one, for instance—a dish made of bulls' eyes, that was called "Waking up in the morning."

"And did you have cutlets *maréchal* then?" asked Nikolay.

"No."

Nikolay shook his head scornfully and said:

"Ah-h! Fine cooks you were!"

The little girls, who were sitting or lying on the stove, stared down without blinking; there seemed to be a lot of them, like cherubs in the clouds. They liked the stories; they sighed, and shuddered and turned pale with rapture or terror, and to Granny, whose stories were the most interesting of all, they listened breathlessly, afraid to stir.

They lay down to sleep in silence; and the old people, stirred up and troubled by their reminiscences, thought what a fine thing it was to be young: youth, whatever it may have been like, left nothing in the memory but what was buoyant, joyful, touching; and death, they thought, how terribly cold was death, which was not far off—better not think of it! The little lamp went out. The darkness and the two little windows brightly lit by the moon, the stillness and the creak of the cradle for some reason made them think of nothing but that life was over and that there was no way of bringing it back. . . . You doze off, you sink into oblivion, and suddenly someone touches your shoulder or breathes on your cheek—and sleep is gone; your body feels numb, as though circulation had stopped, and thoughts of death keep coming into your head. You turn on the other side, and you forget about death, but old, dull, dismal thoughts of want, of fodder, of how dear flour is getting stray through the mind, and a little later you remember again that life is over and there is no way of bringing it back. . . .

"Oh, Lord!" sighed the cook.

Someone rapped gently, ever so gently, at the window. It must have been Fyokla, come back. Olga got up, and yawning and whispering a prayer, unlocked the door, then pulled the bolt of the outer door. But no one came in; only there was a cold draught of air from the street and the entry suddenly grew bright with moonlight. Through the open door could be seen the silent, deserted street, and the moon itself floating across the sky.

"Who's there?" called Olga.

"Me," came the answer, "it's me."

Near the door, hugging the wall, stood Fyokla, stark naked. She was shivering with cold, her teeth were chattering, and in the bright moonlight she looked very pale, strange, and beautiful. The shadows and the bright spots of moonlight on her skin stood out sharply, and her dark eyebrows and firm, young breasts were defined with peculiar distinctness.

"The ruffians over there stripped me and turned me out like this," she muttered. "I had to go home without my clothes . . . mother-naked. Bring me something to put on."

"But come inside," Olga said softly, beginning to shiver, too.

"I don't want the old folks to see." Granny was, in fact,

already stirring and grumbling, and the old man asked: "Who's there?" Olga brought out her own shift and skirt, dressed Fyokla, and then both went softly into the house, trying to close the door noiselessly.

"Is that you, you slick one?" Granny grumbled angrily, guessing who it was. "Curse you, you night-walker! . . . Why don't the devil take you!"

"It's all right, it's all right," whispered Olga, wrapping Fyokla up; "it's all right, dearie."

All was quiet again. They always slept badly; each one was kept awake by something nagging and persistent: the old man by the pain in his back, Granny by anxiety and malice, Marya by fear, the children by itch and hunger. Now, too, their sleep was restless; they kept turning from one side to the other, they talked in their sleep, they got up for a drink.

Fyokla suddenly burst out into a loud, coarse howl, but checked herself at once, and only sobbed from time to time, her sobs growing softer and more muffled until she was still. Occasionally from the other side of the river came the sound of the striking of the hours; but the clock struck oddly—first five and then three.

"Oh, Lord!" sighed the cook.

Looking at the windows, it was hard to tell whether the moon was still shining or whether it was already dawn. Marya got up and went out, and could be heard milking the cows and saying, "Stea-dy!" Granny went out, too. It was still dark in the cabin, but already one could distinguish all the objects in it.

Nikolay, who had not slept all night, got down from the oven. He took his dress coat out of a green chest, put it on, and going to the window, stroked the sleeves, fingered the coattails—and smiled. Then he carefully removed the coat, put it away in the chest, and lay down again.

Marya came in again and started to light the stove. She

was evidently half asleep and was waking up on her feet. She must have had some dream, or perhaps the stories of the previous night came into her mind, for she stretched luxuriously before the stove and said:

"No, freedom is better!"

VII

"The master" arrived—that was what they called the district police inspector. When he would come and what he was coming for had been known for a week. There were only forty households in Zhukovo, but they had accumulated more than two thousand rubles of arrears in zemstvo and other taxes.

The police inspector stopped at the tavern. There he drank two glasses of tea, and then went on foot to the elder's house, near which a crowd of tax defaulters stood waiting. The elder, Antip Sedelnikov, in spite of his youth —he was only a little over thirty—was strict and always sided with the authorities, though he himself was poor and remiss in paying his taxes. Apparently he enjoyed being elder and liked the sense of power, which he could only display by harshness. At the village meetings he was feared and obeyed. Occasionally he would pounce on a drunken man in the street or near the tavern, tie his hands behind him, and put him in jail. Once he even put Granny under arrest and kept her in the lock-up for a whole day and a night because, coming to the village meeting instead of Osip, she started to curse. He had never lived in a city or read a book, but somewhere or other he had picked up various bookish expressions, and loved to employ them in conversation, and people respected him for this although they did not always understand him.

When Osip came into the village elder's cabin with his tax book, the inspector, a lean old man with long gray side whiskers who wore a gray tunic, was sitting at a table in a corner writing something down. The cabin was clean; all the walls were bright with pictures clipped from magazines, and in the most conspicuous place near the icons there was a portrait of Prince Battenberg of Bulgaria. Beside the table stood Antip Sedelnikov with his arms folded.

"He owes one hundred and nineteen rubles, your Honor," he said, when Osip's turn came. "Before Easter he paid a ruble, and he's not paid a kopeck since."

The inspector looked up at Osip and asked:

"Why is this, brother?"

"Show heavenly mercy, your Honor," began Osip, growing agitated. "Allow me to say, last year the master from Lutoretzk said to me, 'Osip,' he says, 'sell your hay . . . you sell it,' says he. Well, why not? I had a hundred poods * for sale; the women mowed it on the water-meadow. Well, we struck a bargain. . . . It was all right and proper. . . ."

He complained of the elder, and kept turning round to the peasants as though inviting them to bear witness; his face got red and sweaty and his eyes grew sharp and angry.

"I don't know why you're saying all this," said the inspector. "I am asking you . . . I am asking you why you don't pay your arrears. You don't pay, any of you, and am I to have to answer for you?"

"I just can't."

"These words are of no consequence, your Honor," said the elder. "The Chikildeyevs certainly are of the needy class, but please just inquire of the others, the root of it all is vodka, and they are a disorderly lot. With no understanding at all."

The inspector wrote something down, and then said to Osip quietly, in an even tone, as though he were asking him for a drink of water:

"Get out."

* A *pood* is a little over 36 pounds. *Ed's note.*

Soon he drove off; and as he was climbing into his cheap buggy, coughing as he did so, it could be seen from the very look of his long lean back that he no longer remembered Osip or the village elder or the Zhukovo arrears, but was thinking of his own affairs. Before he had gone two thirds of a mile Antip was already carrying off the samovar from the Chikildeyevs' cabin, while Granny followed him, screaming shrilly, straining her lungs:

"I won't let you have it! I won't let you have it. God damn you!"

He walked rapidly with long strides, and she ran after him, panting, almost falling down, a hunched infuriated creature; her kerchief slipped onto her shoulders, her gray hair with a greenish tint to it blew in the wind. She suddenly stood still and, like a real insurgent, fell to thumping her breast with her fists and shouting louder than ever in a singsong voice, seeming to sob:

"Christians, all you who believe in God! Friends, they've done me wrong! My dears, they've ruined me! Oh, oh, my dears, come and help me!"

"Granny, Granny!" said the village elder sternly, "get some sense into your head!"

With no samovar it was hopelessly dismal in the Chikildeyevs' cabin. There was something humiliating in this deprivation, something insulting, as though the honor of the house were lost. It would have been better, had the elder carried off the table, all the benches, all the pots— the place would not have seemed so bare. Granny screamed, Marya cried, and the little girls, seeing her tears, cried too. The old man, feeling guilty, sat in the corner, silent, with hanging head. Nikolay too was silent. Granny loved him and was sorry for him, but now, forgetting her pity, she fell upon him with abuse, with reproaches, shaking her fist right in his face. She screamed that it was all his fault; indeed, why had he sent them so little when he bragged in his letters that he was earning fifty rubles a month at the Slavyansky Bazar? Why had he come, and with his family, too? If he died, where would the money come from for his funeral? And it was pitiful to look at Nikolay, Olga, and Sasha.

The old man sighed hoarsely, took his cap, and went off to the elder. It was getting dark. Antip was soldering something by the stove, puffing out his cheeks; the air was full of fumes. His children, thin and unwashed, no better than the Chikildeyev brood, were scrambling about on the floor; his wife, an ugly, freckled, big-bellied woman, was winding silk. They were a wretched, unlucky family, and Antip was the only one who looked sturdy and handsome. On a bench stood five samovars in a row. The old man muttered a prayer to Battenberg and then said:

"Antip, show heavenly mercy, give me back the samovar! For Christ's sake!"

"Bring three rubles, then you can have it."

"I just can't."

Antip puffed out his cheeks, the fire hummed and hissed, and was reflected in the samovars. The old man kneaded his cap and said after a moment's thought:

"You give it back to me."

The dark-skinned elder looked quite black and resembled a magician; he turned round to Osip and said sternly, speaking rapidly:

"It all depends on the district magistrate. On the twenty-sixth instant you can state the grounds of your dissatisfaction before the administrative session, verbally or in writing."

Osip did not understand a word, but he was satisfied with that and went home.

Some ten days later the police inspector came again, stayed for an hour and drove away. During those days it had been cold and windy; the river had been frozen for a long time, but still there was no snow, and people were worn to a frazzle because the roads were impassable. On the eve of a holiday some of the neighbors came in to Osip's to sit and have a chat. They talked in the dark, because it was a sin to work and so they did not light the lamp. There were scraps of news, all rather unpleasant. In two or three households hens had been taken for the arrears, and had been sent to the district office, and there they had died because no one had fed them; sheep had been taken, and while they were being carted away tied to one another, and shifted into another cart at each village, one of them had died. And now the question was being discussed: who was to blame?

"The zemstvo," said Osip. "Who else?"

"Of course, the zemstvo."

The zemstvo was blamed for everything—for the arrears, the unjust exactions, the failure of the crops, though no one of them knew what was meant by the zemstvo. And this dated from the time when well-to-do peasants who had factories, shops, and inns of their own served as members of the zemstvo boards, were disgruntled, and took to berating the zemstvos in their mills and taverns.

They talked about how God was not sending the snow; wood had to be hauled for fuel, yet there was no driving or walking over the frozen ruts. In former days, fifteen to twenty years ago, talk had been much more interesting in Zhukovo. In those days every old man looked as though he were guarding some secret; as though he knew something and were waiting for something. They used to talk about a charter with a golden seal, about the division of land, about new settlements, about treasure troves; they hinted at something. Now the folk of Zhukovo had no secrets at all; their whole life lay bare and clear to all, as though on the palm of your hand, and they could talk of nothing but want, food and fodder, the absence of snow.

There was a lull. Then they recalled the hens again, and the sheep, and began arguing once more as to who was at fault.

"The zemstvo," said Osip dejectedly. "Who else?"

VIII

The parish church was nearly four miles away at Kosogorovo, and the peasants only attended it when they had to do so, for christenings, weddings, or funerals; for regular services they went to the church across the river. On holidays in fine weather the girls dressed up in their best and went to Mass in a crowd, and it was a cheering sight to see them walk across the meadow in their red, yellow, and green frocks; when the weather was bad they all stayed home. To confess and to take the communion, they went to the parish church. The priest, making the round of the cabins with the cross at Easter, collected fifteen kopecks from each of those who had not managed to take the sacrament during Lent.

The old man did not believe in God, for he had hardly ever given Him a thought; he acknowledged the supernatural, but felt that it could be of concern to women only and when religion or miracles were discussed in his presence and a question about these matters was put to him, he would say reluctantly, scratching himself:

"Who can tell!"

Granny did believe, but somehow her faith was hazy; everything was mixed up in her memory, and no sooner did she begin to think of sins, of death, of the salvation of the soul, than want and cares took possession of her mind, and she instantly forgot what she had started to think about. She remembered no prayers at all, and usually in the evenings, before lying down to sleep, she would stand before the icons and whisper:

"Virgin Mother of Kazan, Virgin Mother of Smolensk, Virgin Mother of the Three Arms . . ."

Marya and Fyokla crossed themselves regularly, fasted, and took communion every year, but quite ignorantly. The children were not taught any prayers, nothing was told them about God, and no moral precepts were given them; they were merely forbidden to take certain foods on fast days. In other families it was much the same: there were few who believed, few who had any understanding. At the same time all loved the Holy Scripture, loved it tenderly, reverently; but they had no books, there was no one to read the Bible and explain it, and because Olga sometimes read them the Gospels, they respected her, and they all addressed her and Sasha in the deferential second-person plural.

For local holidays and special services Olga often walked to neighboring villages and to the county seat, in which there were two monasteries and twenty-seven churches. She was abstracted, and when she went on these pilgrimages she quite forgot her family, and only when she was on her way home would suddenly make the joyful discovery that she had a husband and daughter, and then she would say, smiling and radiant:

"God has blessed me!"

What went on in the village seemed to her revolting and was a source of torment to her. On St. Elijah's Day they drank, at the Assumption they drank, at the Exaltation of the Cross they drank. The Feast of the Intercession was the parish holiday for Zhukovo, and on that occasion the peasants drank for three days on end; they drank away fifty rubles belonging to the communal fund, and on top of that collected money for vodka from each household. On the first day the Chikildeyevs slaughtered a sheep and ate mutton in the morning, at noon, and in the evening; they ate large amounts of it, and the children got up at

night to eat some more. Those three days Kiryak was fear-
fully drunk; he drank away all his belongings, even his cap
and boots, and beat Marya so terribly that they had to pour
water over her to revive her. Afterwards they were all
ashamed and felt sick.

However, even in Zhukovo, in this "Flunkeyville," once
a year there was a genuine religious event. It was in August,
when they carried the icon of the Life-Bearing Mother
of God from village to village throughout the district. The
day on which it was expected at Zhukovo was windless
and the sky was overcast. The girls, in their bright holiday
frocks, set off in the morning to meet the icon, and they
brought it to the village towards evening, in solemn procession, singing, while the bells pealed in the church across the
river. A huge crowd of villagers and strangers blocked the
street; there was noise, dust, a crush of people. The old man
and Granny and Kiryak all stretched out their hands to the
icon, gazed at it greedily and cried, weeping:

"Intercede for us! Mother! Intercede!"

All seemed suddenly to grasp that there was no void
between earth and heaven, that the rich and powerful had
not seized everything, that there was still protection from
abuse, from bondage, from crushing, unbearable want,
from the terrible vodka.

"Intercede for us! Mother!" sobbed Marya. "Mother!"

But the service ended, the icon was carried away, and
everything went on as before; and again the sound of
coarse, drunken voices came from the tavern.

Only the well-to-do peasants were afraid of death; the
richer they grew, the less they believed in God and in the
salvation of the soul, and only through fear of their earthly
end did they light candles and have Masses said, in order to
be on the safe side. The poorer peasants did not fear death.
The old man and Granny were told to their faces that they
had lived too long, that it was time they were dead, and

they did not mind. They did not scruple to tell Fyokla in Nikolay's presence that when Nikolay died her husband Denis would be discharged from the Army and return home. And Marya, far from dreading death, regretted that it was so long in coming, and was glad when her children died.

Death they did not fear, but they had an exaggerated terror of every disease. The merest trifle—an upset stomach, a slight chill, and Granny would lie down on the stove, wrap herself up, and start moaning loudly and incessantly: "I am dy-ing!" The old man would hurry off for the priest, and Granny would receive the sacrament and extreme unction. They often talked of colds, of worms, of tumors that shifted about in the stomach and moved up close to the heart. Most of all they feared catching cold, and so dressed in heavy clothes even in summer and warmed themselves on the stove. Granny was fond of doctoring herself and often drove to the dispensary, where she always said she was fifty-eight instead of seventy; she supposed that if the doctor knew her real age he would not treat her, but would say it was time she died instead of doctoring herself. She usually went to the dispensary early in the morning, taking with her two or three of the little girls, and came back in the evening, hungry and cross, with drops for herself and salves for the little girls. Once she had Nikolay go along with her, too, and for a fortnight afterwards he took drops and said he felt better.

Granny knew all the doctors, medical attendants, and quacks for twenty miles round, and not one of them she liked. On the Feast of the Intercession, when the priest made the round of the cabins with the cross, the deacon told her that in the town near the prison lived an old man who had been an army surgeon's assistant and who worked many cures, and advised her to turn to him. Granny took his advice. After the first snowfall she drove to the town and fetched a little bearded old man, in a long coat, a converted Jew, whose face was covered with a network of tiny blue veins. Just then there were people working in the house: an old tailor, in terrifying spectacles, was cutting a waistcoat out of some rags, and two young men were making felt boots out of wool; Kiryak, who had been sacked for drunkenness and now lived at home, was sitting beside the tailor mending a horsecollar. And the place was crowded, stuffy, and evil-smelling. The converted Jew examined Nikolay and said that it was necessary to cup the patient.

He put on the cups, and the old tailor, Kiryak, and the little girls stood round and looked on, and it seemed to them that they saw the disease coming out of Nikolay; and Nikolay, too, watched how the cups sucking at his breast gradually filled with dark blood, and felt as though there really were something coming out of him, and smiled with pleasure.

"That's fine," said the tailor. "Please God, it will do you good."

The convert put on twelve cups and then another twelve, had tea and drove away. Nikolay began shivering; his face took on a drawn look, and, as the women put it, shrank up into a little fist; his fingers turned blue. He wrapped himself up in a quilt and a sheepskin coat, but felt colder and colder. Towards evening he began to feel very ill, asked to be laid on the floor, begged the tailor not to smoke; then he grew quiet under the coat, and towards morning he died.

IX

Oh, what a hard, what a long winter it was!

Already by Christmas their own flour had given out and they started buying flour. Kiryak, who lived at home now, was disorderly in the evenings, terrifying everyone, and in the mornings he was tormented by headache and shame, and it was pitiful to look at him. Day and night the bellowing of the starved cow came from the barn—breaking the heart of Granny and Marya. And as though out of spite, the frosts were bitter the whole time and the snowdrifts high; and the winter dragged on. At Annunciation there was a regular blizzard and snow fell at Easter.

But after all, the winter did end. At the beginning of April there were warm days and frosty nights; winter would not yield, but one warm day overpowered it at last, and the streams began to flow and the birds to sing. The whole meadow and the shrubs that fringed the river were submerged by the spring floods, and the area between Zhukovo and the farther bank was one vast sheet of water, from which wild ducks rose up in flocks here and there. Every evening a fiery spring sunset, with superb clouds, offered new, extraordinary, incredible sights, just the sort of thing that one does not credit afterwards, when one sees those very colors and those very clouds in a painting.

The cranes flew swiftly, swiftly, uttering mournful calls, and there seemed to be a summoning note in their cries. Standing on the brink of the slope Olga stared for a long time at the flooded meadow, at the sunshine, at the church that looked bright and rejuvenated, as it were; and her tears flowed and she gasped for breath: so passionate was her longing to go away, anywhere, to the end of the world. It was already decided that she should return to Moscow to go into service as a chambermaid, and that Kiryak should set off with her to get a job as a porter or something of the sort. Oh, to get away quickly!

As soon as the ground was dry and it was warm, they made ready to leave. Olga and Sasha, with bundles on their backs and sandals of plaited bast on their feet, left at daybreak: Marya came out, too, to see them off. Kiryak was not well and remained at home for another week. For the last time Olga, looking at the church, crossed herself and murmured a prayer. She thought of her husband, and though she did not cry, her face puckered up and turned ugly, like an old woman's. During the winter she had grown thinner and plainer, her hair had gone a little gray, and instead of her former attractive appearance and pleasant smile her face now had the sad, resigned expression left by the sorrows she had experienced, and there was something obtuse and wooden about her gaze, as though she were deaf.

She was sorry to leave the village and the peasants. She kept remembering how they had carried Nikolay down the street, and how a Mass for the repose of his soul had been said at every cabin, and how all had wept in sympathy with her grief. During the summer and the winter there had been hours and days when it seemed as though these people lived worse than cattle, and it was terrible to be with them; they were coarse, dishonest, dirty, and drunken; they did not live at peace with one another but quarreled continually, because they feared, suspected, and despised each other. Who keeps the tavern and spreads alcoholism among the people? The peasant. Who embezzles and drinks away the funds of the community, the schools, the church? The peasant. Who steals from his neighbors, sets fire to their property, bears false witness at court for a bottle of vodka? At meetings of the zemstvo and other local bodies, who is the first to raise his voice against the peasants? The peasant. Yes, to live with them was terrible; but yet, they were human beings, they suffered and wept like human beings, and there was nothing in their lives for which one could not find justification. Crushing labor that made the whole body ache at night, cruel winters, scanty crops, overcrowding; and no help, and nowhere to look for help. Those who were stronger and better-off could give no assistance, as they were themselves coarse, dishonest, drunken, and swore just as foully. The most insignificant little clerk or official treated the peasants as though they were tramps, and addressed even the village elders and church wardens as inferiors, and as though he had a right to do so. And indeed, can any sort of help or good example be given by lazy, grasping, greedy, dissolute men who only visit the village in order to outrage, to despoil, to terrorize? Olga recalled the wretched, humiliated look of the old folks when in the winter Kiryak had been led off to be flogged . . . And now she felt sorry for all these people, it hurt her, and as she tramped on she kept looking back at the cabins.

After walking two miles with them Marya said goodbye, then she knelt, and pressing her face against the earth, began wailing:

"Again I am left alone. Poor me! Poor unhappy soul that I am! . . ."

And for a long time she went on wailing like this, and for a long time Olga and Sasha could see her still on her knees, as she kept bowing sideways, clutching her head in her hands, while the rooks flew over her.

The sun rose high; it turned hot. Zhukovo was left far behind. Walking was pleasant; Olga and Sasha soon forgot both the village and Marya; they were cheerful and everything entertained them: an ancient burial-mound, a row of telegraph posts marching one after another into the distance and disappearing on the horizon, the wires humming mysteriously; a farmhouse, half hidden by green foliage, and with a scent of dampness and hemp coming from it, a place that for some reason seemed inhabited by happy people; a horse's skeleton making a lonely white spot in the open fields. And the larks trilled tirelessly, quails called to one another, and the corn-crake cawed as though someone were jerking an old cramp-iron.

At noon Olga and Sasha came to a large village. There in the broad street they encountered the little old man who had been General Zhukov's cook. He was hot, and his red, perspiring bald spot shone in the sun. At first he and Olga failed to recognize each other, then they looked round at the same moment, did recognize each other, and went their separate ways without saying a word. Stopping before the open windows of a cottage which looked newer and more prosperous than the rest, Olga bowed down and said in a loud, thin, sing-song voice:

"Orthodox Christians, give alms, for Christ's sake, as much as you can, and in the Kingdom of Heaven may your parents know peace eternal."

"Orthodox Christians," Sasha echoed her chant, "give alms, for Christ's sake, as much as you can, and in the Kingdom of Heaven. . . ."

x

Olga's sister, Klavdia Abramovna, lived in one of the lanes near the Patriarchs' Ponds in a two story frame house. The ground floor was occupied by a laundry; the entire upper story was rented by an elderly maiden lady, a quiet and modest woman who sublet the rooms to lodgers and supported herself that way. As you entered the dark foyer, you saw two doors, on the right and on the left. One led into a small room occupied by Klavdia Abramovna and Sasha; the other opened into the room of a man who worked in a printing office. There was also a parlor, which held a divan, armchairs, a lamp with a shade, had pictures on the walls—all as it should be, but there was a smell here of wet wash and steam, which came from the laundry, and all day long the sound of singing kept floating up from below.

The parlor, which was used by all the lodgers, led into three flats. One was occupied by the landlady herself, another by the old waiter, Ivan Makarych Matveichev, a native of Zhukovo, the same who had once found a position for Nikolay. A large padlock hung on his door, which was painted white and was always kept closed. In the third flat lived a young, sharp-eyed, thick-lipped woman with three children who were always crying. On holidays she was visited by a monk. All day long she walked about in a petticoat, unwashed, uncombed, but when she expected her monk, she would curl her hair and put on a silk dress.

Klavdia Abramovna's room was so small that, as the saying goes, you could hardly turn around in it. Although it contained nothing but a bed, a chest of drawers, and one chair, it was crowded. Nevertheless it was tidy, and Klavdia Abramovna called it her boudoir. She herself was very much pleased with the furnishings and particularly with the objects on the chest of drawers: a looking glass, face powder, lip rouge, a cosmetic containing white lead, scent bottles, little boxes and other luxury items, which she considered essential to her profession and on which she spent almost all her earnings. Here too were framed photographs which showed her in various poses. There was a picture of her with her husband, a postman. She had left him after a year, because she had no vocation for family life. She was photographed in such poses as women of that sort usually affect: with a roll of hair on her forehead, with her hair in a poodle cut, wearing a soldier's uniform with a naked sword, dressed like a page astride a chair, so that her thighs in tights lay on the chair like a pair of big boiled sausages. There were also portraits of men—she called them her guests and did not know the names of all of them. Among them was Kiryak too, in the capacity of a relative. He had had himself photographed full length in a black suit which he had rented for the occasion.

Formerly Klavdia Abramovna had frequented masked balls and Filippov's restaurant, and she spent whole evenings on Tverskoy Boulevard. As the years went by, however, she became more and more a stay-at-home, and now that she was forty-two, she received guests very seldom, mostly the few she had known in the past and who came to her for old time's sake and who—alas!—had themselves grown old. The visits grew rarer because with each year the number of these men diminished. She had only one new guest, a beardless youth. He would enter the foyer quietly, sullenly, like a conspirator, the coat collar of his high school uniform turned up, and trying not to be seen from the parlor. Before leaving he would lay a ruble on the chest of drawers.

For days Klavdia Abramovna would sit indoors, doing nothing. Sometimes, when the weather was fine, she promenaded on Malaya Bronnaya Street or Tverskaya, with head proudly lifted, feeling like a lady of dignity and importance, and only when she stepped into a drugstore to ask in a whisper for an ointment against wrinkles or red hands, did she feel ashamed. In the evening she sat in her room without a light, waiting for a guest. About eleven o'clock—this happened rarely now, perhaps once or twice a week—someone would be heard on the stairs, and then fumbling at the door, looking for the bell. The door would open, there would be mutterings, and a guest would hesitatingly step into the foyer, usually an elderly, fat, bald, homely man, and Klavdia Abramovna would hasten to take him into her room. She adored the right kind of guest. For her no creature ranked higher or was more deserving. To receive the right kind of guest, to treat him considerately, to humor him, to please him, was the need of her soul, her duty, her pride, her happiness. She was unable to refuse a guest, to treat him coldly, even when she prepared for the holy sacrament by prayer and fasting.

When Olga returned from the village, she placed Sasha with her sister. She thought that the child was still too young to understand, even if she noticed anything *bad*. But now Sasha had turned thirteen, the time had really come to find other living quarters for her, but she and her aunt had become attached to each other and it was hard to separate them. Besides, what could Olga do with the child, when she herself had no home and slept on chairs in the hallway of the boarding house where she was in service? Sasha spent the day with her mother, or in the street, or downstairs in the laundry. She slept on the floor in her aunt's room between the bed and the chest of drawers, and if a guest came, she lay down in the foyer.

In the evening she loved to go to the restaurant where Ivan Makarych worked and to watch the dancing from the kitchen. There was always music there, it was bright and lively, a savory smell surrounded the cook and the dishwashers, and Granddaddy Ivan Makarych would give her a glass of tea or a little ice cream, and would slip into her hand tidbits from the plates which he carried back to the kitchen.

Late one autumn evening, she brought back from the restaurant in a paper bag some sturgeon, the drumstick of a chicken and a piece of cake . . . Her aunt was already in bed.

"Auntie dear," said Sasha sadly, "I've brought you something to eat."

Klavdia Abramovna lit the lamp. She sat up in bed and started eating. Sasha, seeing her curl-papers, which gave her a terrifying appearance, and her withered, old shoulders, gazed at her long and mournfully, as at a sick person, and suddenly tears streamed down her cheeks.

"Auntie dear," she brought out in a trembling voice, "auntie dear, this morning the girls in the laundry were saying that when you were old you would be begging in the street and you'd die in a hospital. This isn't true, auntie, it isn't true," Sasha went on, sobbing now. "I'm not going to leave you, I'll see that you have something to eat. . . . I won't let them take you to the hospital. . . ."

Klavdia Abramovna's chin quivered and tears came into her eyes, but she controlled herself at once, and said, looking sternly at Sasha:

"It's indecent to listen to washerwomen."

XI

Gradually the lodgers in "The Lisbon" boarding-house quieted down. There was a smell of extinguished lamps in the air, and the tall waiter stretched out on the chairs that formed his bed. Olga took off her beribboned white cap and her apron, put on a kerchief, and went to the Patriarchs' Ponds district to see her daughter. At "The Lisbon" she was on duty every day from morning till late in the evening, so that she could seldom visit her sister and then only at night. Her job took up all her time, leaving her not a free moment, and since her return from the country she had not been to church once.

She was in a hurry because she wanted to show Sasha the letter that Marya had sent her from the village. The letter contained nothing but ceremonious greetings and complaints: Marya wrote about their troubles, about the want of money, about the fact that the old people were still hanging on to life and eating away without doing a stroke of work. But for some reason these crooked lines, in which each letter resembled a cripple, seemed to hold a peculiar, secret fascination for Olga. In addition to the greetings and complaints, the letter seemed to bring her word that in the country the days were now warm and clear, that the evenings were still, the air was fragrant, and you could hear the bells ringing the hours in the church beyond the ravine. She pictured to herself the village churchyard where her husband was buried: the green graves breathed quiet, you envied the dead—and what a sense of spaciousness and freedom! Strange: when they were in the country, they longed for Moscow, now, on the contrary, they were drawn to the countryside.

Olga woke up Sasha and read the letter to her twice, agitated and anxious, afraid that the whispering and the light might disturb someone. Then the two of them descended the dark, foul stairway and went out of the house. Through the open windows they could see that the ironing was being done in the laundry. In front of the gates stood two washerwomen, with cigarettes between their teeth. Olga and Sasha were walking rapidly down the street and saying how nice it would be to save up two rubles and send them to the village: one ruble for Marya, the other to pay for a Mass to be said on Nikolay's grave.

"Oh, did I have a scare the other day!" Olga was saying, striking her hands together. "No sooner did we sit down to our meal, darling, when suddenly Kiryak turned up—drunk as a lord! 'Olga,' said he, 'gimme money!' And he yelled and stamped his feet—'gimme' and that's all! And where was I to get money? They don't pay me any wages, I live on charity, all that I have is what kind gentlemen give me. . . . He wouldn't listen—'gimme!' The lodgers looked out of their doors, the boss came—it was dreadful, it was a shame! I wheedled thirty kopecks out of the students and gave them to him. So he left. All the rest of the day I kept going about, whispering: 'Lord, soften his heart!' That's what I kept whispering. . . ."

The streets were quiet; now and then a cabby drove by; far off, apparently in a beer garden, music was still playing and rockets were exploding with a muffled crackle.

a visit to friends

The morning mail brought this note:

Kuzminki, July 7

Dear Misha!

    You have completely forgotten us, come to see us, we want to have a glimpse of you. Both of us entreat you on our knees, come today, show us your fair countenance. We are waiting for you impatiently.

Ta and Va.

The letter was from Tatyana Alexeyevna Loseva, whom they had called Ta for short a dozen years previously, when Podgorin was staying at Kuzminki. But who was Va? Oh, yes, it was Varya, or Varvara Pavlovna, a friend of Tatyana's. Podgorin recalled the long talks, the gay laughter, the flirtations, the evenings walks, and the flower garden of girls and young women who were then staying at Kuzminki, and he also recalled the plain, animated, intelligent face and the freckles that went so well with Varya's dark-red hair. Since then she had graduated from medical school, taken a position as a doctor in a factory somewhere near Tula, and now was apparently visiting Kuzminki.

"Dear Va!" thought Podgorin, giving himself up to reminiscences. "How nice she is!"

Tatyana, Varya and he were almost of the same age. But at the time he had been only a student, and they marriageable girls. He had been considered a mere boy. And now, although he was already an established lawyer and his hair was beginning to turn gray, they still called him Misha, thought of him as a young man and declared that he had not lived.

He loved them dearly, but it would seem rather as memories than in actuality. The present was scarcely real to him, was incomprehensible and alien. Alien also was this short, playful letter. Much time and effort must have gone to composing it, and as Tatyana was writing it, her husband, Sergey Sergeich, must have been standing behind her. The Kuzminki estate had become Tatyana's property six years ago when she was married, but this Sergey Sergeich had already succeeded in ruining it, and now every time payment to the bank or on a mortgage fell due, they turned to Podgorin, as a lawyer, for advice. Besides, they had already tried to borrow from him twice. Apparently, now too they wanted money or advice from him.

He was no longer drawn to Kuzminki, as he used to be. There was something melancholy about the place. The laughter, the clamor, the bright carefree faces, trysts on still moonlit nights—all that was gone, above all, youth was gone; and, furthermore, all this was probably fascinating only in retrospect. . . . In addition to Ta and Va, there had then been Na, Tatyana's sister Nadezhda. Half in jest, half in earnest they had called her his fiancée. She had grown up before his eyes, everyone thought that he would marry her, and indeed at one time he had been in love with her and was ready to propose to her. Yet she was already in her twenty-fourth year, and he hadn't proposed to her.

"Strange, how it all turned out," he reflected, rereading the note with embarrassment. "But I can't *not* go, they'll be offended. . . ."

The fact that he hadn't been to see the Losevs for a long time lay like a weight on his conscience. And after he had paced the room for a while and turned the matter over in his mind, he overcame his reluctance and decided to go to Kuzminki for a stay of two or three days, and then be free from any sense of obligation at least until the following summer. And as he was getting ready to drive to the Brest Station after breakfast he told the servants that he would return in three days.

There was a two hours' train ride from Moscow to Kuzminki and a twenty minutes' drive from the station to the estate. When one got off the train, Tatyana's forest came into view, as well as three summer cottages, which Losev had started building but had not completed—during the first years of his marriage he had had all kinds of schemes. He was ruined by these summer cottages and other money-making enterprises, and by frequent trips to Moscow, where he lunched at the Slavyansky Bazar, dined at the Hermitage and at the close of the day wound up on Malaya Bronnaya Street or at the Gypsy place known as The Slaughterhouse (he called this "getting shaken up"). Podgorin himself drank, sometimes rather heavily, took up with all kinds of women, but indolently, coldly, without enjoyment, and he was disgusted when in his presence others gave themselves over to that sort of thing passionately; he did not understand men who were more at ease at The Slaughterhouse than at home, in the company of decent women, and he disliked such men. It seemed to him that all kinds of dirt clung to them like burrs. He disliked Losev and considered him a dull fellow, lazy and without ability, and more than once he felt a sense of distaste for his company . . .

Sergey Sergeich and Nadezhda were waiting for him just beyond the forest.

"My dear fellow, why have you been completely neglecting us?" asked Sergey Sergeich, kissing him three times and putting both arms around his waist. "You don't love us any more, old man."

He had massive features, a fleshy nose, a rather thin blond beard, and he combed his hair to one side, like a merchant, to give himself a simple, typically Russian appearance. He had a way of breathing in the face of the person he was speaking to, and when he was silent he breathed heavily, through his nose. His obesity and his habit of overeating made it hard for him to fill his lungs, and in consequence he kept thrusting out his chest, which gave him an air of haughtiness. Beside him, Nadezhda, his sister-in-law, seemed ethereal. She was a pale, slim blonde with kindly eyes that seemed to caress you. Whether she was beautiful or not Podgorin could not tell, for he had known her since childhood and he took her for granted. She wore a white dress, open at the neck, and the sight of her long, white, naked throat was strange to him and affected him disagreeably.

"Sister and I have been waiting for you since morning," she said. "Varya is with us, and she has been waiting for you, too."

She took his arm, laughed abruptly without any reason, and gave a light, joyous cry, as though suddenly struck by some pleasant thought. The field of flowering rye, motionless in the still air, the forest lit by the sun, were beautiful, and it seemed as though Nadezhda had noticed it just now, as she walked beside Podgorin.

"I can stay three days," he said. "Forgive me, I couldn't get away from Moscow any sooner.'

"It's wrong, wrong, you've completely neglected us," said Sergey Sergeich, in good-natured reproach. "*Jamais de ma vie!*" he said suddenly and snapped his fingers.

He had a way of astonishing the person to whom he was speaking by an exclamation that had no bearing whatever on the talk, at the same time snapping his fingers. And he was always aping someone. If he rolled his eyes, or nonchalantly tossed back his hair, or turned bathetic, it meant that the previous evening he had been to the theatre or had attended a banquet with speeches. He was now walking mincingly like a victim of gout without bending his knees—apparently imitating someone.

"You know, Tanya didn't think that you would come," said Nadezhda. "But I had a premonition that you would, and so did Varya; for some reason I knew that you would come on this train."

"*Jamais de ma vie!*" repeated Sergey Sergeich.

The ladies were waiting on the terrace in the garden. Ten years back Podgorin, then a needy student, had tutored Nadezhda in mathematics and history for room and board. He had also given Latin lessons to Varya, a medical student. As for Tanya, at the time already a grown girl and a beauty, she had thought of nothing but love, and had wanted only love and happiness, passionately wanted and hoped for a husband, of whom she dreamed day and night. And now when she was over thirty and just as beautiful as ever, in a loose tea gown, with her full, white arms, she had thoughts for nothing but her husband and her two little girls. She wore an expression which seemed to say that although there she was talking and smiling so casually, she was nevertheless on guard, she stood prepared to defend her love and her right to this love, and at a moment's notice she was ready to pounce on an enemy who wanted to take away her husband and her children. She loved devotedly and she believed that she was loved in the same way, but jealousy and fear for her children constantly tormented her and interfered with her happiness.

After a clamorous reunion on the terrace, everyone went

off to Tatyana's room, with the exception of Sergey Sergeich.

The lowered blinds kept out the sun and created a twilight in the room, so that all the roses in a large bouquet seemed to be of the same color. They made Podgorin sit down in an old armchair at the widow. Nadezhda sat on a low stool at his feet. He knew that in addition to friendly reproaches, jokes, laughter, which so keenly reminded him of the past, there would also be an unpleasant conversation on the subject of promissory notes and mortgages—that was unavoidable—and it occurred to him that it would be best to have the business talk at once, without delay, to put it behind them and then go out into the open, to the garden. . . .

"Shouldn't we first talk about business?" he said. "What's new at Kuzminki? There's nothing rotten in the state of Denmark?"

"Things are out of joint at Kuzminki," replied Tatyana, sighing sadly. "Oh, the situation there is bad, so bad that I don't think it could be worse," she said, agitatedly pacing the room. "The estate is to be sold, August 7th is the date of the auction; the announcement has already been published, and buyers have started coming here, they walk through the house, they stare . . . Anyone has the right to come into my room now, and look. Perhaps according to law this is as it should be, but it humiliates me, it offends me deeply. We have no money and there is no one we can borrow from. It's simply terrible, terrible! I swear to you by all that's holy," she continued, halting in the middle of the room, her voice breaking and her eyes filling with tears, "I swear to you by the happiness of my children, I cannot live without Kuzminki! I was born here, it's my home, and if it's taken from me, I shan't be able to go on, I shall die of despair."

"It seems to me you are taking too black a view of the

matter," said Podgorin. "Things will arrange themselves. Your husband will find a position, you will adjust yourself to a new setting and live a new life."

"How can you say such a thing?" cried Tatyana. As she spoke, she looked very beautiful and strong, and her readiness to pounce instantly on the enemy who would take her husband, her children, her home away from her was very evident in her face and in her whole bearing. "A new life, indeed! Sergey is busy trying to make connections, he has been promised the post of tax collector somewhere in the province of Ufa or Perm. I am prepared to go anywhere, even to Siberia, I am ready to live there ten years, twenty, but I must know that sooner or later I'll return to Kuzminki. Without Kuzminki I cannot live. I can't and I don't want to. I don't want to!" she cried, and stamped her foot.

"You are a lawyer, Misha," said Varya, "you know how to turn a trick, and it's your business to advise us what to do."

There was only one piece of sensible advice that he could offer: "Nothing can be done," but Podgorin did not have the heart to blurt it out, and he mumbled hesitantly:

"I'll have to give the matter some thought. . . . I'll think it over."

There were two men in him. As a lawyer he occasionally had to deal with pretty ugly affairs. At court and with clients he behaved haughtily and spoke his mind bluntly. With casual acquaintances he could be rather cutting. But with intimates or friends of long standing he was exceedingly delicate, shy and sensitive, and could not speak harshly. A tear, a sidelong glance, a lie, or even an unseemly gesture was sufficient to make him flinch and lose his self-possession. Nadezhda was still sitting at his feet, and her bare throat offended him. This was a source of distress, so that he even thought of going home. The previous year he had happened to run into Sergey Sergeich in the flat of a certain lady on Bronnaya Street, and now he felt embarrassed in Tatyana's presence, as if he himself had been party to her husband's infidelity. And this conversation about the estate placed him in a very awkward position. He was used to having all thorny and unpleasant questions settled by judges or jurymen, or simply by some statute. But when a matter was put up to him personally for decision, he was lost.

"Misha, you're our friend, we all love you as one of our own," continued Tatyana, "and I'll be frank with you: you are our only hope. For God's sake, tell us what to do. Maybe an appeal is possible? Perhaps it isn't too late to put the estate in Nadya's name, or Varya's? What shall we do?"

"Come to our rescue, Misha, do," said Varya, lighting up. "You were always so clever. You haven't really lived, you've had no experience, but you've a good head on your shoulders. You'll help Tanya, you know you will."

"I must think it over. . . . Maybe, I'll come up with some scheme."

They all went out for a walk in the garden, and then they wandered off into the fields. Sergey Sergeich went along. He took Podgorin by the arm and tried to walk ahead of the rest, apparently intending to broach the subject of his financial straits. To walk beside him and talk to him was torment. Now and then he would kiss his guest, always three times, put his arms around his waist, breathe in his face, and it seemed as though he were covered with a sweet glue and would actually stick to his companion. And that expression of his eyes, which showed that he wanted something from Podgorin, that he was going to ask him for something, had a painful effect, as if he were aiming a gun at his guest.

The sun set, it was getting dark. Here and there along

the railway line lights appeared, green, red. . . . Varya
halted, and looking at the signals, recited:

"There is a straight and shining road,
With rails and posts, a bridge afar,
On either side lie Russian bones,
Oh, what huge heaps of them there are! . . .

How does it go on? Oh, good Lord, I can't remember any
of it!

We labored in the heat, the cold,
Our heads were bowed, our backs were bent . . ."

She recited with deep feeling, in a magnificent chest-
voice. Her face grew flushed and tears came into her eyes.
It was the old Varya, Varya the student, and as he listened
to her Podgorin thought of the past and recalled that as a
student himself he had known many fine poems by heart
and had liked to recite them.

"And even now his back is bent,
His silence stolid as before . . ."

Varya could not remember any more. She fell silent and
smiled uncertainly and faintly, and the green and red signals had a melancholy look.

"Oh, I've forgotten it!"

But Podgorin recalled the way it went on—somehow the
lines had remained in his memory from his student days,
and he recited quietly, under his breath:

"The Russian folk have borne enough,
This road-building—a fearful load—
They've borne and more will they endure,
And build themselves a glorious road.
The pity is . . ."

" 'The pity is,' " Varya broke in, having remembered:

"The pity is that neither you nor I
Will be alive to greet that glorious time."

She laughed and slapped him on the back.

They returned to the house and sat down to supper. Aping someone, Sergey Sergeich carelessly stuck a corner of his napkin into his collar.

"Let's have a drink," he said, pouring some vodka for himself and Podgorin. "In our student days we knew how to drink, how to make a speech, how to work seriously. I drink your health, friend, and you drink the health of an old fool of an idealist and wish him this: that he die an idealist."

All during supper Tatyana kept looking tenderly at her husband, fretting lest he eat or drink something that might disagree with him. It seemed to her that he was weary, that he was spoiled by women—she liked this in him, but at the same time she suffered from jealousy. Varya and Nadya, too, were tender with him and looked at him anxiously, as though afraid that he would suddenly get up and leave them. When he wanted to pour himself a second glass of vodka, Varya made an angry face and said:

"You're poisoning yourself, Sergey Sergeich. You're a nervous, impressionable sort, and you can easily become an alcoholic. Tanya, tell them to remove the vodka."

Sergey Sergeich was generally very successful with women. They loved his stature, his build, his massive features, his idleness, his misfortunes. They said that he was very kind and therefore a spendthrift, an idealist and therefore impractical, that he was honest, pure of heart, that he could not adjust himself to people and circumstances, and so owned nothing and could find no definite occupation. They believed him implicitly, adored him, and so spoiled him by their admiration that he himself became convinced that he was idealistic, impractical, honest, pure of heart, and that he was superior to these women and that they should look up to him.

"Why don't you say a word of praise about my little girls?" asked Tatyana, feasting her eyes on her two little daughters and piling high with rice the plates of these healthy-looking, well-nourished children, who made one think of dinner rolls. "Just look at them! They say that all mothers dote on their children, but I assure you I'm unbiassed, my little girls are extraordinary. Particularly the elder."

Podgorin smiled at her and at the little girls, but he found it odd that this young, healthy, rather intelligent woman— a big complex organism—should spend all her energy, all her vital forces on such a simple, petty job as the building of this nest, that in any case was complete.

"Perhaps that's as it should be," he reflected, "but it's dull and stupid."

"*Before the clumsy churl could gasp,
Old Bruin had him in his grasp,*"

said Sergey Sergeich, and snapped his fingers.

Supper was over. Tatyana and Varya made Podgorin sit down on a divan in the drawing room and again started talking to him about business matters.

"You must rescue Sergey Sergeich," said Varya. "It is your moral duty. He has his weaknesses, he's not thrifty, he doesn't plan for a rainy day, but that's because he is kind and generous. He has the soul of a child. Present him with a million, and in a month there'll be nothing left of it, he will have given it all away."

"It's true, it's true," said Tatyana, and tears streamed down her cheeks. "He has made me suffer very much, but I must admit, he's a wonderful human being."

And neither of them, Tatyana or Varya, could refrain

from the little cruelty of saying to Podgorin reproachfully:
"Your generation, Misha, is different!"

"What has my generation to do with it?" thought Podgorin. "Losev isn't more than half a dozen years older than
I. . . ."

"Life is not easy," said Varya, and sighed. "You are always threatened by a loss. They want to take your property away, or someone close to you falls ill and you fear
for his life—and so on, day after day. But what's to be done,
my dears? One must submit to the higher Will without a
murmur, one must remember that in this world nothing is
accidental, everything has its purpose, no matter how re-
mote. You haven't really lived, Misha, and you haven't
suffered much, and you will laugh at me; laugh, but I will
say this, nevertheless: during the period when I was most
anxious, I had several experiences of clairvoyance, and the
result has been a spiritual revolution within me, and now I
know that nothing is accidental, and that everything that
happens to us is necessary."

How different she was, this Varya, already gray-haired,
corseted, wearing a fashionable dress with puffed sleeves,
rolling a cigarette in long, thin fingers, that trembled for
some reason, this Varya, easily falling prey to mysticism,
speaking in such a weak, monotonous voice, how different
she was from Varya, the medical student, the gay, noisy,
bold red-head. . . .

"What has time done to them?" Podgorin wondered,
listening to her with boredom.

"Sing us something, Va," he said, to put an end to the
talk about clairvoyance. "You used to sing beautifully."

"Oh, Misha, that's all past and gone."

"Or recite something by Nekrasov."

"I don't remember any of it. It was just an accident that
I recalled those lines earlier in the evening."

In spite of the corset and the fashionable sleeves, it was

plain that she was far from prosperous and that she lived
meagerly at the factory beyond Tula. It was noticeable,
too, that she was overworked. Heavy, monotonous work
and the constant concern with other people's affairs, her
fretting about other people had been a strain on her, and
had aged her prematurely, and Podgorin, looking now at
her sad face, already faded, thought that not Kuzminki, not
Sergey Sergeich, but she herself who was so concerned
about them, was in need of help.

Higher education and the fact that she was a physician
did not seem to have affected the woman in her. Like
Tatyana, she took pleasure in weddings, births, baptisms,
lengthy conversations about children, she liked terrifying
novels with happy endings; when she took up a newspaper
it was to read only about fires, floods and public ceremo-
nies. She was dying to have Podgorin propose to Nadezhda,
and were it to happen, she would burst into tears.

He did not know whether it was by chance or whether
Varya had arranged it, but he found himself alone with
Nadezhda. The mere suspicion that he was being watched
and that something was wanted of him constrained and
embarrassed him, and sitting beside Nadezhda, he felt as
though the two of them had been placed in a cage.

"Let us go down to the garden," she said.

They went off to the garden: he, disgruntled, vexed, not
knowing what to talk to her about, she—joyous, proud of
having him at her side, obviously happy that he would stay
there another three days, and perhaps full of sweet reveries
and hopes. He did not know if she was in love with him,
but he was aware that she had long since grown used to
him and was attached to him, that she still saw her tutor in
him, and that she was just the way Tatyana used to be,
that is, she thought of nothing but love, of how to get
married as soon as possible, to have a husband, children, a
nook of her own. She had preserved that feeling about

friendship which is so intense in children, and it was possible that she merely respected Podgorin and was fond of him as of a friend, that she was in love not with him, but with her dreams of a husband and children.

"It's getting dark," said he.

"Yes. The moon rises late now."

They kept strolling along one alley, near the house. Podgorin was loath to go far into the garden: it was dark there, he would have to take her by the arm, be very close to her. Shadows were moving on the terrace, and it seemed to him that Tatyana and Varya were watching them.

"I must ask your advice," said Nadezhda, halting. "If Kuzminki is sold, then Sergey Sergeich will take a position, and our life will be completely changed. I'm not going to stay with sister, we shall separate, because I don't want to be a burden on the family. One must work. I'll find some employment in Moscow, I'll earn money and be able to help sister and her husband. You'll advise me, won't you?"

Knowing nothing at all about it, she was now animated by the idea of working and of independence, she was making plans for the future—this was written on her face, and the prospect of working and helping others seemed to her beautiful, poetical. He saw her pallid face and dark eyebrows at close range and recalled what an intelligent, keen, capable pupil she had been, and how pleasant it had been to tutor her. And it might well be that now she was not simply a young lady who wanted a husband, but a high-minded girl, of extraordinary kindness, with a gentle, pliable soul, which could be molded into any shape, like wax, a girl who, given proper surroundings, could grow into an admirable woman.

"Why not marry her, really?" thought Podgorin, but was immediately frightened by the thought and began walking in the direction of the house.

When they entered the drawing room, they found

Tatyana sitting at the piano, and her playing vividly brought back the past, when in this very drawing room there was playing, singing and dancing late into the night, with the windows open, and the birds in the garden and on the river singing, too. Podgorin brightened, grew playful, danced with Nadezhda and with Varya, and afterwards he sang. A corn on his foot annoyed him, so he asked if he might wear Sergey Sergeich's slippers, and, strange to say, in slippers he felt like one of the family, a relative ("like a brother-in-law" flashed through his mind) and he grew even gayer. This made all of them come to life, they brightened, were rejuvenated, as it were; hope shone in everyone's face: Kuzminki was saved! It was a simple matter: all that was needed was to think up something, dig up a law, or if Podgorin were to marry Nadya . . . And, obviously, the affair was under way. Nadya, pink-cheeked, happy, her eyes shining with tears in the expectation of something extraordinary, circled in the dance, her white dress billowing and showing glimpses of her slim, pretty legs in their flesh-tinted stockings. Varya, thoroughly contented, took Podgorin by the arm and said to him under her breath with a significant expression:

"Misha, don't run away from your happiness. Take it while it offers itself to you freely, later you will be running after it, but you won't overtake it."

Podgorin wanted to promise, to be encouraging, and he himself believed that Kuzminki was saved, and that it could all be arranged very simply.

"And thou shalt be queen of the world," he broke into song, striking a pose, but suddenly remembering that he could do nothing for these people, nothing at all, he fell silent like one stricken with guilt.

And there he sat in a corner, mute, cross-legged, with his feet in another man's slippers.

At the sight of him, the others understood that nothing

could be done, and fell silent, too. The piano was closed.
Everyone noticed that it was late, time to go to bed, and
Tatyana put out the big lamp in the drawing room.

A bed was made up for Podgorin in the same wing in
which he used to live years back. Sergey Sergeich went to
see him settled, holding the candle high above his head,
although the moon had risen and it was light. They walked
between lilac bushes, and the gravel of the path crunched
under their feet.

> *"Before the clumsy churl could gasp,*
> *Old Bruin had him in his grasp."*

said Sergey Sergeich.

It seemed to Podgorin as if he had heard these lines a
thousand times. He was fed up with them. When they
reached the wing, Sergey Sergeich produced a bottle and
two glasses from the pocket of his ample jacket and put
them on the table.

"It's cognac," he said. "Number zero-zero. Varya's in
the house, you can't drink in her presence, she'll start
squawking about alcoholism, but here we're free. It's excellent cognac."

They sat down. The cognac was indeed excellent.

"This time we must finish the bottle," continued Sergey
Sergeich, biting into a lemon. "I haven't forgotten my
student days, sometimes I like to let myself go. One has
to."

But there was that look in his eyes that said he needed
something from Podgorin and was about to ask for something.

"Let's drink, old chap," he continued, sighing, "life is
getting too hard for me. My kind is finished, for good.
Idealism is out of fashion. The ruble is king nowadays, and
you have to kneel down and worship it if you don't want to
be kicked out, left nowhere. I can't do it. It's disgusting!"

"When is the auction?" asked Podgorin, to change the subject.

"The seventh of August. But I have no hope of being able to save Kuzminki, my dear friend. The arrears are enormous, and the estate brings in nothing, there are only losses every year. The game isn't worth the candle. . . . Of course, Tanya is cut up, it's her patrimony, but as for me, to be frank, I'm rather glad. I don't care for the country. Give me the big, bustling city, with its struggle—then I'm in my element!"

He kept on talking, but he didn't say what he wanted to say, and he watched Podgorin intently, as though looking for an opportune moment. And suddenly Podgorin felt the man's eyes peering closely into his and the man's breath on his face.

"My dear fellow, save me!" Sergey Sergeich brought out, breathing heavily. "Give me two hundred rubles! I implore you!"

Podgorin wanted to say that he was short of funds, and it flashed through his mind that it would be better to give the two hundred rubles to some poor devil or even lose them at cards, but he became terribly embarrassed, and feeling himself trapped in this little room with the one candle, and wishing to rid himself as soon as possible of this breath on his face, these soft, sticky arms which clasped his waist and already seemed glued to him, he began to rummage hastily in his pockets for his wallet.

"Here . . ." he mumbled, taking out a hundred rubles. "The rest later. I don't have any more on me. As you see, I can't refuse," he went on with irritation, beginning to get angry. "I have an insufferably flabby character. Only, please, consider this a loan. I'm hard up myself."

"Thank you! Thank you, old chap!"

"And please, stop imagining that you're an idealist. You

are as much of an idealist as I am a turkey. You are just an unthinking loafer and nothing else."

Sergey Sergeich drew a deep sigh and sat down on the couch.

"You're angry, my dear fellow," he said, "but if you knew what I'm going through! I'm having a hellish time. My dear fellow, I swear to you—it's not myself I'm sorry for, not a bit of it! I'm only sorry for my wife and the children. If it weren't for my wife and the children, I'd have committed suicide long ago."

And suddenly his head and shoulders began to shake, and he burst into sobs.

"That's all that was wanting," said Podgorin, dreadfully vexed, pacing the room in agitation. "Well, what am I to do with a man who has behaved like a rascal and then starts to sob? Your tears disarm me, I can't say anything to you. You sob, therefore you are right."

"I behaved like a rascal?" asked Sergey Sergeich, getting up, and looking at Podgorin in amazement. "My dear fellow, how can you say such a thing? I behaved like a rascal? Oh, how little you know me! How little you understand me!"

"Very well, I don't understand you, only please stop blubbering. It's disgusting."

"Oh, how little you know me!" Losev repeated, quite sincerely. "How little you know me!"

"Look at yourself in the mirror," Podgorin continued, "you're no longer young, soon you will be an old man, it's high time for you to come to your senses, to realize who you are and what you are. All your life you've done nothing, all your life—this idle, puerile chatter, these airs, these affectations—aren't you fed up with all this, aren't you sick of it all? It's painful to be with you! And so dreadfully boring!"

With this, Podgorin left the room, banging the door.

Almost for the first time in his life he had been completely sincere and had said what he wanted to say.

A little later he was sorry that he had been so harsh. What good was it to speak seriously to or argue with a man who lied constantly, ate a lot, drank a lot, spent a lot of money belonging to other people and at the same time was convinced that he was an idealist and a martyr? You were dealing with stupidity or with inveterate bad habits, which are as firmly lodged in the organism as an incurable disease. At any rate, indignation and severe reproaches were useless. It would have been better to laugh at it all; one good gibe could do more than ten sermons!

"Still better, pay no attention," thought Podgorin, "and, above all, don't lend him money."

A little later, Sergey Sergeich and his hundred rubles were far from his thoughts. There was something pensive about the night, which was still and brilliant. When Podgorin looked at the sky on moonlit nights, it seemed to him that only he and the moon were awake, while everything else was either asleep or drowsing; he didn't think of people or of money, and gradually a quiet, peaceful mood possessed him; he felt alone in the world, and in the nocturnal silence the sound of his own footsteps seemed melancholy to him.

The garden was enclosed by a white stone wall. In the right corner of the side facing the fields there was a tower, built a long time back, in the days of serfdom. The lower part of the tower was of stone, the upper was built of wood, and had a balcony; from the conical roof rose a tall spire topped by a black weathervane. Below there were two doors, so that one could either pass from the garden into the fields or reach the balcony by a stairway that creaked underfoot. Under the stairs old broken armchairs were lying about; the moonlight, coming through the door, made them gleam, so that with their crooked legs sticking up they seemed to have come to life in the night and to be lying in wait for someone there in the stillness.

Podgorin walked up the stairs and sat down on the balcony. Just beyond the wall there was a ditch with an embankment marking the boundary of the property. Farther off, were the broad fields, flooded with moonlight. Podgorin knew that there was a forest straight ahead, about two miles from the house, and it seemed to him that he saw a dark stripe in the distance. Quails and corn crakes were calling, and from time to time the voice of the cuckoo, which was also still wakeful, came from the direction of the woods.

There was the sound of footsteps. Someone was walking in the garden, approaching the tower.

A dog barked.

"Beetle!" a woman's voice called gently. "Beetle, come back!"

One could hear below someone entering the tower, and after a moment a black dog, an old friend of Podgorin's, appeared on the embankment. It stood still and, looking up to where Podgorin was sitting, wagged its tail in a friendly fashion. A little later a white figure rose like a shadow from the black ditch and also stood still on the embankment. It was Nadezhda.

"What do you see up there?" she asked the dog, as she too looked up.

She did not see Podgorin, but apparently felt his presence: she was smiling, and her pale face, lighted by the moon, seemed happy. The black shadow of the tower that stretched far out over the field, the motionless white figure and the pale face smiling happily, the black dog, the shadows cast by the two—it was all like a dream.

"There is someone there . . ." said Nadezhda softly.

She stood and waited, hoping that he would either come down or call her to him, and that he would finally propose to her, and they would be happy in this still, beautiful night. White, pale, slim, very lovely in the moonlight, she was longing for caresses. Her continual dreams of happiness and love had wearied her, she could no longer hide her feelings, and her whole posture, the brilliance of her eyes, her fixed, blissful smile, betrayed her sweet thoughts. As for him, he was ill at ease, he shrank together, he froze, not knowing whether to say something so as to turn it all into a joke, or to remain silent, and he was vexed, and could only reflect that here in the country, on a moonlit night, with a beautiful, enamored, dreamy girl so near, his emotions were as little involved as on Malaya Bronskaya Street—clearly this fine poetry meant no more to him than that crude prose. All this was dead: trysts on moonlit nights, slim-waisted figures in white, mysterious shadows, towers and country houses, and "types" like Sergey Sergeich, and like himself, Podgorin, with his chilly boredom, constant vexation, his inability to adjust himself to real life, inability to take from it what it had to offer, and with an aching, wearying thirst for what was not and could not be on earth. And now, sitting here in this tower, he would have preferred a good display of fireworks or a procession in the moonlight, or to have Varya recite Nekrasov's "Railroad" again, or some other woman, who, standing there on the embankment where Nadezhda was standing, would speak of something absorbing, novel, having no relation to love or happiness, or if she did speak of love, it would be a call to a new kind of life, exalted and yet reasonable, a life on the threshold of which we live and of which we sometimes have a premonition. . . .

"No one there," said Nadezhda.

And, after waiting another moment, she walked off slowly with lowered head in the direction of the woods. The dog ran in front of her. For quite a long while Podgorin could see a white spot moving in the distance.

"Strange, how it all turned out," he kept repeating to himself, as he went back to his room.

He could not picture what he would talk about to Sergey Sergeich, to Tatyana, the next day, and the day after that, how he would behave toward Nadezhda—and in anticipation he felt embarrassment, fear and boredom. How was he going to fill the interminable three days that he had promised to stay on? He recalled the talk about clairvoyance, Sergey Sergeich's phrase:

"Before the clumsy churl could gasp,
Old Bruin had him in his grasp."

He recalled that the next day, to please Tatyana, he would have to smile at her plump, well-fed little girls—and he decided to leave.

At half past five Sergey Sergeich, wearing a Bokharan dressing-gown and a fez with a tassel, appeared on the terrace of the big house. Without losing a moment's time, Podgorin went up to him and began his farewells.

"I have to be in Moscow at ten," he said, without looking at his host. "I had completely forgotten that they would be waiting for me at the notary public's. Please, don't detain me. When the family is up, give them my apologies, I am terribly sorry . . ."

He did not hear what Sergey Sergeich was saying to him, and hurried off, and kept looking back at the windows of the big house, afraid that the ladies would wake up and try to detain him. He was ashamed of his nervousness. He felt that this was his last visit to Kuzminki, that he would not come there again. Several times, as he was driving off, he looked back at the wing in which he had spent so many happy days, but his heart was unmoved and he did not grow melancholy.

When he reached home, the first thing he noticed on his table was the note he had received the previous day. "Dear

Misha," he read, "you have completely forgotten us, come as soon as possible. . . ." And for some reason he recalled how Nadezhda had circled in the dance, how her dress billowed, showing her legs in the flesh-tinted stockings.

Ten minutes later he was at his desk, working, and without a thought of Kuzminki.

1898

de-compensation

Vigil Service was being celebrated in the home of the district marshal of the nobility, Mikhail Ilyich Bondaryov. The officiating priest was a fair-haired, rotund young man with long curls, a broad nose and a leonine profile. A deacon and the clerk did the chanting.

Mikhail Ilyich, who was seriously ill, sat in an armchair, motionless, pale, with closed eyes, like a corpse. Next to him stood his wife, Vera Andreyevna, her head bent to one side, in the passive, indolent pose of a person indifferent to religion but obliged to stand up and make the sign of the cross from time to time. Vera Andreyevna's brother, Alexander Andreyevich Yanshin, and his wife Lenochka stood next to each other behind the armchair. It was the eve of Pentecost. In the garden the trees were rustling gently and half the sky was blazing festively with a gorgeous sunset.

Whether the chimes of the monastery bells or those of the town churches floated in through the open windows, or a peacock screamed in the yard, or someone coughed in the anteroom, involuntarily the thought occurred to everyone that Mikhail Ilyich was gravely ill, that the doctors had ordered him to go abroad as soon as he got better, but that his condition changed from day to day so that it was all very baffling, and meanwhile time was passing and the uncertainty was trying. Yanshin had come at Easter to be of help to his sister when she went abroad with her husband, but he had stayed on here with his wife nearly two months, he was already witnessing the third Mass, and still the future was clouded and there was no understanding anything. And what assurance was there that this nightmare would not drag on till autumn?

Yanshin was annoyed and bored. He was fed up with the daily preparations for the trip abroad, and he wanted to return to Novosyolki, his own estate. True, it wasn't jolly at home either, but then Novosyolki didn't have this huge drawing room with columns in the four corners, these white armchairs upholstered in gold brocade, these yellow portieres, this chandelier, all this vulgar exhibition of bad taste masquerading as magnificence, this echo repeating every step of yours at night, and above all—it didn't have this sickly, yellow, bloated face with closed eyes. . . . At home you could laugh, talk nonsense, quarrel openly with your wife or your mother—in a word, live as you pleased. But here it was like a boarding school, you had to go on tiptoe, speak in whispers, make only sensible remarks, or else you had to stand up and listen to Mass, which was served not because of any religious sentiment, but, as Mikhail Ilyich himself said, for the sake of tradition. . . . And nothing is more tiring and humiliating than having to kowtow to a man whom at heart you consider a nonentity, and having to nurse a patient for whom you are not sorry. . . .

Yanshin's mind was busy with another matter: the previous night Lenochka had told him that she was pregnant. This news was interesting only in so far as it complicated the question of the trip abroad. What was to be done? Take Lenochka abroad with them, or send her back to Novosyolki? But in her condition it was unwise to travel, and she would by no means consent to go home, because she didn't get along with her mother-in-law and would not be willing to live in the country alone, without her husband.

"Or shall I use this as a pretext and go home with her?" Yanshin asked himself, trying to close his ears to the deacon. "No, it's awkward to leave Vera alone," he decided, glancing at his sister's slim figure. "So what shall I do?"

He was pondering and asking himself: "What shall I do?" and his life seemed to him very involved and complicated. The trip, his sister, his wife, his brother-in-law, and so on, were so many problems; each one of them separately could perhaps be easily and comfortably solved, but they were linked up together and formed an impassable jungle, and to get rid of one of them was merely to entangle the others all the more.

When, before starting to read the Gospel, the priest turned around and said: "Peace be unto all!" the patient suddenly opened his eyes and began to fidget in the armchair.

"Sasha!" he called.

Yanshin quickly stepped forward and leaned over him.

"I don't like the way he conducts the service," said Mikhail Ilyich under his breath, but so that everyone in the room heard his words clearly. He breathed heavily, making a whistling, rattling sound. "I want to go inside. Help me, Sasha."

Yanshin helped him get up and took him by the arm.

"You stay here, darling . . ." said Mikhail Ilyich in a weak, imploring voice, as his wife made a move to take his other arm. "Stay here!" he repeated irritably, glancing at her indifferent face. "I'll make it!"

The priest stood with the Gospel open, waiting. In the

silence that followed a chorus of male voices sounded clearly and harmoniously. People were singing somewhere beyond the garden, perhaps on the river. It was very delightful when suddenly the bells in the neighboring monastery began to ring, and the soft, melodious chimes mingled with the singing. Yanshin's heart contracted with the sweet premonition that something good was going to happen, and he almost forgot that he was helping the patient out of the room. For some reason, the sounds that had floated into the drawing room reminded him of how little joy and freedom there was in his life now, and how petty were the problems with which he struggled so desperately every day from morning till night. As he walked along slowly, supporting the patient, and the servants, stepping aside and making way for them, eyed them with the gloomy curiosity with which country people look at a dead body, he was suddenly seized with hatred, with acute, overpowering hatred for the sick man's bloated face, clean-shaven like an actor's, for his waxen hands, his plush dressing gown, his stertorous breathing, the tapping of his black cane. This emotion, which he had never before experienced and which possessed him so unexpectedly, made his heart pound and his hands and feet turn cold. He was overwhelmed by the passionate wish that Mikhail Ilyich should die that very minute, that he should cry out for the last time and flop down on the floor, but the next moment he visualized this death and turned away from it in horror. When they had left the drawing room, what he desired was not the death of the patient but life for himself: to pull his own hand away from the warm armpit and run, run, run without looking back.

A bed was made up for Mikhail Ilyich on a Turkish divan in his study. The patient found his bedroom hot and uncomfortable.

"Either one thing or the other: be a pope or an Hussar!"

he said, lowering himself heavily onto the divan. "What manners! Oh, my God . . . If I had my way, a fop like that would never be a priest, he'd be nothing but a deacon."

The capricious expression on the unhappy face made Yanshin want to object, to be impertinent, to confess his hatred, but he recalled the doctors' orders not to irritate the patient, and held his peace. However, it was not the doctors that stopped him. What wouldn't he say, what wouldn't he shout at him, if his sister Vera's lot weren't eternally and hopelessly tied to this hateful man? Mikhail Ilyich had a habit of constantly pursing his lips and moving them from side to side as though he were sucking at a candy, and Yanshin was further irritated by this movement of the full, shaven lips.

"Go back, Sasha, go . . ." said Mikhail Ilyich. "You are in good health, and apparently you are indifferent to the Church. . . . It doesn't matter to you who officiates."

"But you too are indifferent to the Church . . ." Yanshin brought out quietly, controlling himself.

"No, I believe in Providence and I recognize the Church."

"Exactly. It seems to me that what religion means to you is not God, not the truth, but such words as 'Providence,' 'Heaven.' . . ."

Yanshin wanted to add: "Otherwise you wouldn't have been so rude to the priest just now," but he cut himself short. It seemed to him that as it was he had allowed himself to say too much.

"Please, go!" said Mikhail Ilyich impatiently. He did not like to be contradicted or to be the subject of discussion. "I don't wish to be in anybody's way. . . . I know how hard it is to be around a sick person. . . . I know, my dear fellow! I have always said and I always will say: there is no harder and more saintly work than that of a nurse. Do me a favor, go!"

Yanshin left the study and went down to his own room; there he put on his coat and hat and, passing through the main entrance, walked out into the garden. It was already after eight o'clock. Upstairs they were chanting the Canon. Making his way among flower beds, rose bushes, patches of heliotrope set out to form the initials V and M, past marvelous blossoms, which gave no one on this estate any pleasure, and which apparently grew and bloomed "for the sake of tradition" too, Yanshin walked hurriedly, afraid that his wife might hail him from upstairs. She could easily have seen him. But now, having cut across the park, he reached the fir-tree alley, long and dark, which was the usual frame for the sunset. Here the aged, decrepit firs always rustled lightly and sternly, even on windless days, there was a smell of resin, and your feet slipped on dry needles.

As Yanshin strolled along, he was thinking that he was not going to get rid of the hatred which had suddenly taken possession of him during the Mass, and that it would be necessary to reckon with it. This brought a new complication into his life and boded ill. But the firs, the distant sky and the festive sunset breathed a blessed peace. He listened with pleasure to his own muffled footsteps, which sounded lonely in the dark alley, and he no longer asked himself: "What shall I do?"

Almost every evening he walked to the railway station to fetch the newspapers and his mail, and this was his sole distraction while he was staying at his brother-in-law's. The mail express arrived at 9:45, precisely when the period of intolerable evening boredom began in the house. There was no one with whom to play cards, supper was not served, you didn't want to sleep, so that you were reduced to sitting up with the patient or reading aloud to Lenochka the translated novels of which she was so fond. The station was a large one, with a buffet and a book stall. One could have a snack here, a glass of beer, and one could browse among the books. Yanshin especially liked meeting the train; he envied the passengers who were going somewhere and seemed happier than he was.

When he arrived at the station, the public which he was accustomed to see there every evening was already promenading on the platform while waiting to see the train come in. Here were the summer residents who lived near the station, two or three officers from the town, a country gentleman wearing one spur and followed by a Great Dane, its head drooping sadly. The summer people, men and women, apparently well acquainted with each other, were talking loudly and laughing. As usual, the most lively person there and the one who laughed loudest was an engineer, a very corpulent man of about forty-five, distinguished by side whiskers and a broad pelvis, who wore a cotton shirt over his wide velveteen pants. When, thrusting his large paunch forward and stroking his whiskers, he passed by, and Yanshin caught a cordial glance from his oily eyes, it seemed to him that this man had a keen zest for living. The engineer's face wore a particular expression that could only be interpreted as: "Ah, how delicious!" He had a bizarre, triple surname, and Yanshin remembered it only because the engineer, who liked to discuss politics in loud tones, would often swear to the truth of a statement with the phrase: "Or may my name not be Bitnyi-Kushle-Suvremovich!"

People said that he was fond of fun, very hospitable and a passionate card player. For a long time Yanshin had wanted to get acquainted with him, but could not bring himself to accost him and talk to him, although he suspected that the man would not be averse to the acquaintance. For some reason every time that Yanshin strolled on the platform alone and listened to the summer residents, it occurred to him that he was already thirty-one, and that

since the age of twenty-four, when he graduated from the
university, he had not spent one pleasurable day: he was
either engaged in litigation with a neighbor over a boundary, or there was his wife's miscarriage, or it seemed to him
that his sister Vera was unhappy, or again Mikhail Ilyich
was ill and it was necessary to go abroad with him. He
reflected that this sort of thing would be repeated in various forms endlessly, and that at forty and fifty he would
be plagued by the same thoughts and worries as at thirty-
one—in a word, that until he died he would be encased in
that hard shell. To believe otherwise was to deceive one-
self. And he yearned to cease to be an oyster at least for an
hour, yearned to peer into other people's worlds, to be
carried away by what did not concern him personally, to
talk to strangers, for instance to this fat engineer or to the
women of the summer colony who, in the twilight, all
looked so pretty, gay and, above all, young.

The train pulled in. The gentleman farmer with one spur
met a plump elderly lady, who embraced him and repeated
"Alexis!" several times in an agitated voice. Ceremoniously,
like a *jeune premier* in a ballet, he clinked his spur, offered
her his arm, and said to the porter in a velvety, sugary
baritone: "Be so good as to fetch our luggage!"

In a few minutes the train left. The summer residents got
their newspapers and mail and went home. Silence fell.
Yanshin strolled a little longer, and then went into the
first-class waiting room. He was not hungry, but he ate a
veal cutlet and had a beer. The exquisite, ceremonious manners of the gentleman with the spur, his mawkish baritone,
and that sophisticated civility of his made a morbid impression on him that he could not shake off. He kept recalling the man's long moustaches, his kind, rather intelligent, yet strangely inscrutable face, his way of rubbing his
hands as if it were cold, and reflected that if the plump
elderly lady were really this man's mother, she was proba-

bly very unhappy. Her agitated voice uttered only one word: Alexis! But her timid, distraught face and her fond eyes said everything else.

II

Vera Andreyevna had seen through the window that her brother had gone out. She knew that he was bound for the station, and she saw in her mind's eye the long alley of fir trees, the slope falling away toward the river, the broad prospect and that sense of simplicity and peace that rivers always gave her. She pictured to herself the meadows under water and beyond them the station, the birch woods where the summer residents lived, and far away to the right the town and the monastery with its golden cupolas. . . . Then once more she summoned up the alley, the darkness, her fear and shame, the sound of familiar footsteps, and everything that could occur again, perhaps even that very night. . . . She left the drawing room to see about tea for the Father, and when she reached the dining room she took out of her pocket a stiff envelope with a foreign stamp, folded once. The letter had been delivered to her a few minutes before the Mass, and she had already read it twice.

"My dear, my darling, my torment, my longing," she read, holding the letter in both hands so as to give both of them the ecstasy of touching those precious burning lines. "My dear," she read the first words over again and went on, "my darling, my torment, my longing, you write persuasively, but I don't know what to do. At the time you said that you were positively leaving for Italy, and like a madman I dashed here ahead of you, to meet you and to love you, my dear, my joy. I thought that here you would not be in terror on moonlit nights, afraid your husband or your brother might see my shadow through the window. Here we could walk in the streets, and you would not be afraid that Rome or Venice might discover that we loved

each other. Forgive me, my treasure, but there are two
Veras: one, timid, faint-hearted, hesitant; the other, indifferent, cold, proud, who addresses me formally in the presence of strangers and makes believe that she hardly notices
me. I want this proud, beautiful woman to love me. . . .
I do not want to be an owl, entitled to pleasure only when
evening comes. Give me light! Darkness oppresses me, my
dear, and this love that we steal in snatches leaves me half-
starved, and I am irritated, I suffer, I go mad . . . Well,
in a word, I thought that here, abroad, where it is easier to
hide from observation, *my* Vera, the second one, would
give me at least one hour of complete love, real love, without looking back, so that for once I would feel that I was
a lover, not a smuggler, so that as I embraced her the
woman would not say: 'It's time for me to go!' That is
what I thought, but here I have been in Florence a whole
month, yet you are not here, and there is no knowing when
you will come. You write: 'We are not likely to leave this
month.' What am I to make of this? My despair, what are
you doing to me? Get it into your head, I cannot be without you, I can't, I can't!!! They say Italy is beautiful, but
I am bored here, as if I were in exile, and my strong love *is*
languishing like an exile. You will say that my pun is not
funny. Very well, but *I* am ridiculous, like a clown. I dash
off to Bologna, to Venice, to Rome, and everywhere I go
I look for a woman in the crowd who resembles you. Out
of sheer boredom I have made the rounds of all the picture
galleries and museums five times, but in every canvas I see
only you. In Rome I ascend Monte Pincio, panting, and
from there look at the eternal city, but eternity, beauty,
the sky—all that melts into one image that has your face
and wears your dress. And here, in Florence, I walk into
shops where they sell sculpture, and when the place is
empty, I embrace the statues, and it seems to me that I am
embracing you. I need you now, this minute . . . Vera,

I am acting insanely, but, forgive me, I cannot help myself. Tomorrow I will be on my way to you . . . This letter is unnecessary, but I am mailing it anyway! My dear, and so it is settled: tomorrow I take the train."

(Unfinished)

Written in 1902-3
Published posthumously in 1905

2 other writings

on the harmful effects
of tobacco [FIRST VERSION]

a monologue for the stage

Delivered by Markel Ivanych Nyukhin, the husband of his wife, who keeps a boarding school for girls.

The stage represents a rostrum in a provincial club.

Nyukhin (enters with great dignity, bows, pulls down his waistcoat, and begins majestically): Ladies and gentlemen! It was suggested to my wife that I deliver a popular lecture in the interests of charity. True learning is modest and does not like to make a show of itself, but because of the worthy end in view, my wife agreed, and here I am before you. I am not a professor and learned degrees are not in my line, but it is no secret to any of you that . . . that . . . (fidgets and glances at a scrap of paper that he pulls out of his pocket) that for the last thirty years, untiringly and at the sacrifice of my health and life's other blessings, I have been at work on problems of a strictly scientific nature and have even contributed scientific papers to the organ of the local press. The other day I delivered to the editor a long article entitled: "On the mischievousness of coffeeism and teaism for the organism." As the subject of today's lecture I have chosen the injury that the use of tobacco causes mankind. Of course, it is difficult to exhaust the importance of the subject in one lecture, but I shall endeavor to be brief and mention only what is most essential. As an enemy of popularization, I shall be strictly scientific, and as for you, my listeners, I suggest that you appreciate the full significance of the subject and that you treat this lecture of mine with due seriousness. The frivolous person, the person who shrinks from the dryness of a strictly scientific address need not listen—he may depart. (Makes a dignified gesture and pulls down his waistcoat). And so, I commence . . .

Your attention, please. I particularly crave the attention of Messrs. the physicians here present, who may obtain much useful information from my lecture, since tobacco, aside from its harmful effects, is also employed in medicine. Thus, on February 10, 1871, the doctor prescribed that my wife use it in enemas. (Glances at his notes). Tobacco is an organic substance. In my opinion, it is obtained from the plant Nicotiana Tabacum, of the Solaneae family. It grows in America. Its chief ingredient is the terrible, pernicious poison, nicotine. Chemically it consists, in my opinion, of ten atoms of carbon, fourteen atoms of hydrogen . . . and . . . two . . . atoms of nitrogen. (Gasps and clutches his chest, dropping his paper). More air! (To keep from falling, teeters on his heels and waves his arms). Oh! Let me catch my breath! One moment . . . just wait . . . I'll get over the attack by sheer will power (thumps his chest with his fist). Enough! Ouf! (A pause, in the course of which Nyukhin paces the platform, breathing heavily). I have been suffering from attacks of asthma for years. My first seizure occurred on September 13, 1869, on the very day when my wife gave birth to our sixth daughter, Veronica. My wife has given birth to nine daughters and not one son, a fact in which my wife rejoices, since, in a boarding school for girls, sons would in many respects be awkward. In the entire boarding school there is only one man—it is me. . . . But the eminently respectable, highly esteemed families that have entrusted the fate of their daughters to my wife, can be completely easy in their minds with regard to me. However . . . as time is short, don't let us digress from the subject of our lecture. . . . And so,—where was I? Ouf! The attack of asthma interrupted me at the most interesting point. But there's no ill wind that brings nobody good. For me and for you and particularly for Messrs. the physicians here present, this attack may serve as an admirable lesson. In nature there are no events without a cause. Let us, then, look for the cause of my attack. (Puts one finger to his forehead and ponders). I have it! The only remedy for asthma is refraining from rich and stimulating foods, but before coming to this lecture I allowed myself a dietary indiscretion. You see, in my wife's boarding school pancakes are being served today at dinner instead of a roast. Each pupil is served one pancake. Inasmuch as I am the husband of my wife, it does not behoove me to praise this high-minded lady, but I take my oath that no other boarding school offers meals so sensible, so hygienic, and so well planned. I can personally testify to that, since in this boarding school of ours I have been entrusted with the responsibility for the housekeeping. I buy provisions, keep an eye on the servants, present the daily accounts to my wife every evening; I stitch the notebooks together, invent insecticides, freshen the air with an atomizer, I count the linen, I see to it that no more than five pupils use one toothbrush and no more than ten young ladies dry themselves with one towel. Today my duty was to issue to the cook an amount of butter and flour corresponding to the number of pupils. And so, today pancakes were baked. I must note that the pancakes were to be served to the pupils only. The members of my wife's family were to have roast meat, for which purpose we had the hind leg of a calf that had been in the cellar since last Friday. My wife and I had arrived at the conclusion that we must not fail to roast the leg today: tomorrow might be too late. But let us proceed. Listen to what happened. When the pancakes had been baked and counted, my wife sent word to the kitchen that five pupils were to be punished for bad manners by being deprived of pancakes. Thus it turned out that we had baked five pancakes too many. What would you have us do with them? Give them to our daughters? But my wife forbids them to eat doughy foods. Well, what do you suppose? What did we do with them? (Sighs, and shakes his head). Oh, loving heart! Oh, angel of kindness! She said: 'Eat these pancakes yourself, Markesha dear!' And I ate them, after emptying a glass of vodka. That's what caused the attack. *Da ist der Hund begraben!* However (looks at his watch), we have been carried away and have strayed from our subject. Let us proceed.—And so nicotine consists of . . . of (nervously rummages in his pockets and looks around for his notes). I suggest that you remember this formula . . . A chemical formula is a lodestar . . . (Discovering the paper on the floor, he drops a handkerchief on it, and picks up the two together). I forgot to tell you that in my wife's boarding school, aside from being in charge of the housekeeping, I teach mathematics, physics, chemistry, geography, history, and object lessons. In addition to these sciences, the following subjects are taught in my wife's boarding school: French, German, English, religion, handicrafts, drawing, music, dancing, and deportment. As you see, the curriculum is above that of a secondary school. And the food! And the comforts! And what is most remarkable: all this for such a modest fee. Pupils taking the full course pay 300 rubles, those taking only half pay 200 rubles, day pupils—100. Dancing, music and drawing are extra—by arrangement with my wife . . . An excellent boarding school! The address is: corner Cat Street and Five Dog Lane, the house belonging to the widow of Captain Mamashechkin. My wife can be seen at home at any time for an interview. And you can purchase the prospectus of the boarding school from the porter for only 50 kopecks. (Looks at his notes). And so I suggest that you commit the formula to memory! Chemically, nicotine consists of ten atoms of carbon, fourteen atoms of hydrogen and two of nitrogen. Be good enough to write it down. It is a colorless liquid with an ammoniacal odor. Properly speaking, for us the important thing is the action of nicotine (looks into his snuffbox) on the nerve centers and the muscles of the digestive tract. Oh, Lord! They've put something into it again! (Sneezes). Well, what is one to do with these nasty, wicked girls? Yesterday they put face powder into my snuffbox, and today it's something sharp and stinking (sneezes and scratches his nose). It's infamous! This powder is doing the devil knows what to my nose. Brr! Nasty, wicked girls! Perhaps in this mischief of theirs you will perceive evidence of insufficient discipline in my wife's boarding school. No, gentlemen, it isn't the fault of the school. No! Society is at fault! You are at fault! The family must go hand in hand with the school, but, instead, what do we see? (Sneezes). But let us forget it! (Sneezes). Let us forget . . . Nicotine throws the stomach and intestines into a tetanic condition, that is, into a condition of tetanus. (Pause). But I notice smiles on many faces. Obviously, some of my listeners have not sufficiently appreciated the high importance of the subject under discussion. There are even individuals who are capable of laughter when truths consecrated by exact science are announced from the rostrum. (Sighs). Of course, I dare not reprove you, but . . . to my wife's daughters I always say: 'Children, do not laugh at what is above laughter!' (Sneezes). My wife has nine daughters. The eldest, Anna, is twenty-seven, the youngest—seventeen. Gentlemen, whatever Nature holds of beauty, purity, and high-mindedness resides in these nine young, immaculate creatures. Forgive me my agitation and the tremor in my voice: you see before you the happiest of fathers (sighs). But how hard it is nowadays to marry off daughters! Terribly hard. It's easier to arrange for a third mortgage than to find a husband for only one daughter! (Shakes his head). Ah, young men, young men! By your stubbornness, your materialistic inclination, you deprive yourselves of one of the loftiest pleasures, the pleasure of family life! If you only knew how wonderful that life is! I have lived with my wife thirty-three years, and I can say that these have been the best years of my life. They have flown by like one happy moment. (Weeps). How often have I distressed her by my weaknesses! The poor darling! Although I accepted punishment submissively, yet how did I reward her anger? (Pause). My wife's daughters are so slow in getting married because they are shy, and because men never see them. My wife cannot give evening parties, she never invites anyone to dinner, but . . . I can tell you confidentially (comes closer to the footlights and whispers) that my daughters may be seen on high holidays at the home of their aunt, Natalya Semyonovna Zavertyakhina, the same that suffers from epilepsy and collects old coins. She serves refreshments, too. Time is getting short, however, and we must not stray from our theme. We were on the subject of tetanus. However (looks at his watch), good-bye for the present! (Pulls down his waistcoat and stalks out majestically).

1886

on the harmful effects
of tobacco [FINAL VERSION]

A monologue for the stage in one act

Delivered by Ivan Ivanovich Nyukhin, husband of a wife who keeps a music school and a boarding school for girls. The stage represents a rostrum in a provincial club.

Nyukhin (sporting Dundreary whiskers, his upper lip shaven, and wearing an old, threadbare frock coat; enters majestically, bows, and pulls down his waistcoat). Ladies and, as it were, gentlemen (Combs his whiskers). It was suggested to my wife that I deliver a popular lecture here in the interests of charity. Well, so let us have a lecture— it is all one to me. Of course, I am not a professor and learned degrees are not in my line, nevertheless for the past thirty years I have been working untiringly and, I might even say, at the sacrifice of my health and so forth, on problems of a strictly scientific nature. I engage in meditation and sometimes, think of it, I even write learned papers, that is not exactly learned, but, pardon the expression, very nearly learned. Among other things I recently composed

an enormous article entitled: "On the harmfulness of certain insects." My daughters liked it very much, particularly
the section on bedbugs, but I read it over and tore it up.
For, write what you may, you cannot dispense with Persian
powder.* We have bugs even in the piano. . . . As the
subject of my lecture today I have chosen, so to speak, the
injury that the use of tobacco inflicts on mankind. I myself
smoke, but my wife has ordered me to lecture today on
the harmful effects of tobacco, and therefore there is no
help for it. If it must be tobacco, it must—it's all one to me.
As for you, gentlemen, I suggest that you treat my present
lecture with due seriousness, or something untoward may
occur. But anyone who shrinks from a dry scientific lecture, who doesn't care for it, need not listen—he may leave
(pulls down his waistcoat). I particularly crave the attention of Messrs. the physicians here present, who may obtain
much useful information from my lecture, since tobacco,
aside from its injurious effects, is also employed in medicine. Thus, for instance, if you place a fly in a snuffbox, it
will expire, probably from nervous prostration. In the main,
tobacco is a plant. . . . When I deliver a lecture, I usually
wink my right eye, but pay no attention to it: it is due to
agitation. Generally speaking, I am a very nervous man, and
I started to wink my eye on September 13, 1889, on the
very day when my wife gave birth, as it were, to her fourth
daughter, Varvara. All my daughters were born on the
thirteenth. However (glances at his watch), as the time at
our disposal is short, don't let us stray from the subject of
the lecture. . . . I must tell you that my wife keeps a
music school and a private boarding school, that is: not
exactly a boarding school but something of that description. Between ourselves, my wife likes to complain of
straitened circumstances, yet she has something salted away,
about forty or fifty thousand, while I haven't a kopeck to
* An insecticide. Ed.'s note.

bless myself with, not a groat—but what's the use of talking about it! At the boarding school I am in charge of the housekeeping. I buy the provisions, look after the servants, keep the accounts, stitch the exercise books together, exterminate bedbugs, walk my wife's lapdog, catch mice. . . . Last night it was my duty to issue butter and eggs to the cook, because we were going to have pancakes. Well, in a word, today when the pancakes had already been fried, my wife came into the kitchen to say that three pupils would not be able to eat their pancakes because they had swollen glands. Thus it turned out that we had fried several pancakes too many. What would you have us do with them? At first my wife ordered them taken to the cellar, but then she thought and thought, and said: "You eat these pancakes yourself, you dummy." When she is in a bad humor she addresses me thus: "dummy," "viper," or "Satan." Now, what kind of Satan am I? She is always in a bad humor. And you couldn't say that I ate the pancakes—I swallowed them without chewing them, because I'm always hungry. Yesterday, for example, she gave me no dinner. "No use feeding you, dummy that you are," she said. However (looks at his watch), we have been carried away and have strayed somewhat from our theme. Let us proceed. Though, of course, you would rather listen to a love song, now, or some symphony or other, or an aria. (Breaks into song): 'In the heat of battle we shall not blink an eye . . .' I don't recall where that comes from. . . . Incidentally, I forgot to tell you that at my wife's music school, in addition to being in charge of the housekeeping, I teach mathematics, physics, chemistry, geography, history, solfeggio, literature, and so forth. For dancing, singing, and drawing my wife charges extra, though I am also the one who teaches dancing and singing. Our music school is located at Five Dog Lane, No. 13. Probably my life is a failure because the number of the house that we live in is 13. Besides, my daughters were born on the thirteenth, and our house has thirteen windows. . . . But what's the use of talking? My wife can be seen at home at any time for an interview, and the prospectus of the school may be had from the porter at 30 kopecks a copy. (Produces several copies from his pocket). I can let you have some, if you like. Thirty kopecks a copy! Anyone wants a copy? (Pause). No one? Well, I'll make it 20 kopecks! (Pause). How annoying! Yes, house no. 13! Nothing succeeds with me, I've grown old, stupid. . . . Here I am delivering a lecture, outwardly I am cheerful, but privately I long to cry out at the top of my voice or fly to the ends of the earth. And there's no one to complain to, I could burst into tears. You will say: daughters . . . But what are daughters? I talk to them, but all they do is laugh . . . My wife has seven daughters . . . No, I am sorry, six, I believe. (Quickly) Seven! The eldest, Anna, is twenty-seven, the youngest, seventeen. Gentlemen! (Looks round). I am wretched, I have turned into a fool, a nonentity, but actually you see before you the happiest of fathers. Actually, that's how it ought to be, and I daren't say it is not. If you only knew! I have lived with my wife thirty-three years, and I can say that those were the best years of my life, that is, not the best, but just generally speaking. They have swept by, in a word, as one happy moment; strictly speaking, a curse on them. (Looks round). I believe she hasn't come yet, she isn't here, and I may say what I please. I am in terror of her . . . in terror when she looks at me. Well, as I was saying: my daughters are so slow about getting married, probably because they are bashful and also because men never see them. My wife doesn't want to give evening parties, she never invites anyone to dinner, she is a very stingy, ill-tempered, quarrelsome lady, and that is why no one ever comes to the house, but . . . I can tell you confidentially (comes close to the footlights). My

wife's daughters may be seen on high holidays in the home
of their aunt, Natalya Semyonovna, the same that suffers
from rheumatism and wears a yellow dress with black dots
as if cockroaches were crawling all over her. Refreshments
are served there, too. And when my wife isn't on the scene,
one can . . . (raises his fist to his lips). I must tell you
that I get drunk on one glass, and then I have such a wonderful feeling, and at the same time I am so sad, I can't tell
you how awfully sad; for some reason I recall my youth,
and for some reason I am seized with a desire to run away,
oh, if you knew how I long to do it! (Enthusiastically).
To run away, to throw everything over and run away
without looking back . . . Where to? No matter where
. . . only to run from this cheap, trashy, vulgar life that
has turned me into a pitiful old fool, a pitiful old idiot, to
run away from that stupid, petty, mean, mean, mean skin-
flint, my wife, who has tormented me for thirty-three
years, to run away from the music, the kitchen, my wife's
money, from all this pettiness, all these vulgarities . . .
and to come to a halt somewhere far, far away, in the fields,
and to stand there like a tree, a post, a scarecrow in a
kitchen garden, under the wide sky, and all night long
watch the bright, still moon hanging overhead, and forget,
forget . . . Oh, how I long not to remember anything!
How I long to tear off this vile old frock coat that I wore
at my wedding thirty years ago . . . (tears off his frock
coat) in which I constantly give lectures in the interests
of charity . . . Take that! (Tramples on the frock coat).
Take that! I am old, poor, pitiful, like this waistcoat with
its shabby, threadbare back . . . (Turns round to show
its back). I want nothing! I'm better than this, superior to
this, I was once young, intelligent, I was a university student, I dreamed, I considered myself a human being . . .
Now I want nothing. Nothing but rest . . . rest! (Glancing aside, quickly dons the frock coat). My wife is standing

in the wings. She has come and she's waiting for me there. (Looks at his watch). Time is up . . . If she asks you, please, I beg you, tell her that the lecture was . . . that the booby, that is me, behaved with dignity. (Glances aside, clears his throat). She is looking in my direction. (Raising his voice). Starting from the premise that tobacco contains a terrible poison, of which I have just spoken, one should on no account indulge in smoking, and I allow myself to hope, as it were, that my lecture on the harmful effects of tobacco will be of help. That is all I had to say. *Dixi et animam levavi!* (Bows, and stalks out majestically).

1902

Moscow hypocrites

Last spring the central administration, the mayor, the clergy and the press brought pressure to bear on the Moscow Municipal Council, three quarters of the members of which are merchants, to adopt regulations limiting trade on Sundays and holidays. As a result, on those days stores were open not ten to twelve hours, but three only. The other day the same Council, apparently taking advantage of the temporary absence of certain persons who had at heart the welfare of the salesclerks, resolved almost unanimously: "The regulations affecting the urban population with regard to the limitation of trade on Sundays and holidays are to be abolished."

And they were abolished. The grocers, dry goods merchants and fishmongers who attended the hearing shouted "Bravo!" in unison so vociferously that twice the police had to eject them. Bravo, indeed! Only brave and thoroughly unabashed people can publicly and without blushing utter the poppycock that was spouted by the Messrs. merchants who, come what may, want to do business on

Sunday. One of them observed: "Only intellectuals go to church, not salesclerks." Someone else, whose intake amounts to two groats a day, spoke of a loss of millions. A third, Merchant Lanin, who in his own person is at once a proprietor and salesclerk (he is a member of the Salespeoples' Society) said, in the tone of an objective man to whom the interests of both parties are equally dear, that the regulations were unnecessary, that one could at the same time keep the stores open and give the clerks an opportunity to rest—in other words, one could both make money and preserve one's virtue. He had been abroad and had observed that there on holidays the wives and daughters of the shopkeepers were on duty instead of the clerks. This custom could very well be introduced in Russia, provided the regulations were promptly rescinded and the proprietors "evinced the desire to tend store themselves or to put their wives, sons or daughters behind the counter." This Lanin evidently studied foreign commerce in Moscow, at lemonade stands and cheap sausage stalls, where, indeed, one is served by the wives and daughters of the owners. Instead of citing foreign customs, it would have been simpler for this Mr. Lanin to have looked into his own champagne establishment.* Does he have enough sons and daughters to replace the scores of people he employs? If he were childless, or a bachelor, whom would he put behind the counter? And why, may I ask, must his family tend store while he and his clerks take the air? What nonsense!

A man says foolish things when he is wrong or stupid. Every day and every hour many absurdities are uttered in Moscow, in Niżhny, in Kazan. There aren't enough "Bless yous" for all the sneezes, and similarly you can't counter

* Mikhail Petrovich Lanin was a pioneer in the manufacture of artificial mineral waters in Russia. *Ed.'s note.*

all the absurdities. But the nonsense of the Moscow Lanins has such a sharp, specific smell that it can't be ignored. One is too keenly aware of the fox that hides behind the mask of a Moscow fool and simpleton when he rambles on at a fair or at a session of the Municipal Council.

Is it not hypocrisy to speak of the Church in defending trade on holidays? Is it not hypocrisy when a shopkeeper on the look-out for the main chance calls himself a clerk and speaks, as it were, in the name of the salespeople? Is it not hypocrisy to raise a scare about a loss of millions or the antagonism between clerks and proprietors? Don't these losses of millions and clerkly revolutions resemble "the peaceful conquest of Siberia by the British" which the Nizhny economists have recently held up as a bugaboo to harass the imagination of the Minister of Commerce? London's trade is ten, or perhaps twenty or thirty times the total amount of Moscow's; nevertheless, on Sundays London stores are closed. The proprietors rest and so do the clerks. Why speak of the family? Mr. Lanin knows very well that after the regulations have been rescinded neither his wife nor his daughters will be behind the counter, but the clerks. And strangely enough, all these advocates of holiday trade, turning the clerks' arguments against them, try to give their own pretensions a religious air. They say that on holidays a salesperson with free time on his hands will haunt the taverns, and so forth, and thereby desecrate the holy day. What saintly people! But why don't they start their sermons with the fourth commandment? Then this problem of the salesclerks would be crystal-clear from the religious viewpoint, and there would be no need to insult publicly thousands of workers, young and old, by accusations of dissolute living, impiety, and the like. If the bigots are so eager to make an intimate connection between the problem of the salesclerks and these accusations, let them do it more intelligently, more tactfully. And further, let them remember that thousands of dissolute canaries and rabbits are much better than one pious wolf.

1888

good news

Since the end of last year a course in elocution has been part of the curriculum of the University of Moscow. One can only rejoice at this admirable new departure. We Russians are fond of talking and listening, but the art of oratory is neglected among us. At zemstvo meetings, at assemblies of the nobility, at sessions of learned societies, at public banquets, we are bashfully silent or we speak indistinctly, flatly, dully, mumbling in our beards, not knowing what to do with our hands. One word is addressed to us and we respond with ten, because we do not know how to be concise, and we lack that grace of speech which effects most with the least effort—*non multum sed multa.*

We have many advocates, prosecutors, professors, preachers, who, because of the very nature of their calling, may be assumed to possess a certain eloquence, and we have many institutions where, for official reasons, much talk is indulged in, but there are none among us who can express their thoughts clearly, briefly, and simply. In both capitals there are perhaps no more than half a dozen really fine speakers, and as for our provinces, they don't seem to have any golden-tongued orators at all. Our university chairs are occupied by stammerers and whisperers who can be understood only after you have accustomed yourself to them. People who speak execrably are allowed to appear at literary evenings, because the public is used to it, and when a poet reads his verse, the audience looks at him, instead of listening to him. They tell an anecdote about a captain who was to deliver a long funeral oration over the grave of his friend, but only brought out: "Be well!" hawked, and said no more. Then there is the incident of our estimable art critic, V. V. Stasov, who was scheduled to give a lecture at the Artists' Club. For several minutes he stood on the platform, a silent, embarrassed statue; then he uttered some inarticulate sounds and stepped down, without having said a word. And how many stories could be told about counsel so tongue-tied that they make their own clients laugh, about lecturers who bore their students to death and in the end make learning distasteful to them!

We Russians are dull people, lacking passion. The blood in our veins has long since coagulated with tedium. We do not chase after pleasures, we do not seek them out, and we are therefore not at all disturbed by the fact that our indifference to the art of eloquence deprives us of one of the noblest and most exalted delights accessible to man. But if the pleasure does not attract us, we should at least recall that in every age richness of language has gone hand in hand with the art of eloquence. In a society where true eloquence is despised, what thrives is rhetoric, verbal bigotry, or the vulgar gift of gab. In antiquity, as in modern times, eloquence was one of the most powerful instruments of culture. It is unthinkable that a preacher of a new religion should not be a captivating speaker. All the greatest statesmen, when the state was flourishing, the greatest philosophers, poets, reformers, were also great orators. The road to every career was strewn with "flowers" of eloquence, and mastery of the art of speaking was considered obligatory. Perhaps we too shall live to see the day when our jurists, professors, and functionaries whose official duty it is to speak not only learnedly, but perspicuously and beautifully, will cease excusing themselves on the grounds that they "do not know how." At bottom, you see, it should be as unbecoming for an educated person to speak badly as to be unable to read or write. Elocution should be an obligatory subject of instruction. And so the pioneering effort of the University of Moscow is a serious forward step.

1893

across Siberia

"Why is it so cold in this Siberia of yours?"

"It's God's will," answers my coachman.

Yes, already it is May, in Russia the forests are green and nightingales are singing at the top of their voices, in the South lilac and acacia have been in blossom for some time, but here, between Tyumen and Tobolsk, the earth is brown, the woods are bare, lusterless ice covers the lakes, on the shores and in ravines there is still snow.

But never in my life have I seen such an abundance of game. Wild ducks waddle in the fields, swim in the pools and in the ditches beside the road, they take wing almost at the very carriage wheels and fly off lazily into the birch grove. The silence is suddenly broken by the familiar melodious cry, you look up and you see a pair of cranes flying low, and for some reason you are saddened. Here are wild geese winging their way, a string of snow-white beautiful swans sails by. . . . Everywhere woodcocks moan, gulls wail.

We overtake a crowd of peasants and their women walking behind two carts. They are migrants.

"Where are you from?"

"From the province of Kursk."

A muzhik, quite unlike the rest, trudges along in the rear. He has a shaven chin, a white moustache, and a strange flap at the back of his coat made of coarse, drab stuff. Under each arm is a fiddle wrapped in a piece of cloth. Needless to ask who he is and how he had come by these violins. Sickly, sensitive to cold, rather partial to vodka, timid, shiftless, wayward, he has lived all his life as a superfluous, useless fellow, first under his father's, later under his brother's roof. No allotment of land was set aside for him, he was not married off. . . . A worthless sort! Work did not agree with him, two glasses made him tipsy, he talked too much and aimlessly. All he could do was play the fiddle and fool with the children on the stove. He fiddled in taverns, at weddings, and in the fields, and, oh, how he fiddled! But now his brother has sold his log cabin, his livestock and all his property, and with his family is removing to distant Siberia. The derelict is with them—he has nowhere else to go. And he has taken his two fiddles with him. When they reach their destination, he will prove unequal to the Siberian cold, he will sicken and die quietly, unnoticed by anyone, and the fiddles with which he used to gladden and sadden his native village will go to a clerk or a deportee for a twenty kopeck piece. The man's boys will pull off the strings, break the bridges, and pour water into the slits . . . Go back, uncle!

I had seen migrants before, when I was on a Kama river steamer. I remember a peasant of about forty with a flaxen beard. He sat on a bench, at his feet were sacks filled with his household goods, on the sacks his children, in bast shoes, lay huddled together against the cold, biting wind that was blowing from the desolate banks of the river. His face wore an expression which said: "I have given in." There was irony in his look, but it was irony directed inward, it played over his own soul and had to do with his past life, which had so cruelly deceived him.

"It can't be worse!" he says, and he smiles with his upper lip only.

You make no comment and you ask no questions, but a moment later he repeats:

"It can't be worse!"

"It will be worse!" says a voice from another bench. The speaker is a red-headed, sharp-eyed peasant, not a migrant. "It will be worse!"

These migrants, who are footing it along the road behind their carts, are silent. Their faces have a serious, concentrated look. I watch them and reflect that it requires heroic strength of character to pull up stakes and say goodbye to a home, a region, a familiar way of life.

A little later we overtake a party of convicts. With a clanking of irons, thirty to forty men walk along the road; on either side of them are soldiers with rifles, behind them two carts. One convict looks like an Armenian priest; another, a tall man with an aquiline nose and a large forehead, I seem to have seen somewhere behind a counter in a drugstore; a third has the pallid, grave, emaciated face of an ascetic monk. I haven't the time to scrutinize all of them. Both the prisoners and the convoy are exhausted, the road is bad, they do not have the strength to go on. There are still ten versts to cover before they reach the village where they will spend the night. And when they get there, have a hasty bite, drink their brick tea, and immediately drop off to sleep, they are at once attacked by bedbugs, the most vicious and formidable enemy of the drowsy and the dog-tired.

By nightfall the ground begins to freeze and the mud hardens into ridges. The carriage lurches and bumps along, grinding and creaking. It is cold! Not a house in sight, not a wayfarer . . . Nothing stirs in the dark air, there is not a sound except the noise of the carriage rumbling over the frozen earth, and when I light a cigarette, two or three ducks, startled by the light, fly up from the roadside.

Here is the river. We must cross it by ferry. There is not a soul on the bank.

"They've gone to the other side, a plague on their souls!" exclaims my coachman. "Let's roar, your Honor."

To scream with pain, to cry, to summon help, to call generally—all that is described here as "roaring." In Siberia not only bears roar, but sparrows and mice as well. "The cat got it, and it's roaring," they say of a mouse.

We begin to "roar." The river is broad, in the dark the farther shore is invisible. . . . Night dampness chills your feet and your whole body. For half an hour we keep shouting, for an hour—still no trace of the ferry. I am sick and tired of the river, the stars that strew the sky, this heavy, funereal silence. To while away the time, I talk to my coachman, who looks like an old man, and I learn that he was married at sixteen, that he had eighteen children, of whom only three had died, and that his father and mother are still living. Neither of them, he says, has ever seen any town except Ishim. They are Old Believers and don't use tobacco, but he, as a young fellow, allows himself a smoke. He tells me that this dark, forbidding river abounds in sterlet, white salmon, eel-pout, pike, but that there is no one to catch the fish, and no tackle to catch it with.

Finally we hear measured splashes, and something dark and clumsy heaves into view on the river. It is the ferry. It looks like a small barge; there are some five men rowing, and their long oars with broad blades resemble a lobster's claws.

The oarsmen no sooner put in to shore than they start cursing. They curse viciously, without the slightest provocation, apparently because they haven't had enough sleep.

Listening to their choice swearing, you might think that
not only my coachman, they themselves, the horses have
mothers, but also the water, the ferry, the oars.* The oarsmen's lightest and most innocuous curse is "A plague on
you!" or "A plague on your mouth!" Which particular
plague was meant I could not discover, though I made inquiries. I wore a sheepskin coat, high boots, and a cap, and
in the darkness one could not see that I was the kind of
person addressed as "your Honor," and one of the oarsmen
shouted at me hoarsely:

"Hey, you, plague take you, why do you stand there
gaping? Unhitch the outrunner!"

We drive onto the ferry. The ferrymen, still cursing,
take the oars. They are not local peasants, but men deported here for misdemeanors by order of their communi-
ties. They do not like to stay in the villages where they
are registered. It is boring there, they do not know how
to till the soil, or they have lost the habit. Besides, they
have no love for this alien land, and so they have hired
themselves out as ferrymen. Their faces are wasted, emaciated, and show marks of beatings. And their expression! It
is clear that the men were utterly brutalized while they
were being transported here aboard special convicts' barges,
handcuffed together in pairs, and then traveling on foot in
parties along the highways, sleeping in huts where bedbugs
mercilessly set their bodies on fire. And now that they
shuttle between the bare banks across the cold water, they
have completely lost all human feeling, and only one thing
remains for them in life: vodka, wench; wench, vodka. . . .
In this world they are no longer human beings but beasts,
and, in my coachman's opinion, in the world to come, too,
it will go badly with them: they will go to hell for their
sins.

* Obscene references to mother abound in Russian profanity. *Ed.'s note.*

II

It is the night of May 6th, and I have behind me the large
village of Abatskoe, 375 versts east of Tyumen. My coachman is a man of sixty. Before hitching up the horses, he
steamed himself in a public bath and cupped himself. Why
cupping-glasses? He says he has a backache. He is spry for
his age, nimble, talkative, but his gait is unsteady: I think
he has locomotor ataxia.

My tarantass, a small, springless, high-hung carriage, is
drawn by a pair of horses. At first, the old man swung his
whip and urged the horses on with shouts, now he no
longer shouts, but only groans and moans like an Egyptian
pigeon.

On both sides of the road and in the distance—serpentine
fires: what is burning is last year's grass, which they purposely set on fire. It is damp and slow in yielding to the
flames, and so the fiery snakes creep unhurriedly, now
breaking into segments, now vanishing, now flaring up
again. The fires send up sparks, and above each flare there
is a white cloud of smoke. When the flame suddenly en-
folds tall grass, the spectacle is striking: a six-foot fiery
column shoots up into the air, spouts a great roll of smoke,
and promptly drops, as though sinking through the ground.
The effect is even more beautiful when the snakes creep
into a birch grove; it is all lit up at once, the white trunks
are distinctly visible, the shadows of the birches play against
patches of light. There is something eery about this illumination.

A mail coach drawn by a three-horse team is coming
straight toward us at full speed, thundering over the bumps
of the road. My coachman quickly pulls over to the right,
and the next moment the huge, heavy vehicle flies by. But
presently there is thunder again: another troika comes
straight toward us, also at full speed. Again we pull over

to the right, but to my great amazement and horror the troika for some reason turns left and flies straight at us. What if we collide head-on? As the thought flashes through my mind, there is a crash, our two horses and the troika's team are one dark mass, my tarantass rears up, I drop to the ground, and all my bags and bundles fall on top of me. . . . While I lie on the ground, stunned, I hear a third troika driving toward us. "This one," I say to myself, "will surely kill me." That instant I realize that, thank God, I have no broken bones, I haven't been badly hurt, I can get up. I jump up, scramble off the road and shout wildly: "Stop! Stop!"

A human form stands up in the empty carriage, grasps the reins, and the third troika halts close by my scattered luggage.

For a while there is silence. We seem to be dumbfounded and unable to make out what has happened. The shafts are broken, the harness torn, shaft-bows with bells are lying around on the ground. The horses pant heavily, they too are stunned and apparently badly hurt. My old man, groaning and grunting, rises from the ground. A fourth and fifth troika arrive on the scene of the collision.

Then ferocious cursing breaks out.

"Plague strike you!" shouts the driver who has collided with us. "A plague on your mouth! Where were your eyes, you old cur?"

"And who's to blame?" cries my old man in a whining voice. "You're to blame and then you swear!"

As far as one can gather from the exchange of profanity, the cause of the collision was as follows. Five troikas, having delivered mail, were returning, empty, to Abatskoe. According to regulations, such vehicles must travel slowly, but the foremost driver, fed up with the slow pace and eager to reach his warm hut as soon as possible, whipped up his horses, and they raced forward. The drivers of the other four coaches were asleep, and the horses were left to themselves. When the head troika dashed forward, they followed, and soon all the five troikas were traveling at breakneck speed. If I had fallen asleep in my tarantass, or if the third troika had been close to the second, then of course I shouldn't have got off so lightly.

The drivers curse at the top of their voices, so that they are probably heard within a radius of ten versts. They curse horribly. How much cunning, viciousness and grossness of spirit it must have taken to think up those foul words and phrases, meant to insult and drag through the mud everything man holds precious and sacred. It is said that the Siberian drivers and ferrymen have learned from convicts to swear as they do.

The driver who is at fault, a mere boy of about nineteen, swears more loudly and viciously than the rest.

"Don't you curse, you fool!" my old man tries to silence him.

"And what if I do?" asks the boy, walks over to him threateningly and, stopping before him, thrusts his face into the old man's. "What if I do?"

"Pipe down!"

"And what if I don't? Tell me: what'll you do? I'll grab one of these broken shafts and give it to you, you plague!"

A fight is brewing. In the small hours, surrounded by this savage swearing horde, within view of the flames devouring the grass but failing utterly to lend any warmth to the cold night air, near the disturbed horses which are restively crowding together and neighing, I am overcome by an indescribable sense of desolation.

The fight has not come off. The old man, grumbling, and lifting his feet high—a symptom of his illness—stalks around the tarantass and his team, and unties pieces of thong and rope wherever possible, in order to use them to fasten together the two halves of the broken shaft; then, lighting match after match, he crawls along the road on his stomach looking for the traces. My luggage straps are also turned to account. Already there are signs of dawn in the east, the wild geese have long since departed, and we are still stuck on the road, trying to get repaired. We attempt to move on, but the shaft that had been bound up breaks again, and once more we must stop. It's cold!

Somehow or other, we slowly make our way to a village. We halt before a two-story cottage.

"Ilya Ivanych, are the horses here?" my old man shouts.

"They're here!" comes a muffled answer from behind the window.

In the cottage I am met by a tall, barefoot, sleepy man wearing a red shirt, who is smiling at something in his half-awake state.

"The bedbugs have got me down, friend," he says, scratching himself and smiling more broadly. "We don't heat the room, on purpose. When it's cold, they don't walk."

In Siberia bedbugs and cockroaches don't creep, but walk; travelers do not ride, but run. "Where are you running, your Honor?" they ask you. That means: "Where are you going?"

While the carriage is being greased and, as they putter about it, the bells on the shaftbow ring; while Ilya Ivanych, who will now be my coachman, is getting dressed, I find a comfortable place in the corner, rest my head on what seems to be a sack of grain, and immediately fall into a sound sleep. I dream of my own bed, my own room, I dream that I am back home, sitting at the table and telling my people how my carriage collided with the mail troika. But two or three minutes pass and I hear Ilya Ivanych saying, as he tugs me by the sleeve:

"Get up, friend, the horses are ready."

What disregard for indolence, for aversion to the chill

which creeps snake-like up the spine and all through you! I am again on the road. It is already light, and golden tones in the sky announce sunrise. The road, the grass in the fields, the sorry-looking young birches are covered with hoarfrost as with powdered sugar. In the distance heath cocks utter mating-calls.

III

Along the Siberian highway, from Tyumen to Tomsk, there are no solitary homesteads, no hamlets, but only large villages, separated by 20, 25, and even 40 versts. On the way you will come across no manors, since there are no gentry here. Nor will you see any factories, mills, inns. As you travel, the only thing that reminds you of man are mileposts and telegraph wires humming in the wind.

In each village there is a church, sometimes two; there are also schools, I think, in every village. The houses, which are of wood, often have two stories and the roofs are shingled. Near each cottage on the fence or on a birch tree there is a birdhouse for starlings, placed low enough to be within arm's reach. Everyone here loves starlings, and even the cats don't touch them. There are no gardens.

About five o'clock in the morning, after a frosty night and a tiring ride, I sit having tea in the cottage of a peasant whose services, with those of his horses and his carriage, are for the traveler's hire. We are in the *gornitza*, the better of his two rooms; it is light and spacious, furnished in a way of which our Kursk or Moscow peasant can only dream. The cleanliness is astonishing: nowhere a spot or a speck of dust. The walls are whitewashed, the floors are of wood, either painted or covered with colored sacking; there are two tables, a couch, chairs, a cupboard containing china, pots of flowers on the window sills. In the corner stands a bedstead, upon it a mountain of feather beds and pillows in red pillow slips; you have to use a chair to get up on that mountain, and, when you lie down on it, you sink. Siberian folk like to sleep soft.

The icon in the corner is flanked on both sides by cheap prints; here are invariably two or more portraits of the czar, a picture of St. George, "European sovereigns," including the Shah of Persia, next to these—images of saints bearing Latin and German legends, half length portraits of Prince Battenberg and General Skobelev, and more saints. . . . To relieve the bareness of the walls, candy wrappers, vodka labels, and cigarette wrappers are turned to account, and these pitiful decorations are strikingly out of keeping with the solid bed and the painted floors. But what's to be done? The demand for art is great here, but the Lord hasn't provided any artists. Observe the door on which is painted a tree with red and blue flowers and birds that look more like fish. The tree grows out of a vase, and to judge by the way it is painted, the whole thing is the product of the brush of a European, that is: a deportee. It was a deportee, too, who had daubed a circle on the ceiling and a design on the stove. A crude enough sort of painting, but beyond the powers of the native peasant. For nine months he does not take off his mittens and does not straighten out his fingers. Either it is 40 degrees below or the meadowlands are flooded within a radius of twenty versts. And when the short summer comes, your back aches with labor, and your sinews feel as if they were being pulled apart. How is a man to think of painting? The year round he is engaged in a cruel struggle with nature, and so he is no painter, no composer, no singer. In a village you will rarely hear a concertina, and don't expect your driver to break into song.

The door is open, and one can see across the entry into the other room, which is also bright and has a wooden floor. Work is in full swing there. The wife, a tall slim woman of about twenty-five, with a kind, gentle look, stands at the table kneading dough. The morning sun streams over her brow, her breast, and her hands, and it looks as though she were kneading sunlight into the dough. A girl, her sister, is frying pancakes, a cook is pouring boiling water over a freshly slaughtered sucking pig, the master of the house is making *valenki* (felt boots). Alone the old folk are idle. Grandmother sits on the stove, with her legs hanging down, moaning and groaning; grandfather is lying on the high sleeping platform and coughing away, but on noticing me, he climbs down and walks through the entry into the *gornitza*. He wants to talk. . . . He begins by saying that for many years they haven't had such a cold spring. Think of it, tomorrow is St. Nicholas' Day (May 9), the day after is Ascension,* but last night it snowed, and on the road to the village a woman was found, frozen; the livestock is getting lean for want of fodder, the frosts give the calves loose bowels. Then he inquires where I come from, whither I am bound, and for what purpose, if I am married, and whether the women are telling the truth when they say that war is coming.

I hear a baby crying. Only now do I notice that between the bed and the stove there is a small cradle, suspended from the ceiling. The woman of the house leaves the dough and runs into the room.

"Ain't we the lucky ones, mister!" she says with a gentle smile, as she rocks the cradle. "About two months ago a woman came here from Omsk with a little baby. . . . She was of plain folk, but she was dressed like a lady. . . . Her baby was born at Tyukalinsk, and she had it baptized there; on the road, just out of childbed, she got sick, and we put her up here with us. She said she was married, but who knows? It ain't written on her face, and she has no passport. Maybe, the baby's illegitimate. . . ."

"It ain't for us to be sitting in judgment," Grandfather mutters.

* A movable feast, celebrated forty days after Easter. *Ed.'s note.*

"She stopped with us a week," the woman goes on, "and then she said: 'I'll go back to Omsk, to my husband, but let my Sasha stay with you; I'll come to fetch him next week. I'm afraid he might freeze to death on the road.' So I says to her: 'Listen, lady, God sends people children, some ten, some twelve, but me and my man the Lord has punished, He hasn't given us any; you leave us your Sasha, we'll take him and he'll be our little son.' She didn't answer for a bit, thinking, and then she said: 'You wait, I'll ask my husband; and I'll write you in a week. I don't dare do it without my husband.' So she left Sasha with us and went away. And now it's two months and she hasn't come back and she hasn't written. It's a punishment from heaven! We've come to love Sasha as if he was our own, but we don't know if he is ours or not."

"You must write a letter to this woman," I venture to advise her.

"Indeed, we ought to," says the master of the house, who has come into the entry.

He walks into the *gornitza* and looks at me silently, as if expecting me to offer some further advice.

"But how can we write to her?" asks the wife. "She didn't tell us what her family name is. Marya Petrovna—that's all we know. And Omsk, of course, is a big city, how are you to find her? It's like looking for a needle in a haystack."

"No way of finding her," the man agrees, and looks at me as if he wants to say: "Help us, for God's sake!"

"We've got so used to Sasha," says the wife, giving the baby the usual bit of bread tied in a rag to suck on. "When he starts to peep, whether it's daytime or at night, my heart's lighter, and it's as if we'd come to live in a new cottage. But if that woman comes back, God forbid, and takes him away. . . ."

The wife's eyes fill with tears and redden, and she hurries out of the room. The husband cocks his head towards her, gives a crooked smile, and says:

"She's got used to it. . . . Of course, it's a pity!"

He too has grown accustomed to the baby, he too is sorry, but he is a man, it's awkward for him to admit it.

What wonderful people! I have tea, and listen to more talk about Sasha. My belongings are in the carriage out in the yard, and I wonder if someone will steal them. When I say so, I am told with a smile:

"Who should steal them? There is no stealing in these parts even at night."

And, indeed, all along the highway I have heard of no case of theft from a traveler. In this respect the ways of the people hereabouts are admirable, the traditions good. I am convinced that if I had left my wallet in the carriage, the coachman on finding it would have returned it without even looking into it. I traveled very little in post chaises, and about their drivers I can only say that in all the books for complaints which I read at the stations out of boredom I noticed only a single complaint of theft: one traveler lost a boot bag. No action was taken, as appears from the official entry in the book, for the reason that the bag was soon found and restored to the owner. As for robberies on the road, they are unheard of. The tramps you run into, against whom I was warned so emphatically just before I left Moscow, frighten the traveler as little as hares and ducks do.

They served me wheaten pancakes with my tea, as well as pies with curds and eggs, fritters and *kalachi*, made with butter. The pancakes are thin and dripping with fat, the *kalachi* look and taste like the yellow, spongy ring-shaped rolls that Little Russians sell on the market place in Taganrog and Rostov-on-the-Don. All along the Siberian highway you can get excellent bread; large quantities of it are baked daily. Wheat flour is cheap here: thirty to forty kopecks a *pood* (thirty-six pounds).

Bread alone will not satisfy your appetite. If at noon you ask for some hot food, you are served "duck soup" and nothing more. But you can hardly swallow this broth: it is a turbid liquid in which bits of wild duck and guts imperfectly cleaned are swimming. It turns your stomach to look at it, and it is far from tasty. In every log cabin there is game. In Siberia hunting laws are unknown, and game birds are shot all year round. But it is not likely that game will soon be exterminated here. Between Tyumen and Tomsk, a distance of fifteen hundred versts, there is an abundance of game, but you will scarcely find a decent fowling piece, and only one out of a hundred huntsmen can bring down a bird on the wing. As a rule, a hunter out for duck crawls on his stomach over hillocks and wet grass and, crouched behind a bush, shoots at a distance of twenty to thirty paces. His wretched shotgun will repeatedly hang fire, and when it discharges it kicks your shoulder and cheek painfully. If the target is hit there is still trouble: take off your boots and pants and plunge into the icy water. There are no retrievers here.

IV

A cold, biting wind has arisen, and the rains have started —it pours continually, day and night. We have reached a village within eighteen versts of the Irtysh river. Fyodor Pavlovich, a peasant with a fresh troika to whom my coachman has brought me, says that it is impossible to go on, because the rains have flooded the meadows along the Irtysh. The previous day Kuzma's team had almost been drowned on the way from Pustynskoe; we must wait.

"How long must I wait?" I inquire.

"Who can tell? Ask God."

I enter the cottage. In the better room sits an old man, breathing heavily and coughing. I make him swallow a dose of Dover's powder, and he is relieved, but he does not believe in medicine and says he is better because he has been "quiet."

I sit and ponder: shall I stay overnight? But all night long the old man will keep on coughing, and of course there will be bedbugs, and, besides, who will guarantee that to-morrow the flood will not spread? No, it is better to go on!

"Let's go on, Fyodor Pavlovich!" I say to the head of the house. "I don't want to wait."

"Just as you say, your Honor," he assents meekly. "Only I hope we don't have to spend the night in the water."

We drive off. It rains cats and dogs, and my tarantass is without a hood. The first few versts we drive along a muddy road, but still at a trot.

"What weather!" exclaims Fyodor Pavlovich. "I must say I haven't been up that way for a long time, I haven't seen the flood, and Kuzma scared me. Well, maybe with God's help we'll get through."

But here before us is a broad lake: the flooded meadows. The wind sweeps over it, howling and raising ripples as it blows. Here and there small islands are visible, and strips of land still show above the water. The direction of the road is marked by bridges, which are partly washed out, and heaps of brushwood, water-logged and pushed out of place. Far-off, beyond the lake, stretches the steep bank of the Irtysh, brown and sullen, and over it hang heavy, gray clouds; here and there on the bank are white patches of snow.

We start crossing the lake. It is shallow, less than a foot deep. The driving would not be so bad, if it were not for the bridges. At each bridge it is necessary to get out of the carriage and step into the mud or the water; we must first make a ramp with the boards and logs which are lying about on the bridge, in order to drive onto it. We let the horses cross the bridges one by one. Fyodor Pavlovich unharnesses the outriders and puts me in charge of them. I hold on to the cold, dirty halters, and the restive animals back up, the wind tries to strip me of my clothes, the rain lashes my face painfully. Shall we turn tail? But Fyodor Pavlovich holds his peace and probably waits for me to suggest returning; I too hold my peace.

We take one bridge by assault, a second, a third . . . In one spot we are stuck in the mud and the carriage almost turns over, at another point the horses get stubborn, and the ducks and gulls wheel overhead as if jeering at our discomfiture. By the look of Fyodor Pavlovich's face, by his unhurried movements, his silence, I can see that he has been in such a fix before, that in fact he has been in worse predicaments and has long since got used to the bottomless mud, the water, the cold rain. Life is hard on him!

We reach an island. A roofless hut stands there; two wet horses are tramping over wet dung. In answer to Fyodor Pavlovich's call, a bearded peasant with a long switch emerges from the hut and undertakes to show us the way. Silently he moves on in front of us, measures the depth of the water with his switch and tests the ground, and we follow. He takes us to a long, narrow strip of land, which he calls a "ridge"; we must drive along the ridge and at the end of it turn left, then bear right until we strike another ridge, which extends as far as the Irtysh crossing.

It is getting dark; there are no ducks, no gulls. Having given us instructions, the bearded peasant has left us. We come to the end of the first ridge, and once more splash in the water. We bear left, then turn right. Here at last is the second ridge. It runs close to the bank of the river.

The Irtysh is broad. If Yermak * had tried to cross it at flood, he would have drowned even if he had not been

* A Cossack conquistador who added Siberia to the lands ruled by Ivan the Terrible. Legend has it that he was drowned trying to swim across the Irtysh in full armor as he fled from a Tartar force that had massacred his men. *Ed.'s note.*

wearing his coat-of-mail. The farther shore is high and steep, and looks completely deserted. We see a valley. At the bottom of it, says Fyodor Pavlovich, there is the road that leads uphill to the village of Pustynnoe, which is my destination. The hither bank is flat and a little over two feet above the water. It is bare and looks gullied and slippery. Turbid, white-capped billows lash it viciously and promptly recoil, as though they were loath to touch this clumsy, slimy bank, which appears fit only for toads and the souls of great sinners. The Irtysh neither booms nor roars, but seems to knock on the lids of coffins down at the bottom. A dismal effect!

We drive up to the cabin occupied by the ferrymen. One of them comes out and says that the weather is too foul for crossing, and that we must wait till morning.

I spend the night there. All night long I listen to the snoring of the ferrymen and of my coachman, to the rain beating against the windows, the wind roaring, and the sullen Irtysh knocking on the lids of coffins. . . . Early in the morning I go out to have a look at the river; it is still raining, but the wind has abated somewhat; yet it is not safe to cross the river on the ferry. We are taken across in a rowboat.

The ferrymen here are all local peasants, not one of them a convict. They are kind, gentle folk. When, having crossed the river, I climb up the slippery slope where the horses are waiting for me, all wish me a safe journey, good health, and success in my business. . . . Alone the Irtysh is sullen.

v

This flood is a punishment! At Kolyvan they refuse to give me post horses: they say the banks of the Ob are under water and that you can't travel. Even mail has been delayed and they are waiting for special instructions concerning it.

The station clerk advises me to hire horses from a private coachman and proceed to Vyun, and thence to Krasny Yar, then to go on for a dozen versts by rowboat, reaching Dubrovino, where I would be able to hire post horses. I follow his advice and arrive in Krasny Yar. There they take me to a peasant by the name of Andrey, who owns a rowboat.

"There is a boat, so there is," says Andrey, a man of about fifty, rather lean, with a light brown beard. "There is a boat! Early this morning it took the assessor's clerk to Dubrovino, and it'll soon be back. You wait, sir, and in the meantime have some tea."

I have tea, then climb up onto the mountain of feather beds and pillows. When, after a while, I wake up, I ask about the boat—it hasn't come back yet. In order to warm the room, the women are heating the oven and getting ready to bake bread. And now the room is warm and the bread has been baked, and still there is no trace of the boat.

"That fellow we sent can't be trusted!" Andrey sighs, shaking his head. "He's as helpless as a woman, he must be scared of the wind, that's why he isn't coming. The wind *is* pretty stiff. Why don't you have more tea, sir? It must be dull for you."

An idiot boy, wet to the skin, in tatters and barefoot, carries firewood and buckets of water into the entry. From time to time he peers into the room: he shows his unkempt, tousled head, rapidly mutters something, moos like a calf, and then disappears. The sight of his wet face and unblinking eyes, the sound of his voice, is enough to make you soon start raving yourself.

In the afternoon we have a visitor: a tall, obese peasant with a broad bovine nape and huge fists, looking like a Russian barman who has put on flesh. His name is Pyotr Petrovich. He lives in the neighboring village, and he and his brother keep fifty horses. They hire them out to travel-

ers and supply troikas to the postal station. He also farms
and deals in livestock, and is now on his way to Kolyvan
on business.

"Are you from Russia?" he asks me.

"From Russia."

"Haven't ever been there. In these parts a man who has
been to Tomsk puts on airs as if he'd gone round the world.
But now the papers say that they'll soon be building a railroad up here. Tell me, your Honor, how can that be? The
machine works by steam—that I can understand. Well, but
if it has to go through a village, isn't it going to smash the
houses and crush people?"

I explain the matter, and he listens closely, and says:
"Think of that!" From the conversation I learn that this
fat fellow has been to Tomsk, Irkutsk, Irbit, and that he
had taught himself to read and write when he was already
married. He condescends toward Andrey, who has only
been to Tomsk, and listens to him reluctantly. When they
offer him something, or serve him, he says politely: "Don't
trouble yourself."

Host and guest sit down to have tea. A young peasant
woman, the wife of Andrey's son, brings them the tea on a
tray and makes a low obeisance to them. They take the cups
and drink in silence. The samovar is boiling away near the
stove. I climb up onto the mountain of featherbeds and
pillows, I lie and read, then I dismount and write. A long,
long time passes, but the young woman keeps bowing and
the two men keep sipping tea.

"Beh-bah!" the idiot boy cries in the entry. "Meh-mah!"

Still no boat! It's getting dark, and they light a tallow
candle in the room. Pyotr Petrovich questions me at great
length about my destination and the purpose of my journey; he wants to know if there will be war, and how much
my pistol costs. But now he has had enough talk. He sits
silently at the table, his cheeks supported by his fists, and is

lost in thought. The wick of the candle becomes crusted with soot. The door opens noiselessly, and the idiot enters and sits down on a chest. He has bared his arms to the shoulder, they are as thin as little sticks. He sits and stares at the candle.

"Get out of here, out!" says the head of the house.

"Meh-mah!" he moos and, stooping, slouches into the entry. "Beh-bah!"

The rain beats against the window panes. Host and guest sit down to eat duck soup. They are not hungry, and eat only out of boredom. Then the young woman makes up a bed on the floor with feather beds and pillows; host and guest undress and lie down side by side.

How tiresome! In an effort to escape the ennui, I betake myself, in thought, to the home scene. It is spring there and cold rain does not lash the windows. But, as if intentionally, I can recall only a gray, flabby, useless existence. It seems to me that there too the wick of the candle is crusted with soot and that someone is mooing: "Meh-mah! Beh-bah!" I lose all desire to turn my thoughts toward what lies behind me.

I spread my sheepskin coat on the floor, lie down, and place a candle near my head.

Pyotr Petrovich half raises his head and looks at me.

"This is what I'd like to make plain to you," he says below his breath, so as not to be heard by the master of the house. "Here in Siberia people have dark minds, they're a helpless lot. They get sheepskin coats, cotton goods, crockery, nails from Russia—they can't make anything themselves. All they do is till the soil and drive horses, nothing else. . . . They can't even catch fish. Dullards, what dullards they are, God help them! You live with them, and all you do is grow bloated with fat, and as for getting something for the soul, for the mind—no, nothing! It's a crying shame, mister! And, you know, a Siberian is a good man, he's soft-hearted, he won't steal, he won't hurt anyone, and he don't drink overmuch. A treasure, not a man, and yet he's just wasted, without doing any good to anyone, like a fly, or, let's say, a mosquito. What does he live for? Ask him!"

"Well, a man works, he has something to eat, something to put on his back," I observe. "What more does he want?"

"Still, he ought to understand what he lives for. I bet, in Russia he understands!"

"No, he doesn't."

"That's not possible," says Pyotr Petrovich, after a pause. "A human being is not a horse. For instance, in all of our Siberia there is no righteousness. If it ever was here, it froze to death a long time ago. Well, man ought to search for this righteousness. I am a well-to-do peasant, I've got power, the official is a friend of mine, and tomorrow I can do whatever I please with my host: I can work it so that he rots in jail, I can make beggars of his children. And he can't stop me, he has no protection, because—we live without righteousness. . . . So, we're human beings only on our birth certificates, Pyotrs and Andreys, but as a matter of fact, we're wolves. Or again, in respect to God . . . It's no small matter, it's an awesome thing, yet our host here lay down and all he did was to cross his forehead three times, as though this was enough. He makes money and he hides it away, I'm sure; he must have put aside some eight hundred, he keeps buying horses. But he should ask himself: what is it all for? Yes, he should, but he hasn't the brains to do it."

Pyotr Petrovich keeps on this way for a long time. . . . But now he is done. It is beginning to grow light, and the cocks are crowing.

"Meh-mah!" the idiot moos. "Beh-bah!"

And still no trace of the boat!

VI

At Dubrovino they give me post horses and I am on my way. But at a station 45 versts from Tomsk I am told that further travel is impossible, that the Tom river has flooded the meadows and the roads. Once more I must take a rowboat. And here the story is the same as at Krasny Yar: the boat has taken someone to the opposite shore and cannot return because a gale is blowing and raising huge billows on the river. We must wait!

In the morning snow falls and soon it is three inches deep —on May fourteenth! At noon we have rain, which washes away the snow, and at dusk, when I stand on the river bank and watch the approaching boat contend with the current, a mixture of rain and snow comes down. At the same time a phenomenon occurs which doesn't tally with the snow and the cold: I distinctly hear peals of thunder. The coachmen cross themselves and say that this means we shall have warm weather.

The boat is a large one. They load it with twenty *poods* of mail, then put my luggage aboard, and cover it all with wet mats. The man in charge of the mail, a tall, elderly fellow, sits down on a mailbag, I on my suitcase. At my feet squats a diminutive soldier with freckles all over his face and hands. His uniform is wringing wet, and water flows from his cap down his neck.

"May the Lord bless us! Push off!"

We go downstream, keeping close to a thicket of purple willow shrubs. The men at the oars tell us that only ten minutes ago a boy in a cart saved himself from drowning by catching hold of a willow shrub; his team went under.

"Keep rowing, fellows, you'll spin yarns later!" says the man at the helm. "Get on with it!"

As is usual before a storm, a gust of wind sweeps the river. The bare willow shrubs bend toward the water with a rustling sound, the river suddenly grows dark, waves tumble about. . . .

"Head for the shrubs, lads, we'll have to wait till it's over," says the helmsman quietly.

They have barely started turning toward the willows when one of the rowers observes that if there is a storm we shall have to spend the night among the willows and in the end get drowned, so why not go on? We put the matter to a vote and decide to row on.

The river grows even more sinister, a gale-driven rain lashes sideways, and the shrubs to which we could hold on in case of disaster are left behind. The postman, who has seen much in his time, holds his peace and sits tight, like one petrified, and the men at the oars, too, are silent. I notice that the little soldier's neck has suddenly turned purple. My heart grows heavy; and I keep thinking that if the boat capsizes, I will first throw off my sheepskin coat, then my jacket, then . . .

But now the river bank is nearer and nearer, the men pull at the oars more cheerfully; little by little my heart is lightened, and when the bank is only twenty feet away, I am suddenly filled with joy, and I reflect:

"It's good to be a coward! You don't need much to feel very happy all of a sudden!"

VII

I don't like it when a deportee with some education stands at the window and stares in silence at the roof of the neighboring house. What is he thinking about then? I don't like it when he talks to me about trifles and at the same time looks at me with an air that says: "You will be going back home, but not I." I don't like it, because at that moment I pity him immeasurably.

It is often said that nowadays capital punishment is resorted to only in exceptional cases. This is not quite exact.

All the extreme punitive measures which have replaced capital punishment nevertheless continue to be marked by its essential and most important feature, namely they are for life, forever. All of them have the same object, inherited directly from capital punishment—to remove the criminal from his normal surroundings permanently. A man who is thus punished for a grave crime dies to the community in which he was born and in which he grew up, just as in the times when capital punishment prevailed. The extreme penalties provided by Russian legislation, which is relatively humane, are almost all for life. A term of penal servitude is followed by exile for life. Exile is terrible precisely because it is for life. A term in a convict labor gang means Siberian exile for life, if the community with which the criminal is registered does not consent to receive him in its midst; the loss of civil rights is for life, and so forth. In this way all the extreme punitive measures fail to give the criminal eternal peace in the grave, that is, they lack precisely the feature which could make capital punishment acceptable to my moral sentiment. On the other hand, lifelong penalties rob the criminal of all hope of betterment. They implant in him the knowledge that the citizen in him is dead forever, that no personal efforts on his part can resurrect him. My conclusion is that both in Europe and among us capital punishment has not been abolished but has merely been given another shape, less repulsive to human feeling. Europe has been accustomed to capital punishment too long to surrender it without endless and tiresome postponements.

It is my deep conviction that within fifty to a hundred years our life sentences will be regarded with the same bewilderment and dismay with which we nowadays look at such penalties as the tearing of nostrils or the cutting off of a finger of the left hand. And I am also deeply convinced that, no matter how clearly and candidly we recognize that survivals like life sentences are antiquated and unreasonable, we are in no position at all to remedy the situation. We now have neither the knowledge nor the experience, and consequently lack the courage, to substitute for life terms something more rational and more nearly just. All attempts in that direction, hesitant and one-sided, can only lead to serious mistakes and extremes—such is the fate of all efforts not based on knowledge and experience. Sad and strange as it is, we are even unable to settle the now fashionable question as to what is more suitable for Russia—prison or exile, for we are totally ignorant about the true nature of prison and exile. Look at our literature on these subjects —what poverty! Two or three articles, two or three names, and then a blank—as though there were no prisons, no exile, no penal servitude. For twenty or thirty years our thinking intelligentsia has been repeating that a criminal is the product of social conditions, but how indifferent these people are to that product! The cause of this indifference to the fate of those who languish in prison or exile, an indifference incomprehensible in a Christian state and in Christian literature, lies in the fact that the Russian jurist is completely uneducated. He knows little and is ruled by professional prejudices as much as the tribe of pettifoggers of which he is so scornful. He passes his university examinations only in order to know how to try a man and sentence him to prison or exile. When he enters the service and gets his salary, all he does is try cases and sentence criminals, but what happens to the criminal after the trial and why, what prison is and what Siberia is—of that he knows nothing; he is not interested, it is not within his competence, it is the business of guards and red-nosed wardens.

According to the testimony of men in the street, functionaries, coachmen, cabbies, with whom I happened to discuss the matter, exiles from among the educated classes

—all these former army officers, officials, notaries, book-keepers, representatives of the gilded youth, who have been deported for forgery, embezzlement, swindling, etc., lead a secluded and modest life. The exceptions are those individuals who have the temperament of a Nozdryov.* These remain themselves everywhere and in all ages. They are rolling stones, they lead a nomad existence in Siberia, they are so much on the move as to be imperceptible to the observing eye. Besides Nozdryovs there are among educated exiles individuals completely depraved, frankly base, immoral, but everyone knows them, they are pointed out to you. The great majority, I repeat, live modestly.

On reaching their destination, the deportees from the educated classes have at first a perplexed, stunned look; they are timid and appear downtrodden, as it were. For the most part they are without means, without physical strength or endurance, they were badly educated, and their only resource is the ability to write in a hand which is often illegible. Some of them begin by selling their fine linen shirts, sheets, and handkerchiefs, piece by piece, and two or three years later die in complete destitution. Such was the recent case of Kuzovlev, a defendant in the trial of the Taganrog custom-house officials; he died in Tomsk and was buried at the expense of a generous man, also an exile. Others, little by little, find some occupation and get on their feet. They go into business, practice law, write for the local papers, become clerks, and so forth. Their earnings rarely exceed thirty to thirty-five rubles a month.

Their life is dull. Nature in Siberia, compared to what it is in Russia, seems to them monotonous, poor, flat. There is frost at Ascension, wet snow at Pentecost. The city flats are wretched, the streets muddy, everything in the shops is expensive, the goods are stale and the selection is poor;

* The rowdy in Gogol's *Dead Souls. Ed.'s note.*

many articles to which a European is accustomed cannot be had for any amount of money.

The native intelligentsia, both its thinking and its unthinking members, drink vodka from morning till night, they drink crudely, coarsely, stupidly, without knowing when to stop and without getting drunk. After the first two phrases, a native of some education is sure to say: "What about some vodka?" Out of boredom an exile drinks with him. At first he makes a wry face, then he gets the habit, and in the end, of course, he becomes an alcoholic. In the matter of drinking, it's the natives who demoralize the exiles, not the other way around. Women here are as dull as Nature; they are colorless, frigid, they do not know how to dress, they do not sing, do not laugh, are not pretty, and, as one old inhabitant put it, they are "hard to the touch." When, in good time, Siberia gives birth to her own novelists and poets, there will be no heroines in their novels and poems; woman will not inspire, will not arouse men to high deeds, save them, follow them "to the uttermost parts of the earth." Aside from wretched tea-houses, public baths for the family, and the numerous houses of prostitution, both open and clandestine, which so appeal to a Siberian, the cities have no entertainment to offer. On long autumnal and winter evenings, an exile stays at home or visits a native in order to drink. The pair will down two bottles of vodka and half a dozen bottles of beer, and then will come the usual question: "How about driving out to a house?" that is, to a house of prostitution. Tedium, tedium! How can one escape it? An exile will dip into a dog-eared volume that has been lying around, like Ribot's *Diseases of the Will*, or on the first clear spring day will don light-colored trousers—that's the best he can do. Ribot is rather boring, and besides, what is the use of reading about the diseases of the will if you have no will? Light-colored trousers don't keep you warm, but at least they are different!

VIII

The Siberian highway is the longest and, it seems to me, the ugliest road in the whole world. Between Tyumen and Tomsk it is tolerable, not thanks to the administration in charge of it, but because of the nature of the terrain: it crosses a treeless plain. In the morning it rains, but by dusk everything is dry, and if the road is blocked with ice from melting snows until the end of May, you can drive across the trackless meadows, and then you have several byroads to choose from. Beyond Tomsk there are hills, and the *taiga* (vast forest region). It takes a long time for the ground to dry, and there are no byroads to choose from; willy-nilly you must follow the highway. As a result, beyond Tomsk travelers begin to curse and become frequent contributors to the complaint books. The officials read their complaints carefully and invariably write against each: "No action to be taken." Why write? Chinese officials would long since have introduced a stamp.

Two lieutenants and an army doctor travel with me from Tomsk to Irkutsk. One is an infantryman and wears a shaggy *papakha* (Caucasian cap), the other is a topographer and wears a shoulder knot. At each station, dirty, wet, sleepy, worn out by the slow ride and the jolting, we tumble onto the couches and give free rein to our indignation: "What a wretched, horrible road!" At this the clerks and attendants say: "That's nothing, wait till you get to Kozulka."

At each station beyond Tomsk, Kozulka figures as a bugaboo; the clerks smile enigmatically, and travelers going in the opposite direction smirk maliciously, as if to say: "We've been there, now it's your turn!" They have fright-

ened me so that Kozulka appears in my dreams as a bird
with a long beak and green eyes.

Kozulka is the name of a twenty-two verst drive from
the Chernorechenskaya to the Kozulskaya station (between
the cities of Achinsk and Krasnoyarsk). Portentous signs
begin to appear at two or three stations before the dreaded
stretch. One traveler says that he has had four upsets, another complains that he broke an axle, a third keeps a sullen
silence and, when asked how the road is, replies: "A very
good road, devil take it!" Everyone looks at me pityingly,
as at a dead man, because I travel in my own carriage.

"You are sure to smash it and get stuck in the mud,"
they tell me, sighing. "You'd be better off in a post chaise."

The closer to Kozulka, the more terrifying the omens.
At dusk, not far from the Chernorechenskaya Station, the
carriage of my fellow travelers suddenly tips over, and the
lieutenants and the doctor, together with their valises, bundles, sabres, violin case, plunge into the mud. At night my
turn comes. Hard by the Chernorechenskaya Station my
coachman suddenly announces to me that the trigger of
my carriage is bent. The trigger is an iron bolt by which the
front of the vehicle is fastened to the axle; when it is bent
or broken, the carriage falls on its face, hugging the ground.
At the station an attempt is made to repair it. About five
coachmen, who reek so strongly of onion and garlic that
it turns your stomach, lay the muddy carriage on its side
and proceed to straighten the bent trigger by hammering
it. They say that a certain bearing in the carriage is cracked,
another part is out of place, three nuts are missing, but I
understand nothing and indeed have no desire to understand. . . . It is dark, cold, boring, and I am sleepy.

In the station waiting room a little lamp is burning dimly.
There is a smell of kerosene, garlic and onion. One of the
couches is occupied by the lieutenant in the *papakha*, who
is asleep, on another sits a bearded man lazily struggling into

his boots. He has just been ordered to drive off somewhere to repair the telegraph, and he wants to sleep, not to go on the road. The lieutenant with the shoulder knot and the doctor sit at a table, with their heavy heads resting on their hands, and doze. I hear hammering in the yard, and the *papakha* snoring.

People are talking . . . All the station talk along the highway is the same: the local officials are criticized and the road is cursed. The Department of Posts and Telegraphs gets the worst rapping, although on the Siberian highway it reigns, it does not rule. The stories one hears at the stations simply horrify a weary traveler who still has a thousand versts to cover before he reaches Irkutsk. You are told that a member of the Geographic Society who was traveling with his wife smashed his carriage twice, and in the end was forced to spend the night in the woods; that a lady was so violently jolted that her head was cracked; that an excise man was stuck in the mud for sixteen hours and had to pay some peasants twenty-five rubles to pull him out and tow him as far as the station; that not a single owner of a carriage had ever driven to the station in safety. All such stories affect the mind like the cries of an ominous bird.

The mail, it is reported, suffers most of all. If some well-intentioned individual undertook to trace the movement of mail from Perm to Irkutsk and wrote down his findings, the result would be a tale which would bring tears to the readers' eyes. To begin with, all these leather bags and sacks which carry religion, enlightenment, trade, money, order to Siberia stay in Perm needlessly for twenty-four hours because the time-table of the steamboats is not coordinated with that of the trains. Between Tyumen and Tomsk during the spring till June, the post fights the monstrous floods and the bottomless mud. At one station, I remember, I had to wait twenty-four hours; the mail, too, was waiting. Across rivers and flooded meadows heavy parcels are transported in small boats, which don't capsize perhaps only because the mothers of Siberian mailmen ardently pray for them. Between Tomsk and Irkutsk troikas carrying mail stick in the mud for ten to twenty hours near innumerable Kozulkas and Chernorechenskayas. On May 27th at one of the stations I was told that a bridge on the Kacha river had recently collapsed under the mail wagon and that it was a miracle that the horses and the mailbags had not gone under. Such happenings are common with the Siberian post. After I had left Irkutsk the Moscow mail failed to catch up with me for six days. That means that it was more than a week late; for a whole week it had been having who knows what adventures.

Siberian mailmen are martyrs. Theirs is a heavy cross. They are heroes whom the fatherland stubbornly refuses to recognize. They work hard, wage war on Nature like no one else, sometimes suffer intolerable hardships, but they are transferred, fined, and fired more often than they are rewarded. Do you know what wages they get? And have you ever seen a postman with a medal? They may be far more useful than those functionaries who write "No action to be taken," but look how cowed they are, how down-trodden, how timidly they behave in your presence. . . .

But here at last I am informed that my carriage has been repaired. We can proceed on our way.

"Get up!" the doctor wakes the *papakha*. "The sooner we leave this accursed Kozulka behind, the better."

"Gentlemen, the devil isn't as black as he is painted," the bearded fellow tries to reassure us. "Really, Kozulka is no worse than the other stations. Besides, if you're scared, twenty-two versts can be made on foot. . . ."

"Yes, if you don't get stuck in the mud," adds the clerk.

Day is just beginning to dawn. It is cold. The coachmen have not yet left the yard, but already they are saying: "What a road, God help us!" At first we drive through a village. Thin mud, into which the wheels sink, alternates with dry humps and hillocks; like ribs, logs stick out of bridges and brushwood patches drowned in liquid manure. Riding over those logs turns people's vitals inside out and snaps the axles of carriages.

But now we have passed the village and we are on terrible Kozulka. The road here is indeed abominable, but I do not think it is worse than the road at Mariinsk or that same Chernorechenskaya. Imagine a broad lane cleared through the woods, along which stretches an embankment of clay and rubble some thirty feet wide—this is the highway. If you get a lateral view of this embankment, it looks as though from the earth, as from an open music box, a large roll were protruding. On either side of it there is a ditch. The thing is guttered with ruts a foot or more deep that run lengthwise and crosswise in such a way that the embankment forms a system of mountain ridges, among which there are Kazbeks and Elbruzes. The peaks are already dry, and the wheels rattle going over them, but at the base the water makes a squelching sound. Only a very clever magician could place a vehicle on this embankment so that it would stand straight. As a rule, it is in such a position that, until you are used to it, you are forced to cry out every minute: "Coachman, we're tipping over!" Now the right hand wheels are plunged in a deep rut, while the left hand wheels rest on mountain peaks, or else two wheels are stuck in the mud, the third is planted on a peak, and the fourth is suspended in mid-air. . . . The carriage assumes a thousand different positions, while you clasp now your head, now your sides, bow in every direction, as your bags and boxes mutiny and pile upon each other and upon you. And look at the driver: how does this acrobat manage to keep his seat on the box?

Anyone taking a detached view of us would say that we are not riding but going mad. We wish to keep away from the embankment and we drive along a parallel strip looking for a by-road, but here too are ruts, humps, ribs and bridges. Having gone some distance, the coachman halts. He reflects a while and then, with a helpless groan and an air of being about to perpetrate a low-down trick, he heads for the highway, straight into the ditch. There is a crash—bang on the front wheels, bang on the rear wheels! —that means that we are crossing the ditch. Then we climb up on the embankment, with another crash. The horses are steaming, swingletrees break off, breach-bands and shaft bows are askew . . . "Giddap, mother!" shouts the coachman, whipping the horses with all his might. "Giddap, friend! A plague on your soul!" Having dragged the carriage a dozen paces, the horses halt; now, whip them as you may, call them any names you please, they will not budge. There is no help for it, again we head for the ditch, climb down the embankment and drive along the shoulder of the road. Then there is another pause and we turn toward the embankment—and this goes on *ad nauseam*.

The going is hard, very hard, but what makes it worse is the thought that this foul strip of earth, this pock-marked horror is practically the only artery connecting Europe with Siberia. And along this artery, we say, civilization flows into Siberia. So we say, we say a lot. If we were overheard by the drivers, the mailmen or those wet, muddied peasants walking knee-deep in ooze beside their carts, which are loaded with tea for Europe, what would they think of Europe's candor?

By the way, look at this caravan of carts. About forty vehicles carrying tea are going along the embankment. The wheels are half hidden in the deep ruts, the lean nags stretch their necks with the effort. Beside the carts walk the drivers; pulling their feet out of the mud and helping the horses, they have long since strained themselves to the utmost. And now a section of the caravan has stopped. What's the matter? One of the carts has a broken wheel. . . . Well, better not look!

By way of taunting the exhausted drivers, mailmen, and horses, someone has seen to it that heaps of stones and brick rubble have been piled up on either side of the road. This was done in order to remind you constantly that before long the road will be even worse. It is said that in the towns and villages along the Siberian highway there are people who get wages for repairing the road. If that is true, they ought to be given a raise on condition that they should please not exert themselves making repairs, because the more the road is repaired, the worse it gets. According to the peasants, such sectors as the Kozulskaya one are repaired in the following manner: at the end of June or the beginning of July, when the mosquito season—the local version of an Egyptian plague—is at its height, officials dragoon people from the villages and order them to fill in the dry ruts and pits with brushwood, brick rubble, and stone, so soft that it turns to powder between your fingers. This goes on all summer long. Then it snows, and the result is humps and hillocks that are unique in the world and make you sea-sick. Then comes spring and mud, and again repairs—year in and year out.

Before I had reached Tomsk, I made the acquaintance of a local official, who was my traveling companion for two or three stations. I remember, as we sat in a tavern kept by a Jew and ate a fish soup made of perch, a rural constable entered and reported to my fellow traveler that at a certain spot the highway had broken down completely and that the road contractor refused to repair it.

"Tell him to come here!" the official ordered.

After a while a little, wry-faced, shaggy peasant came in. The official leapt up from his chair and pounced on him.

"You rascal you, how dare you? What do you mean by refusing to repair the road?" he shouted, with tears in his voice. "The road is impassable, people break their necks, the governor writes in, the district police officer writes in, they all blame me, and you, plague take your soul, you swine you, you crook, God damn you, what are you waiting for? Eh? You vermin you! By tomorrow the road must be repaired! Tomorrow I'll be driving back, and if I see that the road is not repaired, I'll make a bloody mush of your mug, I'll cripple you, you robber! Get out!"

The little peasant blinked, sweated, screwed up his face worse than before, and darted out of the room.

The official returned to the table, seated himself, and said, with a smile:

"Yes, of course, after the Petersburg and Moscow women, ours cannot please you; still, if you take the trouble to look, you may find a sweet little number even here. . . ."

It would be worth finding out what the diminutive peasant accomplished overnight. What can one achieve in such a short time? I don't know whether or not the Siberian highway profits by it, but road officials do not stay long in one place, the turnover is great. It is said that one such official, having reached his sector, dragooned the peasants and ordered them to dig ditches on the side of the road; his successor, who would not be outdone in originality, dragooned the peasants and ordered them to fill in the ditches; the third man ordered the road surfaced with a layer of clay a foot deep. The fourth, fifth, sixth, seventh official—each brought some honey to the hive.

All year round the highway is in an impossible state: in the spring—mud, in the summer—ruts, pits and repair work, in the winter—hillocks. The swift travel, which years ago took Wiegel's * breath away, and later Goncharov's,† is

* A memoirist of the first half of the nineteenth century. *Ed.'s note.*
† The well-known nineteenth century novelist, author of *Oblomov*, who wrote an account of his voyage around the world. *Ed.'s note.*

nowadays perhaps possible only at the very beginning of winter. True, there are in our own day authors who are enraptured by the speed of travel in Siberia, but this is only because, having been to Siberia, it is awkward for them not to have experienced such speed, at least in their imagination. . . .

It is hard to believe that some day Kozulka will cease breaking wheels and axles. In their lifetime Siberian officials have not seen any better roads. They are pleased with what they have, and the complaint books, the newspaper stories and the critical remarks of travelers are of as little use as the money spent on repairs.

The sun is already high when we reach the Kozulskaya Station. My companions go on, while I remain to have my carriage repaired.

IX

If you are not wholly indifferent to scenery, then in traveling from Russia to Siberia you will be bored all the way from the Urals to the Yenisei River. A chilly plain, crooked birches, puddles, lakes here and there, snow in May, and the desolate, cheerless banks of the Ob's tributaries—this is all that your memory will retain of the first two thousand versts. That Nature, of which the aborigines are in awe, which our escaped convicts respect, and which in time will be an inexhaustible gold mine for Siberian poets, that majestic, beautiful, original Nature begins only at the Yenisei.

Without meaning to offend the jealous admirers of the Volga, let me say that I have never in my life seen a river more magnificent than the Yenisei. The Volga may be a beauty, pranked up, modest, melancholy, but the Yenisei is a fierce, mighty warrior who does not know what to do with his youth and strength. On the banks of the Volga man began boldly, but he ended with a moan that is called song. His golden hopes have been replaced by a malaise which goes by the name of Russian pessimism. On the banks of the Yenisei life began with a moan, but it will end with such prowess as we haven't even dreamed of. Such at least were my thoughts as I stood on the banks of the broad Yenisei and looked eagerly at its waters, which rush toward the stern Arctic Ocean with terrible speed and force. The Yenisei is cramped by its banks. The waves churn and race and crowd each other, and it is strange that this lusty giant hasn't yet washed away its banks and hollowed out its bed. On the hither shore stands Krasnoyarsk, the finest and most beautiful of all Siberian cities. On the farther bank loom mountains which reminded me of the Caucasus, they are just as smoky and have the same air of revery. I stood there and thought: what an ample, bold, intelligent life will one day brighten these shores! I envied Sibiryakov,* who, as I read, had taken a steamer in Petersburg and had traveled by way of the Arctic Ocean to reach the mouth of the Yenisei. I was sorry that the university had been opened in Tomsk, and not here in Krasnoyarsk. Many thoughts passed through my mind and they raced and crowded each other like the waves of the Yenisei, and I was happy . . .

Just beyond Krasnoyarsk begins the famous *taiga*. There has been such a spate of words about it that you expect too much of it. At first you are somewhat disappointed. The road is flanked on either side by an unbroken wall of ordinary woods: pines, firs, larches and birches. There are no trees that it would take five men to encircle, no treetops so high that you get dizzy looking up at them. The trees are no larger than those that grow in the suburbs of Moscow. I was told that the *taiga* is without sound or fragrance. But during my entire journey through these woods birds were

---

* A native of Siberia who owned gold mines there, financed studies of the region, and himself took part in the exploration of the Arctic route to the mouths of Siberian rivers. *Ed.'s note.*

singing at the top of their lungs, insects were buzzing, the
needles, heated by the sun, filled the air with a heavy odor
of resin, clearings in the forest and the borders of the road
were covered with pale-blue, pink and yellow flowers that
caressed more than the eye. Apparently those who wrote
about the *taiga* observed it not in spring, but in summer,
when even in Russia the woods are silent and odorless.

The fascination of the *taiga* lies not in giant trees or in
silence, but in the fact that perhaps alone the migratory
birds know where it ends. The first day you pay no attention, the second and third day you are astonished, the
fourth and fifth you begin to feel that you will never escape
from this monster of a forest. You drive up a tall wooded
hill, you look ahead due east in the direction you are going,
and you see woods below, and farther on, a hill curly with
woods, beyond it another hill, also curly, and beyond *that*
still another hill, and so without end. The next day you look
ahead once more from a hilltop, and the same view unfolds
before your eyes . . . Still, you know that ahead of you
there will be the Angara River and the city of Irkutsk,
but what lies beyond the forest that stretches on both sides
of the road to the north and south, and for how many hun-
dreds of versts it stretches in those directions—that even
the coachmen and the peasants born in the *taiga* do not
know. Their fantasy is bolder than ours, but even they do
not dare take a guess at the size of the *taiga*, and in answer
to our question, they say: "There's no end to it." All they
know is that in winter men from the far north in sledges
drawn by reindeer pass through the *taiga* in order to buy
grain, but who they are and precisely where they come
from even the old men do not know.

There, close to a row of birches, trudges an escaped convict with a knapsack and a kettle on his back. How small
and insignificant appear his crimes, his sufferings, and he
himself, in comparison with the immense *taiga*! He will

perish here in the *taiga*, and there will be nothing complicated or terrible about it, it will be like the death of a gnat.
As long as the population is scarce, the *taiga* is invincible,
and nowhere does the phrase: "man is the king of Nature"
sound so false and timid as it does here. If, let us say, all
the people who now live along the Siberian highway had
conspired to destroy the *taiga* with the aid of fire and the
axe, it would be another case of the titmouse who wanted
to burn up the sea. A forest fire may chance to raze the
trees within a radius of, say, five versts, but this is an insignificant fraction of the total acreage; several decades pass
and where the burnt-out woods had been a young forest
grows up, thicker and darker than what had been there
before. While he was here, one learned traveler who was
on the farther shore accidentally started a forest fire. In a
moment the entire area, as far as the eye could see, was in
flames. Stunned by the extraordinary spectacle, the savant
declared himself "the cause of a terrible calamity." I venture
to say that the learned man's labors probably made a larger
dent on Nature than what he imagined to be a terrible
calamity. On the spot ravaged by fire there probably grows
an impassable thicket, where imperturbable bears ramble
and hazel hens fly. The ordinary human yardstick doesn't
fit the *taiga*.

And how many mysteries does the *taiga* conceal! Here
among the trees a path moves stealthily and vanishes in the
woodsy twilight. Whither does it lead? To a secret still? To
a village, the existence of which is known neither to the
police officer nor the assessor? Or perhaps to a gold mine
discovered by wandering prospectors? And what a captivating, devil-may-care freedom this enigmatic path
breathes!

The coachmen say that in the *taiga* live bears, wolves,
deer, sable, wild goats. Peasants whose homes are along the
highway spend whole weeks in the *taiga* hunting when they

are out of work. The art of venery is very simple here: if the shotgun goes off, you thank God, if it hangs fire, then don't ask mercy of the bear. One huntsman complained to me that his gun hung fire five times on end, and discharged only the sixth time. To go hunting with such a treasure is a great risk, unless you have a knife or a boarspear. Imported rifles are poor and expensive, and for that reason not seldom you come across blacksmiths who can make firearms. Generally speaking, blacksmiths are gifted people, and this is especially noticeable in the *taiga*, where they are not lost in a mass of other talents. Necessity forced upon me the acquaintance of a blacksmith whom my coachman recommended to me in these words: "Oho, he's a great master! He even makes guns!" His tone and facial expression reminded me of our conversation about famous artists. My tarantass had broken down, it had to be repaired, and, summoned by my coachman, there came to the station a pale, lean, nervous individual, who showed all the signs of a gifted man and an alcoholic. Like a physician bored by having to treat a common ailment, he made a cursory examination of my vehicle with an air of condescension, diagnosed the case briefly and clearly, thought a while, and, without saying a word to me, lazily trudged off along the road, then looked back, and said to the coachman:

"Well, take the tarantass to the smithy."

Four carpenters assisted the smith with the operation. He worked negligently, reluctantly, and it seemed that the iron assumed various shapes despite his will. He smoked a good deal, rummaged needlessly in a heap of iron junk, stared at the sky when I tried to hurry him—artists behave thus coyly when urged to sing or recite. Now and then, as if out of coquetry or in order to impress me and the carpenters, he would lift his hammer high and, scattering sparks in every direction, with one blow solve a complicated and difficult problem. Under the heavy clumsy blow which, it seemed, should have shattered the anvil and made the earth quake, the slender iron bar assumed the desired shape, so that the most fastidious couldn't find fault with it.

He received five and a half rubles from me for the work; he took five rubles for himself and let the four carpenters divide the half ruble among them. They said: "Thanks," and dragged the tarantass back to the station. They probably envied the man of talent who in the *taiga* knows his own worth and is as despotic as any in our big cities.

1890

Yegor's story

From *The Island of Sakhalin*

The physician with whom I had been lodging left the island shortly after retiring from service, and I found quarters with a young official, a very decent fellow. He had only one servant, an old woman who hailed from the Ukraine, a convict, and once a day Yegor, also a convict, would come in for a while. He was not accounted my landlord's servant, but "out of respect" he would haul firewood, remove the kitchen slops, and do all the chores that were beyond the old woman's strength. I would sit and read or write, and suddenly I would hear a rustling and panting, and feel a heavy body moving under the table at my feet. Looking down, I would see Yegor, barefoot, picking up waste paper, or dusting.

A man of about forty, he was a clumsy, doltish fellow, with a simple, good-natured look, a face that at once struck you as stupid, and a mouth as wide as an eel-pout's. His hair was red, he had a thin beard and small eyes. He didn't answer a question promptly but would look at you out of the corner of his eye and say: "What?" or "Who do you mean?" He called me "your Honor" but addressed me

familiarly in the second person singular. He had to be doing work of some sort every moment, and he found it
wherever he was. He would be talking to you and at the
same time darting his eyes about to see if there weren't
something to repair or to tidy up. He was occupied so constantly that he slept only two or three hours out of the
twenty-four. On holidays he would put a jacket over a red
shirt and stand on a street corner, his stomach thrust out,
his legs wide apart. This was called "celebrating."

Here, in penal servitude, he had built himself a cabin
with his own hands;* he made buckets, tables, crude
cupboards. He could make any piece of furniture, but
solely "for himself," i.e. for his own use. He had never
been in a fight and had never been thrashed; only a long
time ago in his childhood had his father given him a beating,
because while watching over a crop of peas he had allowed
a cock to get among the plants.

One day I had the following talk with him.

"Why were you sent here?" I asked him.

"What's that, your Honor?"

"Why were you sent to Sakhalin?"

"For murder."

"Tell me how it all happened, from the very beginning."

Yegor took up a position beside the door jamb, put his
arms behind his back, and began:

"We'd been to the Master, to Vladimir Mikhailych, and
we'd settled it about cutting some wood, and about de-
livery to the station. Good. We settled it and went home.
We hadn't got far from the village when the fellows sent
me to the office to witness the paper. I was on horseback.
On the way to the office Andryukha stopped me: there was
a flood, I couldn't make it. 'Tomorrow,' says he, 'I'll be
driving over to the office about my leasehold and I'll have
the paper witnessed.' Alright. So we were stepping along

* Many convicts were allowed to live in homes of their own. *Ed.'s note.*

together, I on horseback, the others on foot. We got to Parakhino. The fellows went into the tavern to get cigarettes, Andryukha and I stayed outside on the sidewalk close by. Then he says: 'Don't you have a five kopeck piece, brother? I'd like a drink,' says he. 'Brother,' I says, 'I know what sort you are: you'll go in to have just one drink, and you'll get stewed to the gills.' 'No,' says he, 'I won't get stewed, I'll have one drink, and go home.' We joined the crowd, agreed on three quarts, all of us chipped in, and we called for the stuff. Then we all sat down at the table to drink."

"Make it shorter," I put in.

"Wait, don't you break in, your Honor. We had the vodka, and then he, Andryukha, called for a half pint of pepper vodka. He poured out a glass for himself and one for me. And we drank together, a glass apiece. Well, now the whole crowd left the pot-house and went home, and the two of us tailed along behind. I got tired riding horseback and got off and sat down on the bank. I sang and cracked jokes. There were no hard words between us. Then we got up and went on."

"Tell me about the murder," I interrupted him.

"You wait. At home I lay down and slept till morning, till they woke me up: 'Get up, who was it beat up Andrey?' Then they brought Andrey, and the constable came, too. He started questioning the lot of us, but none of us said he had any part in the business. Andrey was still alive, and he said: 'You, Sergukha, you hit me with a club, and that's all I remember.' Sergukha don't confess. We all thought it was Sergukha, and began to watch him, so he shouldn't do anything to himself. The next day Andrey died. Now Sergey's folks, his sister, his father-in-law, put him up to this: 'Sergey, don't deny it, because it's all one. Own up, but drag in others. You'll get off easy.' "

"As soon as Andrey died, we all got together at the

village elder's, and we let Sergey know, too. We tried to make him talk, but he wouldn't confess. Then we let him stay the night in our house. We kept a watch on him there, so that he shouldn't do anything to himself. He had a gun. Not safe. Come morning we saw he was gone. The lot of us looked for him in his own house, we looked in the village, we went into the fields, we looked for him high and low. Then someone came from the police station and said Sergey was already there. And now they started pulling us in. What Sergey did was to go straight to the district police officer and to the constable. He got down on his knees and put it on us that as much as three years back we hired him to beat up Andryukha. 'The three of us were walking along,' he said, 'Ivan, Yegor, and me—and we settled it that we'd beat him up. I hit Andryukha,' he said, 'with a stump, not a big one, and Ivan and Yegor jumped on him, and I got scared and ran back,' he said, 'and got behind the other fellows.' Then they took us to town—Ivan, Kirsha, me and Sergey—and they put us in jail there."

"But who are Ivan and Kirsha?"

"My own brothers. Pyotr Mikhailych, the merchant, came to the jail and got us out on bail. And we worked at his place till the Feast of the Intercession of the Holy Virgin (October 1, O.S.). We had it good there. The day after the Feast they tried us in town. Kirsha had witnesses —the men who'd been tailing along stood up for him, but as for me, brother, I got it in the neck. In court I told them just what I'm telling you, just the way it was, but they didn't believe it. 'Everybody here says things like that, and they cross their hearts, and it's all a lie.' Well, they found me guilty and sent me to jail.

"In jail we lived under lock and key, but I had charge of the muck pail, I swept the cells, and took the food round. And for that every man gave me a ration of bread a month. It came to about three pounds from each. We heard we were going to be sent away, so we wired home. That was just before St. Nicholas' Day (December 6, O.S.). The wife and brother Kirsha came to see us and brought us some clothes and other things. The wife howled, but there was nothing for it. When she left I made her a present—two rations of bread. We cried some, and to the children and to all Christian people we sent greetings.

"On the way we were handcuffed together, two by two. I walked with Ivan. In Novgorod they took our pictures, they put us in irons and shaved our heads. Then they marched us to Moscow. In the Moscow jail we put our names to a petition for pardon. How we made our way to Odessa I don't remember. But I had it good. In Odessa they asked us questions in the doctors' room, stripped us to the skin and looked us over. Then they rounded us up and herded us onto a steamer. Cossacks and soldiers led us up steps and had us sit down in the innards of it. We sat on the bunks and that's all we did. Each in his place. There were five of us sitting on the upper bunks. At first we didn't know what was what, then we heard: 'We're off! We're off!'

"We were going along, going along, and then the ship began to rock and pitch. It was so hot the people stood around naked. Some threw up—some—were quiet. Of course, a lot of them just lay there. And it was a bad storm. You were pitched about every which way. We were going along, going along, and then we ran into something. We got quite a jolt. It was a foggy day. It got good and dark. There was this jolt and then the steamer stopped and began to rock on cliffs, you might say. We thought a big fish was churning underneath and making the ship wobble.* They yanked in front, they went on yanking, but they couldn't push it off. Then they started shoving from be-

* The reference is to the shipwreck of the "Kostroma" off the western coast of Sakhalin in 1886. *Author's note.*

hind. They shoved from behind, and broke a hole in the bottom, about the middle. They tried to spread a sail over the hole, they tugged and tugged, but it didn't help. The water came up to the deck where folks were sitting and started to run right under them. The men begged: 'Don't let us perish, your Honor!' At first he said: 'Don't you try to force your way, and don't beg me, I'm not going to let anybody perish.' Then the water reached the lower bunks. The Christian folk cried and tried to force the doors. The master said: 'Well, boys, I'll let you out, but don't start a mutiny—I'll shoot you down, the lot of you.' Then he let us out. The next thing they said a Mass, that the Lord should make the sea quiet down, and that we should not perish. We prayed on our knees. After Mass they gave us hard tack and sugar, and the sea quieted down. Next day they started taking people ashore in barges. On shore Mass was served. Then we were loaded into another boat, a Turkish one,* and were brought here to Alexandrovsk.† They took us to the dock while it was still light, but they kept us there a long time, and when we left the dock it was pitch dark. The Christian folk walked close to the hedges, and some had night blindness, too. We held on to each other: some could see, others couldn't, so we held on to each other. I led a dozen of the Christian folk. They herded us into a prison yard and started to settle us in barracks, some here, some there. Before going to sleep, each man ate what he had with him, and in the morning they started handing out proper rations. Two days we rested, the third day they took us to the baths, the fourth they marched us off to work. First off, we dug ditches for a building, it's the hospital. We cleared the ground, rooted out stumps, dug holes, and such like. This went on for a week or two, maybe a month. Then we hauled logs from Mikhailovka.

* The steamer "Vladivostok" of the Voluntary Fleet. *Author's note.*
† The administrative center of Sakhalin. *Ed.'s note.*

We dragged them a distance of maybe three versts and piled them up at the bridge. Then they herded us into the kitchen gardens to dig for water. And when haying time came, they rounded us all up, and asked us who knew how to mow hay, and, well, whoever owned up, his name was put on a paper. They gave us bread, groats, meat for the whole crew and marched us off with a guard to mow hay at Armudany. I had it good, God gave me health and I mowed well. The guard would thrash some fellows, but there wasn't a hard word said to me. Only the men were cursing me out on account of me working so fast, but that was nothing. When I had time off or when it rained, I wove bast slippers. After work folks would lie down to sleep, but I sat and did my weaving. I would sell the slippers— two rations of meat a pair, worth four kopecks. When the mowing was over, we went home. At home, we were put in jail again. Then Sashka, the settler at Mikhailovka, took me on to work for him. I did all his field work: I reaped, I gathered in the crops, I threshed, dug potatoes, and in return Sashka hauled logs instead of me. I didn't eat Sashka's food, I ate what we got as rations. I worked two months and four days. Sashka promised me money, but he didn't give me none. Only gave me a pood of potatoes. Then Sashka brought me back to the jail and handed me over. They issued me an axe and a rope—and ordered me to haul firewood. I took care of seven stoves. I lived in a yurt and carried water instead of the attendant, and swept the floors. I was in charge of the Tartar's *maidan.** After work he turned it over to me, I did the selling, and for that he paid me fifteen kopecks a day. In spring, when the days got longer, I began to make bast shoes. I got ten kopecks the pair. In summer I floated firewood down the river. I piled up a good bit of it and sold it to the Jew who keeps the

* A kind of miniature and semi-clandestine commissary, pawnshop and gambling den patronized by the convicts. *Ed.'s note.*

baths. And I cut sixty logs and sold them for fifteen kopecks apiece. So with God's help I get along.—Only I have no time to talk to you, your Honor, I must fetch some water."

"How soon will you become a settler?" *

"In about five years."

"Are you homesick?"

"No. There's only one thing—I'm sorry for the children. They've no sense."

"Tell me, Yegor, what were you thinking about when they were taking you to the steamer in Odessa?"

"I was praying to God."

"What for?"

"That He should put sense into the children's heads."

"Why didn't you take your wife and children with you to Sakhalin?"

"Because they're as well off at home."

1893

* After serving his term of penal servitude, a convict lived on the island as a settler. Ed's note.